K.C. MILLS

YOU COULD DO DAMAGE

BLACK
ODYSSEY
MEDIA

WWW.BLACKODYSSEY.NET

Published by
BLACK ODYSSEY MEDIA

www.blackodyssey.net
Email: info@blackodyssey.net

Library of Congress Control Number: 2024916883

First Trade Paperback Printing: March 2025
ISBN: 978-1-957950-70-9
ISBN: 978-1-957950-71-6 (e-book)

Cover Design by Ashlee Nassar of Designs With Sass
To the extent that the image or images on the cover of this book depict a person or persons, such person or persons are merely models and are not intended to portray any character in the book.

10 9 8 7 6 5 4 3 2 1

Manufactured in the United States of America

Distributed by Kensington Publishing Corp.

Dear Reader,

I want to thank you immensely for supporting Black Odyssey Media and our ongoing efforts to spotlight the diverse narratives of blossoming and seasoned storytellers. With every manuscript we acquire, we believe that it took talent, discipline, and remarkable courage to construct that story, flesh out those characters, and prepare it for the world. Debut or seasoned, our authors are the real heroes and heroines in *OUR* story. For them, we are eternally grateful.

Whether you are new to K.C. Mills or Black Odyssey Media, we hope that you are here to stay. Our goal is to make a lasting impact in the publishing landscape, one step at a time and one book at a time. We also welcome your feedback and kindly ask that you leave a review. For upcoming releases, announcements, submission guidelines, etc., please be sure to visit our website at www.blackodyssey.net or scan the QR code below. And remember, no matter where you are in your journey, the best of both worlds begins now!

Joyfully,

Shawanda Williams

Shawanda "N'Tyse" Williams
Founder & CEO, Black Odyssey Media

CHAPTER 1

NARI.

"We have to be out by five. That's all the time they're giving us."

Shayla, my cousin and roommate, never paused her motions as she scrambled around the dingy room that belonged to her, emptying drawers and tossing her belongings into the suitcases wedged open on her tiny twin bed. The mattress was so small that I could barely see it beneath the luggage.

"What the hell do you mean we have to be out by five?"

"You heard me, Nari. *Out*. We don't live here anymore. My God, why do you always act so damn naïve?" Her tone was harsh and condescending even, and most days, I wouldn't react, but today, oh yeah, today was different. I crossed the threshold of her room, barging in like a wild, unexpected storm. My thin fingers gripped her shoulder, spinning Shayla's thick frame in my direction. Her maple-brown eyes went wild from the unexpected attack.

"And you heard me. *Why* do we have to be out by five? We paid our rent for the month. I gave you my half. What the hell is going on?"

She yanked away from me and scoffed. "Yeah, you gave me money but not for rent. It was money you owed me, and I had shit

1

to do, so I handled my business. The rent isn't paid, and we have to be out."

My mind rushed through the month that she'd covered the entire rent. Her boyfriend had offered money to cover it, so he'd technically paid my half. I had just started my job, and they put me in the hole for two weeks before I could get my check. When I did get paid, I still couldn't afford to pay her back because I had to buy suitable clothes and shoes to look the part, or I'd be fired. Shayla promised me it wasn't a big deal and that I could repay her over time.

"Why wouldn't you tell me that? You promised that I could take my time paying you back."

"Yeah, well, things changed. I needed the money. Sticks broke up with me."

"You should've told me. It's been three weeks; you've known for *three weeks* that we'd have to be out by the end of the month. What the hell am I supposed to do?"

"I don't know, Nari, and it's not my problem. I'm not your damn mama. Figure it out. We barely even get along most days. I only made things work because I needed your help to pay the rent." Shayla's confession was like a knife in the gut. I had always known that my cousin didn't care about me. She was my mother's baby sister's child, and I was desperate for any family. She was it, but I knew from the day we met that she would take more than she would give. Either way, to hear the words and the venom behind them still felt painful.

Shayla had been the one who made the connection after we crossed paths on the train. She kept staring at me with this evil scowl, and I didn't understand why until just before I reached my stop and was about to get off the train. Shayla caught my wrist firmly and yanked me back inside just before the doors closed. I missed my stop but gained a cousin. She began her interrogation with basic questions like my name, my parents' names, and where I grew up. It didn't take long for the connection to be made. I explained that I had grown up in foster care and I had never known my parents. The only detail I could offer was my mother's name, Endia Renee Collette. I had her last name because my father's wasn't listed on my birth certificate. The line was blank. Once I provided the golden ticket, my mother's name, Shayla's attitude changed. She smiled and became friendly, telling me we were related and how she had known the minute she laid eyes on me. I looked just like *her*, my mother. My cousin's words, not mine. I had never seen her before.

I never knew the woman but was starved for anything connected to her. My newly identified cousin and I talked, becoming friends, and I learned she hadn't known my mother either. She did, however, know that Endia had a daughter who was placed in foster care at her parents' insistence. At the time, my mother was only sixteen years old. According to Shayla, months after the decision, my mother became seriously depressed and disappeared. She'd packed a bag one night, left the house, and never returned. No one had heard from her since that day, nor did they know if she was dead or alive.

The reality broke my heart. I would never know the woman who gave me life, but the story also gave me a sense of hope that, at the very least, she wanted me, only her parents refused to allow her to keep me. The worst part was that Shayla's mother, who was younger than my mother, had gotten pregnant two years after my mother disappeared . . . and my grandparents embraced her child. They supported her decision to keep Shayla, so she grew up in a loving home with family while I struggled through life with no one. The family I wanted, Shayla was too selfish and spoiled to care about. She made all the wrong decisions to the point where they gave up on her and placed an ultimatum on the table—get it together or get out. At sixteen, she packed her things, like my mother had done, but for different reasons.

She hated her family so much that she would never tell me anything about them. The more we were around each other, the more I realized that Shayla only hated her family because they had expectations. She wanted to run the streets when they demanded she make something of herself. At least they cared. I would've loved to have someone who cared enough to invest in me.

The only proof I had that Shayla and I were related was an old photo of her mother and mine. The woman in the picture, who she identified as my mother, was my twin. Her eyes, nose, lips, round face, and thick, wild hair were identical to what I saw when I looked in the mirror. The only difference was that my mother was fair skinned while my skin was dark and richer with melanin, likely inherited from my father, who I didn't know. Shayla would never introduce me to my family, making clear that she'd told them about our union, and they wanted no part of me. It hurt, but I was used to rejection. Shayla was all I had, so I held on tight, even when she treated me like shit, and now, here we were.

"Are you serious right now? As shitty as this situation is, it's all I have. Where am I supposed to go?"

"I don't know, and I don't care. Grow the fuck up, Nari. It's not my responsibility to take care of you."

"Bitch, you haven't done shit for me—ever. The only reason why I'm here is because you couldn't afford to live on your own, just like me."

She shrugged. "You're right, so why the hell would you want to be around me? Do what you want. I don't care. I have to worry about my damn self."

I watched in astonishment as my cousin acted like I didn't matter now and never really did. Instead of wasting energy on words that wouldn't change the situation or her mind, I crossed the hall to my room and sat on the edge of my twin bed. Our apartment was partially furnished, which was another reason we chose it. Well, that and the fact that we could manage the eight-hundred-dollar rent. Our residence was in a horrible neighborhood, with minimal access to anything, but we could afford it.

Dropping my face in my palms while my sharp elbows dug into my thighs, I fought hard to keep tears at bay. My life, my very complicated and shitty life, was taking a toll on me. I was running low on fight. I had been fighting all my life and, somehow, made it this far. I was twenty-four years old, and I was alive but not living. I'd survived some horrible times and people so that current blow shouldn't have been as devastating as it was, but truthfully, it had completely drained me of any fight I had left.

When Shayla finished packing, she left without saying one word to me. All I was granted was the clang of her keys being tossed on the tiny, wooden dinette in the kitchen and then the door slamming after the thud of her luggage dropping on the other side. My eyes scanned the room, and that was when it hit me. I bolted from the bed and hurried to the dresser. My heart pounded in my chest as I removed the bottom drawer, saying a silent prayer. As I dropped it to the floor, I felt a sharp pain in my chest.

No, no, no, no!

It was gone. My money was gone. I'd saved a little over two grand since working at the club. My goal was to put away enough to get my own place and, hopefully, a decent car. I moved so fast that I almost tripped over my feet, rushing to the window just in time to see Shayla lift her legs into a car and close the door. She was gone, and I had no way of knowing where she was heading. She'd stolen my money. It was all I had to my name. What the hell was I supposed to do now?

I have to be out of here by five and at work by seven.

"You're late, and what's with all that?" Joey, who worked security at the door, along with Ryan, motioned to the two oversized duffels draped over each of my shoulders. I was grateful when he pulled them from my body and gripped each as if they were featherlight. They were heavy, and I was exhausted from having lugged them from the apartment to the car I'd scheduled to get me to work.

"Be right back," he tossed over to Ryan, who was scanning the membership cards of two women waiting in line. Ryan offered a head nod before motioning for the two women to enter. They glided in, looking just as exclusive as the space we were in . . . a club I worked at but couldn't afford membership to.

"Hurry up before Cal sees you. He's in a mood and already asked about you twice."

I frowned at the thought. My boss, Calvetti, wasn't the nicest person. He was all about business, and the club was his baby. It was one of the talking points amongst the elite in our city. I'd serviced some of the wealthiest people who claimed Atlanta as their home, making it harder to work here. They wasted money like it literally grew on trees. For them, I was positive it did.

"I know. I had two rides canceled on me. They're all afraid to come into my neighborhood, and I can't blame them," I mumbled as we entered the employee lounge. He tossed my bags in the corner before pausing to look me over as if he expected something to jump out and explain why I had everything I owned with me when I arrived.

"You going somewhere?" His big body seemed intimidating to most, but he was a big ole softy to me. Joey could snap a neck with his bare hands if he needed to, but he was actually a really nice guy who didn't like confrontation.

"No, well, yeah, but not like what you're asking. I got put out of my place, and well . . . never mind. I need to get to work."

I pushed out a short sigh before hurrying to my locker. My fingers quickly twisted the dial with my combination before digging into the tote I still held. After I pulled out my heels placing them on the floor, I stepped out of my slides and dropped them in. I shoved my things in the locker and turned the dial to secure it.

"What do you mean by 'put out'?"

"Evicted," I mumbled as I bent over to put on my heels.

"How? You just got the place." He and I talked a little, mostly by his doing. The day Shayla and I moved in, I was so relieved to have a solid place to stay that I mentioned it to him. When I was upright again, his thin eyes were narrowed on me.

"By not paying rent."

"If you were short, you could've asked . . ."

I shook my head. "Wasn't me. Shayla screwed me over. I gave her my half, and she didn't pay."

She also stole every penny I had to my name, but I'm too exhausted to be angry right now.

Joey kept a narrowed glare on me while I was on my way to the door. "So, what now? Where are you going to stay?"

"I don't know. I'll figure it out."

"Let me see what I can do."

I quickly shook my head. "No, absolutely not. I'm nobody's charity case, Joey. I'll figure it out," I tossed over my shoulder as we ventured down the hall that would take us back to the main area of the club.

Just before we reached the bar, he caught my wrist. "I know you're not a charity case. That's not what this is. I just want to help because that's what friends do."

I smiled softly before my eyes lowered to where his big hand was gently wrapped around my wrist. He quickly let go.

"I appreciate it, Joey, but we're not really friends, are we? I work here, and so do you, which is the sum total of our affiliation, so anything you do for me will feel like charity. I also promised that I would never owe anybody anything. I have to stick to that because it's all I have."

After a long pause, I walked away but could feel him staring. He was a sweetheart and would never hold anything over my head. Joey had a crush. He never said it, but I could tell by how he hovered, looking out for me the way he did. It was always subtle things, such as walking me to my car at night or handling patrons who got too rowdy or rude, but his efforts didn't go unnoticed. He'd do anything for me. I was sure of it. However, I just couldn't allow myself to become dependent on anyone, especially not after the way I'd just been fucked over by someone who shared the same DNA. My life was my own, and I would have to make it work.

That night, I moved mindlessly through the club, doing what I was paid to do—look pretty and keep the deep pockets happy. It didn't matter whether they were men or women. My job was to make sure the patrons kept a smile on their faces and money flowing. I managed, even though my mind was heavy. Men focused on me and engaged in flirtatious conversation, and I pretended to be interested but wasn't. They were rich, attractive men whose pockets were deep with either legal or illegal money. Politicians would be seated in private sections, next to drug dealers who pushed dope through the same streets those politicians were trying to clean up. They all had a general respect for one another because, in here, none of that mattered. They were on a leveled playing field, which was paved with green. If you could pay, you could play.

I searched the club and realized Joey was no longer at the door. That was usually the case when I worked. He would fade into the shadows, keeping an eye on things. *On me*. I appreciated his presence because there had been a few times when he had to handle clients for getting a little too handsy. I had a feeling that was about to be the case as I approached a section with two men. I had been summoned to them more times than I liked that evening.

There were several women with them as well, but I could tell that they were only sharing space as an alternative option. The man who occupied the section nearby was who they really wanted to spend time with; however, he had ignored advances from everyone who'd approached him throughout the evening.

He denied them all with little effort, choosing to sit by himself, enjoying an exclusive bottle of Gautier Eden Cognac. It was strange, but it wasn't my business. He had been there before but never in my section. I did, however, notice that sitting alone was kind of his thing. Some nights, he was social, but most, he wasn't. I knew for sure that he had spent time with a few of the women who worked there in the private rooms because they all made a point of whispering about him. I didn't care. He wasn't my type if he was there, regardless of how handsome the man was.

What I did gather about him was that he seemed to be important. It wasn't any one thing about him, but then again, it was everything about him that brought me to that conclusion. His presence was dominating, his stature that of a respected man, and his demeanor was intimidating. He communicated and issued demands with a motion of his head or a look of his eyes. I had personally never once spoken a word to him, but I could feel his energy, as could everyone around him, like the two assholes who were in the section next to him. I noticed how they kept their distance, but they watched and whispered about him like the women did. It was odd.

When I paid attention, I noticed he didn't say much to anyone, but he was attentive to everything around him. It was weird in a sense. His presence was a complete contradiction to the other deep pockets that came out to play. They were loud and flashy, attempting to be seen while he barely moved or opened his mouth. The crazy thing was people were drawn to him while the loud and obnoxious were overlooked.

I didn't understand why he had chosen to keep the women at bay who were vying for his attention, but it pissed them off. Men came to the club for a specific reason—women who aimed to please as long as the price was right. If I had to summarize the place, it was like a modern-day brothel. The establishment had two floors. The social club was on the first level, and private rooms were below us. Some women were employed by Cal, the owner, to take care of the clientele who were willing to pay extra for "platinum treatment," but there were also those who showed up with the hopes of being chosen, such as the two women who had arrived the same time I'd showed up late for work. They would look pretty eager to be hand selected by one of these men with deep pockets.

I knew the rules of that place. The black cards with gold writing meant paid memberships to mingle with the rich and elite, such as the *Recluse*. That was what I'd named him.

"I need another bottle," one of the two men who summoned me demanded as soon as I reached their private section. He was medium height and handsome in a generic way, but he was dressed in an expensive suit. They all wore clothes that cost me more than a month's earnings. I'd officially dubbed him as an asshole because the demand for another bottle left his lips as if he had rights to me and my time, like I wasn't worthy of respect.

Plastering on my fake smile, I nodded. "What kind?"

They'd had several throughout the night—champagne, imported Cognac, and aged wine.

His eyes moved from my face down my body, covered in a black form-fitting dress. The front was cut low and the back even lower, exposing skin down to the area just above my ass. Like I said, my job was to look the part.

Seconds later, he moved the woman from his lap and was on his feet. I wasn't allowed time to react before he was on me. My body landed hard against his to the point where I needed his frame to keep me steady until I regained my balance. His hands moved to my ass, and his lips brushed my ear.

"I want to fuck you. I'll pay whatever you want to agree. You get a commission from what I buy, right?"

My body flooded with anger, and I pushed away. Without thinking, my hand landed across his face with so much force that my palm stung immediately after the impact.

His jaw flexed, and he returned the favor by allowing his large hand to connect with the left side of my face before I felt his vise grip around my neck.

I gasped, and my eyes fluttered, but seconds later, they focused on Joey. He was at the man's side with a gun pressed to his temple.

"Let her go—now."

Asshole did as he was told, and the second I was free, Joey flipped the gun in his hand, and it crashed against the side of the man's face. The blow was so forceful that it brought him to his knees.

My eyes doubled in size as I watched what was happening. Two other men appeared, aggressively grabbing ahold of Asshole and his shadow, who'd sprung to his feet as if he planned on defending his friend. It wasn't until then that I noticed Recluse was now nearby. He moved so smoothly that it was as if he glided. His eyes fastened to mine briefly before he reached Joey and spoke lowly. Joey nodded and motioned for both men to be released.

Once they were free, Recluse offered a look that had Asshole and his buddy dropping their eyes. They had somehow pissed him off. He hadn't spoken one word, but something was communicated between them because Asshole and his sidekick hurried out of the section.

Recluse approached me, standing inches away. I should've been alarmed after being assaulted by Asshole, but there was something about him that put me at ease. He wasn't like the two men who'd just left. I instantly felt dwarfed by his height, which wasn't normal because, at five foot nine, I was tall for a woman. He stood six feet plus and had strong arms, a wide chest, and broad shoulders. His dark eyes were serious as they fastened to mine, and my God, that man was gorgeous in a way that I had never seen in a man before. His face was angular, with a strong jaw, and covered in a sheen of inky black hair. It looked slick like oil and matched the organized mass of curls that sprouted from his head. The sides were faded low and lined up clean, giving the appearance that he'd seen his barber that very day. However, the most impressive thing about him at the moment was those lips of his. They were the kind I dreamed about grazing my body while exploring my most intimate parts.

Ten seconds, a minute, a whole year might've passed before he eventually moved, and it was to place his large hand on my chin. He gripped it carefully, being mindful that Asshole had just hit me. Tilting my face slightly to the right, the man examined my features, and his eyes went from relaxed to hard with lightning speed in some kind of shift. I could see the fury behind those serious eyes. He was angry.

"I apologize. He will never step foot in here or anywhere else you are ever again."

The words were eerie and confusing. That was the only place I would ever see the asshole. We ran in different circles. I couldn't imagine being fortunate enough to frequent the same places as him. He might not have been nice, but he was indeed rich.

Recluse stepped away before I could fully process it, moving past Joey and sauntering through the club. I couldn't help but watch as his long legs carried him toward the entrance. His stride was confident. The man moved with purpose, and the funny thing was, it appeared effortless. It wasn't as if he tried. He just existed in all his glory, pulling the attention of everyone he passed, both men and women.

"Hey, you okay?" Joey's tone was low, his eyes soft and apologetic as if it were somehow his fault that Asshole hit me.

"Yeah, I'm good, but what about this? I need my money and can't afford to go in the hole over their tab."

He searched my face for a minute before nodding. "You won't. It's covered."

"How? They left."

"Don't worry about it. The bill is covered, including your tip." Joey stared at me, something moving behind his eyes before he looked toward the door. I sensed he wasn't happy, but I didn't have time to worry about it. I needed to finish my shift and then find somewhere to rest my head tonight. It would likely be a hotel, but that could only be temporary. Unfortunately, I couldn't worry about it now. I had a job to do.

CHAPTER 2

KINCAID.

"What's on your mind?" Aila stared at me with those curious eyes, a look I'd grown accustomed to. I searched her face, trying to decide if I would go through with my plan. I didn't love her, but I did care about her. She would be devastated because, regardless of how little she had rights to my heart, I wholly owned hers.

"Just business," I assured. It was a lie, something I prided myself on avoiding; however, it was necessary and befitting in that situation. Everything about us, our connection, our future . . . was a lie.

"Business," she scoffed after repeating my response, a frown marring her beautiful face. "I know you, Caid. That look in your eyes is not connected to business. It's much heavier than money. What's bothering you?"

Massaging my chin, I lifted my eyes to the corner of the room where my father and hers were puffing on cigars. My mother was at one of her many society or committee meetings, and I was grateful because, had she been here, she and Aila would have been huddled up talking a mile a minute about the wedding they were planning.

Our wedding.

I was annoyed because Aila shouldn't have been here. My father requested I stop by to discuss a few things with him. He informed me that Jabari Kaber, her father, would be in attendance, and I was sure that Aila begged to tag along, hoping to grab a minute of my time. I had been distant over the past few weeks under the guise of being overloaded with business. It was easy for her to accept the explanation as the reason for my absence because I was constantly traveling from one country to the next, either for my corporations or to meet with the underworld that my family had ties to. Changes were happening that were only being whispered about, but we could all feel them.

Either way, she still disliked the distance. We were six months into our courtship and months away from the wedding. The deal was brokered to blend our families, and the closer we drew to the date, the more anxious I became. Marrying a woman I didn't love was a small sacrifice compared to what it would mean for both of our families. The union would give us power like no other, and my father and hers were eagerly looking forward to the merger. I shared the same sentiment at one point, but things had drastically changed in recent weeks.

"It's not important." I stood and kissed her cheek. "I have to go, but I'll see you tonight."

"Wait, you're leaving?" Aila was on her feet in a matter of seconds. The disapproval etched on her pretty face didn't bother me as much as it should've. I cared about her, and had our circumstances been different, I could've possibly learned to love her. She was a genuinely good person, but because her father was stuck in the middle of a complicated situation, she had no idea that the only reason I asked her to marry me was due to a private business deal brokered between our fathers.

I refused to break her heart that way but realized there was no avoiding the detriment. At some point, I'd have to explain why

I wouldn't be her husband. Aila would be devastated, and her father would be furious, but I didn't care. After what I'd learned, my mind was made up. Kaber had been lying to me and my father. He was in debt beyond recovery and was at risk of losing control of his businesses. Not only was he a financial liability, but his relationship with the underworld was also strained. Over the past three years, our families' business was handled solely through me, which was part of the reason my father had no clue about what I'd recently discovered.

The other missing piece was that The Families didn't share details about those they were connected to. If there was an issue, it was handled privately. Sometimes, relationships were severed, and the parties were never spoken of again. Other times, lives ended. I'd witnessed it over the years. Kaber was also aware of that minor detail, which was why he assumed I wouldn't find out that he was a sinking ship. Merging our families would dump his debt on my father, and I refused to allow that to happen. My insider knowledge about Kaber came from someone who wasn't affiliated with The Families, but after a little digging, I verified the information.

"I have a few things to do before I see you later. I wasn't expecting you to be here."

"It can't wait . . ." Her eyes softened. ". . . whatever you have scheduled for today?"

"No, but you'll see me tonight." I pulled Aila to me, delivering a kiss that time to her lips. She relaxed against me until we heard her father's voice.

"Easy, son. She might be your future wife, but she's still my baby," Kaber teased as he and my father approached. Aila blushed, tucking her body at her father's side. She was a daddy's girl after losing her mother before her tenth birthday.

"Daddy, I'm grown."

"You are, sweetheart, but you'll always be my baby." He kissed her cheek, and my pulse thumped. I hated that she was attached to this man. I would protect her as best I could, but I refused to do so by giving her my last name. Her father was a liar who was willing to proxy his daughter to save his ass. She had no idea of the disloyalty. I was sure he loved her, but he loved himself more. He thrived off power, and if handing over his only child to a man he knew didn't love her was the price he had to pay to hold on to that power, then he was going to push for our union.

"I know, Daddy."

"It was good to see you, Kaber." I tossed my chin to him before turning to my father. "I'll see you this weekend."

"I'll walk you out."

I nodded, and my father and I moved through his home toward the front, stopping in the massive foyer just in front of the door. "You okay?"

"Yeah. Why?"

"Not sure. You seem off like something's bothering you. Is it the marriage? You having second thoughts?"

"I'm good, old man. Stop worrying."

He studied my face a few moments longer. "Kincaid, I know what I'm asking of you. Marrying Aila isn't ideal, but it will be good for us. With Akel and Kaber merging as one, we're unstoppable."

"We're unstoppable without him," I made clear without saying too much. My father's face drew in with concern before he smiled.

"True, but this makes it that much better."

I refused to speak on the matter until I had everything in place. That would take a few days. When I had the solid proof I needed to hand over to my father, I would end this charade permanently.

"Later, Pop." I wouldn't agree or disagree. I simply left. As soon as I was in my car, I felt a migraine inching close. I had been having them more frequently over the past few weeks. They were caused by stress, which was also why I wasn't sleeping well. The deal between Kaber and my father had me unsettled, and I wouldn't be at peace until I put an end to this bullshit.

The drive across town seemed to take a lot longer than expected. Maybe it was because the man I was about to see had my blood boiling, and I was ready to draw his. As I moved through the dimly lit building, my fists clenched at my sides, causing my knuckles to crack. I instantly thought of my mother. It was a bad habit of mine—one she hated and wished she could break.

As soon as I pushed through the door, all eyes were on me. I unbuttoned my suit jacket and handed it over to Cast. He was considered my muscle and the first call I made when I needed an extra set of hands.

I walked to the center of the room, standing erect with perfect posture, feet shoulder-width apart and arms folded across my chest. Both men's nervous eyes lifted to me, but neither said a word.

"Do you know why you're here, Mr. Gains?" I addressed the one who had physically assaulted the woman I now knew was named Nari Collette.

It had been a week since the night at the club, and for that entire week, the man who felt bold enough to put his hands on her and his buddy had been there at my establishment with no water or food. That had been more circumstantial than intentional. The morning after I left the club, Cast picked them up. I had to fly out of town on business, so I couldn't handle it personally like I'd wanted. I was gone for four days and then left on a day trip to Miami to handle another business matter. Because of the lapse in time, both men were severely dehydrated and weak.

"I didn't mean to put my hands on her. It was a mistake," Gains mumbled lowly. His head hung before and after he spoke because he didn't have enough strength to hold it steady.

"It wasn't a mistake; it was a choice. You *chose* to put your hands on a woman who hadn't done a damn thing to you. Your arrogance or possibly your inebriated state fueled your ego, and that made you feel as if you had the right to assault her."

My eyes bounced over to his buddy. "And you, Mr. Taylor, do you know why *you're* here?"

"I didn't touch that woman, so no."

I smirked and stared as his eyes were at war with mine. He was angry but more than anything . . . afraid. They were both aware of who I was. It was why they left without argument that night.

"You might as well have since you were in the process of defending the man who assaulted Ms. Collette."

"You know this isn't sanctioned. We work for Manchester." Gains decided to try his hand at an idle threat.

"And that means what? You're allowed to assault women under his protection? Fuck him and you. If he wants to address the issue, he knows how to find me."

Taylor's eyes drifted. His fate had been determined just as Gains's had. One thing I didn't tolerate was disrespect to women. It was a sore point for me.

I glanced at Cast, who reached behind his back and removed a nine millimeter with a silencer affixed. It was at that very moment that both men had a clear understanding of how this would end.

"Come on, Kincaid. I fucked up. I didn't mean anything by it. Let me fix it. I'll apologize and make it right."

The fact that he was now begging for his life irritated me even more. Part of being a man was accepting responsibility for your actions. Whatever that fate may be, you face it head-on. Groveling was for the weak. I hated that shit.

As soon as I took possession of the gun, Gains's eyes grew wide while Taylor began to sniffle. He was fucking crying. That had the gun aimed at his head first, and my finger tugged at the trigger. One shot and his body permanently slumped.

"Kincaid, please, just—"

Before Gains could complete the request, I'd fired my second shot. I didn't flinch, nor did I feel any remorse. They'd both chosen their fate, which wasn't on me but on them.

"What about the girl?" Cast asked as I approached and traded the gun for my jacket. I slipped my arms through the sleeves, fastening the two buttons before tugging at the front.

"What about her?"

He grinned, staring at me for a long moment before turning back. He placed the gun on a workstation lining the closet wall before he lifted coveralls and began stepping into them.

"You tell me." He turned, tugging at the zipper, and then grabbed a gurney, which was covered with a thick layer of plastic. He focused on what he was doing while waiting for me to answer. I knew what he was asking.

I'd given explicit instructions to track down Gains and Taylor after I collected the car's plate number they drove off in. Cast never asked one question. He simply did as he was told and notified me when he had them both. While I was in Chicago, I gave him instructions to pull up on Joey, security, who worked at Salacious, in search of a name and any other information he had on the woman who had been assaulted that night. Cast made clear that Joey wasn't very forthcoming at first but ended up handing over her name, cell number, and schedule. He only had one request, and that was that she go unharmed. His exact words were, *"Tell Kincaid she's a good girl. Not the type to be caught up in the shit he's involved in."*

That was amusing. No one had factual information about what I was caught up in. Joey pushed pills that we supplied, so he had a little insight. Most speculated, and some of what they assumed was true, but nothing could be proved about me or my family. That was by design. We were careful and also protected by years of good business and loyalty to The Families. I respected his concern but didn't give a fuck about what he thought of me or my dealings with Nari Collette. At the moment, none existed, but I wanted to know more about her. She quickly became my obsession after how she looked at me or rather through me that night.

It wasn't my first time seeing her. I'd been to Salacious enough to cross paths with the brown-skinned beauty, but that was the first interaction I'd ever had, and it was one I couldn't wrap my mind around. I felt something odd but welcoming between us, and how she looked at me was unexplainable.

"Tell you what . . ."

Cast removed a hunting knife from the pocket of his coveralls and cut through the zip ties that fastened each man's arms behind their backs and lifted them one by one with ease, tossing their dead, weighted bodies on the gurney. I wasn't surprised by how easy he made it look. Cast was a large man. He was a few inches taller than my six-four frame, but his body was damn near twice the size of mine, and I was pretty damn solid.

"You had me track her down. You just killed two of Manchester's guys because they roughed her up a little. I've followed her for a week while you were gone, all for what?"

I shrugged, my face slipping into a relaxed state, barely exposing a smile. "I don't know. Haven't thought that far ahead."

"Well, you need to."

"Are you telling me what I need to do now?"

"When it means I miss time with women whose specific goal is to please me in every way possible, then, hell yeah, I'm telling you what to do. Figure something out, Caid."

I chuckled at his irritated state. Cast worked for me, but he was also a friend—one of two men I claimed as such. In my line of work, there was little to no trust. Keeping bodies around was risky and something I never did.

"Let me get back to you on that. Right now, I have a meeting, and then I have dinner with Aila and her annoying-ass friends."

Cast chuckled, knowing I hated those damn dinner parties, and Aila seemed to make it a regular occurrence. It was her way of showing me off to her people. She wanted to rub their noses in the fact that she had caught the uncatchable Kincaid Akel.

"So what about the girl?"

"She works tonight. Your babysitting duties are put on hold, at least for tonight," I spoke with amusement while Cast grunted and crossed the room to fire up the cremation chamber. I checked my wrist, realizing I needed to get going or I would be late. There was no need for me to announce my departure. I didn't report to anyone or explain my moves. As much of a friend as I considered Cast, he knew his role and never overstepped. He worked for me and was only privy to the information I provided when I felt it necessary.

My next stop was an office downtown, on the tenth floor of a building I owned. Saulo Perez and Kafi Aku were waiting in one of the conference rooms. Both arrived with security posted up on either side of the door, but I wasn't alarmed. They were always guarded. Saulo and Kafi were heads of The Families, a union of five families of different organizations from five countries who were all tied to an illegal underworld. They worked in tandem to keep order so that no one entity grew in a way that dominated. It upset the balance of things when power was tilted in one direction or the other. Every member had a lot of blood on their hands because of the sacrifices made to maintain the power held between its members. My family had blood on their hands as well, but my sins weren't as egregious as theirs.

"Gentlemen," I greeted in generic form. Saulo stood first, offering a hand. I shook it and then moved to Kafi, who was now on his feet. We shook hands as well, but he embraced me in a brotherly hug.

"Good to see you, Kincaid," Kafi said before returning to his seat.

"Same. I am, however, curious as to what this is about."

They shared a look before Saulo began to speak.

"Your wedding to Aila ... Has anything changed?"

"Why would anything have changed?"

"We're not saying it has; just looking for clarity on the matter."

I stared at them both for a long moment, my expression neutral before I responded.

"I understand that family is important. You've pressed the issue of me taking a wife since my twenty-fifth birthday. I wasn't ready then, but I am now."

The Families had an unspoken rule that family played a role in how everyone operated. Single men moved differently. They had less of an investment when their only responsibility was to themselves. It was a harsh reality, but it was encouraged that anyone connected to The Families had familial liabilities. Husbands with wives and children were more manageable. They had investments that were valued far beyond the net worth of their business dealings. Families also meant heirs to the thrones, which kept a close-knit commitment to loyalty that remained intact throughout generations.

"Indeed. We value marital unions because they keep our ties pure, but unfortunately, that doesn't always solve the problem.

Some just aren't built to handle the privilege and responsibility of being connected."

"I'm not sure I understand where this is going." I needed clarity. I had never been one to dance around what was important.

"Considering what you now know about Kaber, will you follow through with the wedding to his daughter?"

I frowned, my eyes bouncing between both men as I leaned back, extending my legs a little wider for comfort before resting both hands in my lap.

"What is it that you think I know about Kaber?" It felt off. Two bosses from the controlling families came here to ask me about marrying Aila Kaber. That wasn't a standard practice.

"Let me be transparent," Kafi began, his thick Yoruba accent heavy on his tongue. "The proposed union poses an issue for us. The Families have all decided that Kaber is a liability. This isn't typically a conversation we would have—"

"So then, why are you here?"

"Because we hope to change the course of things. It works not only in your favor but ours as well if you back out of the deal with Kaber."

I was extremely uncomfortable with the conversation, which Saulo must've sensed, because he clarified, "Our loyalty is to those who are loyal to us, son. Do you understand what I'm saying?"

"Possibly." I knew exactly what he was saying. He and Kafi were there to express their loyalty to me and my family over Kaber and his.

"You're a man of honor. I would assume that you will follow through with the deal off principle alone. I respect that quality about you. It's why we want to intervene and prevent you from making a terrible mistake."

I'm not marrying her, so fuck principle, but I'll hear you out.

"How? The contract is solid. My lawyer combed through every detail."

"The contract you signed *is* solid; however, there is one loophole."

"And how would you know what I signed?" I felt my nostrils flare.

"I know because he used it as leverage to broker deals behind your back based on his pending merger with your family." Kafi reached inside his jacket pocket and removed a document. It was thick, several pages, which he unfolded and placed on the table, pressing a finger against the paperwork. He then moved them across the table in my direction. I lifted the document, realizing it was the contract I'd signed with Kaber—one my lawyer had thoroughly reviewed.

"It's not the original, only a copy that was obtained by someone we trust after being informed that Kaber presented it as collateral, knowing that your family's name gained him an advantage."

That was news to me. I was privy to the fact that Kaber was in debt but had no idea he was using my family's name in this capacity.

"You didn't know," Kafi spoke with confidence, telling, not asking.

"No."

"As it stands, based on the agreement, if you don't marry Aila, you lose your standing with The Families. Kaber and his poor decisions become yours by affiliation alone. You've considered reneging on the deal, but what you haven't considered is that if you don't marry Aila, you lose controlling interest in everything your family owns, and Kaber takes over in your place."

"So, what's the loophole? How do I walk away from this without marrying Aila and not lose everything?"

"You marry someone else."

I frowned at the idea. It didn't make sense to me.

"I marry someone else?"

"Yes, anyone you choose. We can assist in arranging a union if you would prefer, but you're free to choose whoever you wish. The wording is specific. It states that *you* are to be married within a year of the signed agreement. It does not state *who* you're required to marry. That was understood by both your family and his. If I had to guess, he was attempting to ensure that if the documents surfaced, Aila wouldn't find out that she had been sold to the highest bidder. On his end, it could easily be explained away by the fact that it's an unspoken requirement for you to take a wife and that she was your choice—an egregious error in judgment on Kaber's part. I'm sure he hasn't realized that his attempt to cover his ass left him open to you gaining an advantage. It does not say you have to marry *Aila* specifically within the year, only that you be *married* within a year."

"As long as you're married before the date, you've held up your end of the deal as an honorable member of The Families. Kafi and I make the call, so when it is brought to our attention, we will make clear that you met all requirements and that your family is protected. There's a target on his back. If you marry his daughter, that target lands on your family's backs as well."

"Why not just get rid of him?"

"He's made some bad decisions, but shedding the blood of one of our own without just cause is frowned upon. It's always been blood for blood, which isn't the case here. If we open the door to senseless murders becoming acceptable, then we set the stage for those affiliated to become vigilantes. Kaber will simply be removed, all ties severed, and he's on his own. What happens to him moving forward is no longer our responsibility once the decision is official."

"How can I trust your word?"

"You're a good man, Kincaid. You've always been honorable and smart, and we value your family's commitment to the syndicate. It only felt right to prevent you from suffering at the hand of Kaber."

"Who else knows about this?"

"All The Families know about the marriage. Kafi and I are the only ones who know that we're giving you an out. This remains between us, regardless of what you decide."

"Is that all?"

I stood, letting them know that I was done with the discussion. Kafi and Saulo shared a look before they were both on their feet.

"Yes, yes, that's all. We appreciate you making time to see us today." Kafi was the first to extend a hand, which I shook, and like before, he pulled me into a hug before Saulo extended a hand, which I also shook.

"If you will, please let us know what you decide," were Saulo's parting words.

With a nod, I offered my promise to do so, and they left. I stood, staring into blank space for what felt like an eternity before I lifted the same chair I'd occupied during the meeting with Kafi and Saulo and hurled it across the room. It crashed against the wall, denting the space before landing hard on the floor. I had some decisions to make. I didn't like the fact that I'd left myself open to this type of fuckup, which meant that my moves from here on out had to be a lot less careless.

A few hours later, I found myself struggling. Dinner with Aila and her friends was like suffering through nails on a chalkboard. The reasoning was mostly centered around my mind being preoccupied with other thoughts. Things that felt more like a priority. I needed time to think about what Saulo and Kafi had presented, but every second my mind drifted, my thoughts were interrupted by some pointless interference from Aila or her friends.

That night, it had been Dr. Angela Bowen and her husband, whose name I couldn't recall. She was the breadwinner while he struggled to maintain a bar and grill that she gifted him to keep him out of her hair and fill his time. That much I remembered because the shit was so ridiculous. He was meek and allowed his wife to lead. In just the few hours that I was around them, I knew that she was the man of the house.

It was laughable, and I never would allow myself to be forced into the submissive role that he carried. I had no issue with the woman I chose to be by my side having her own or even earning more than me; however, a man should still be allowed to be a man. In the simplest terms, a man should be the leader of his home. *That man* was definitely *not* in a position of power regarding his role in their union.

After suffering through a meal, wine, and conversation, I cut the evening short by telling Aila that something had come up. She was angry but refused to allow her feelings to show in front of her guests. Not that I would have cared either way, but it did allow me an out without hurting her feelings any more than I already had.

If she would've attempted to argue, I would've shut her down. That was something I did not do. My word was final, which I always made clear, but she occasionally challenged me. It couldn't be helped. Aila was spoiled, considering her father allowed the open space for her to manipulate his emotions to compensate for her mother's absence. I wasn't Kaber and couldn't be manipulated. She had tried and failed many times before and eventually learned not to waste her time.

My original plan was to head to my penthouse in the city after I left; however, once I was in my car, I found myself driving in a completely different direction. Amongst all the weighted thoughts in my mind, *she* managed to shut them down, taking priority over everything else that consumed me. It was why I ended up in the parking lot of Salacious, contemplating my next move. I had no idea what the hell I would say, but I was there . . . and so was she.

CHAPTER 3

NARI.

The night had been terrible. There was no other way to explain the catastrophes that transpired as the night passed. One client complained, stating that I refused to give him the requested section, which, in his words, he had reserved before his arrival. That would have to be done online, and somehow, he blamed me when his reservation didn't show. He'd called for the manager, and when Cal surfaced, eager to please, he allowed the man to verbally demean me in front of all within earshot about my incompetence. He accused me of deleting his reservation, to which Cal refused to defend, knowing good and damn well there was no way in hell I could've done such a thing. He then comped the client for the evening, which meant no commission or tips off his section. Not only that, but Cal also gave me a verbal lashing about how I was to never argue with a customer. They were always right.

Bullshit!

The next issue I had was two women who reserved a section, found deep pockets, and dipped out with the men without paying their tab. Usually, cards are kept on file, but the women didn't have memberships. They only paid to enter that evening, so Cal blamed me for allowing them to leave and deducted the two bottles of overpriced champagne from my earnings.

Now, add on my third and final straw, which was some dickhead who seemed to think that it was okay to put his hands on me since I was dressed the way I was. He owned a technology company that grossed multimillion-dollar government contracts, so, in his eyes, he could afford to pay for the disrespect if I complained. He literally said that he could buy me.

My fists balled at my sides, but I kept a smile on my face, nodded, and walked away. I needed this job. It paid exceptionally well, and the tips were icing on the cake. In the past week, I'd taken home a little over a grand in tips, and in another week, I would receive my check, which was another two grand. We had a base pay since the clientele tipped so high. Cal was smart. He would never allow too much to slip through his hands, but every woman who worked the floor could easily clear five to ten grand a month after probation. My issue was that I was still on probation, which meant that I could be fired at any moment, and 50 percent of everything I earned, tips included, remained in Cal's pocket. It was bullshit, but I kept my head low and stayed out of the way because after my ninety days were up, I could afford to get my own place, a car, and create some normalcy in my life. I had never planned on making my living arrangements with Shayla a forever thing. We simply needed each other. Only she fucked me over before I had the chance to walk away.

Family was bullshit. I didn't have any, didn't need any, and would never claim any if it meant dealing with people like Shayla. I also made a vow that if I ever saw her again, only God could save her from the fury that I would unleash.

"Nari?"

My eyes slammed shut as I heard my name just as I bent the corner to cross through the main area of the club to leave. It was after two a.m., I was exhausted, my feet hurt, and I had a terrible fucking night.

Exhaling a short breath, I turned slowly to see what in the world Cal could possibly want.

"Yes?" I seethed internally but forced a tight-lipped smile. Cal grinned suspiciously as his eyes swept my body. I lifted my phone, noticing I had eight minutes before my ride would be pulling up.

"Joey's gone—family emergency. I'll walk you out. I wanted to talk to you about a few things." I think he sensed that I wasn't in the mood, so he created a reason to be in my personal space. I'd heard stories about Cal from the women who worked there. Several had given me a warning after I was hired; however, since I'd been there, he'd been professional. A little bit anal and rude from time to time, but never had he crossed any lines that made me feel uncomfortable. I prayed that wasn't changing tonight.

He traveled from the hallway that led from his office, nearing my side. I wasn't in the mood but didn't want to rock the boat. The job paid well, and it really wasn't that bad. That night had just been an off night. Cal and I walked to the front of the building, and he pushed the door open, allowing me to exit first. Just as we stepped outside, he got to the point.

"You have another thirty days before you're a permanent hire. I like you a lot. You work hard and keep your nose clean."

"Is there an issue?"

"No, I just want to make sure we understand each other." Cal flashed a smile. He was handsome: midthirties, jet-black hair, decent height, medium build. He had Italian features, which gave him tanned skin and amber eyes. He just wasn't my type.

"I work, you pay me; what more is there to understand?" My body tensed because I felt the bullshit coming. He stepped closer and toyed with a piece of my hair, twirling the coil around his finger.

"In simple terms, that *is* our deal, but . . ."

"Nari . . ."

A deep voice calling my name startled me and interrupted whatever Cal was about to say. I squinted into the darkness of the parking lot, which was now basically empty, aside from the vehicles of the handful of employees who were still inside finishing their closing routines.

The crazy thing was that I could feel him before he stepped out of the shadows, allowing the light from the club to illuminate his face. He stood tall, covered in a suit similar to the one from the other night. His hands were submerged in the pockets of his slacks, and he had a scowl on his face. Silence lingered between the three of us. I knew that Cal was still beside me simply because I was aware of his presence; however, that man I could *feel*. His energy wrapped around me like a blanket.

"Kincaid, we're closed for the night." *His name is Kincaid.* Cal was the first to slice through the awkward tension, but that didn't grant him acknowledgment. With his head tilted to the side, he stared at me with an intensity that made me want to focus on anything *but* him. I was eventually blessed with his voice, but his eyes never left me.

"I'm aware. I'm here to ensure Ms. Collette makes it home safely this evening, and based on the looks of things, I'm right on time." There was a double meaning there. It wasn't just about him showing up in time to catch me leaving. He sensed something was brewing between Cal and me.

Just as he finished explaining his reasoning for being there, my ride pulled in front of the building. The silver Honda was at Kincaid's back because his body was positioned in a way that prevented the car from parking close to the curb.

My eyes darted to the left, where Cal stood with the displeasure of being interrupted plastered all over his face. He looked past Kincaid first before he gave me his attention.

"That's your ride, Nari," he spoke as if concerned when seconds before, I was sure he was about to proposition me with some offer that would threaten my job if I refused.

"So it is," I mumbled, tone flat as I stepped off the curb.

"Tell them to leave." Kincaid's tone was even, but there was no way to miss the command underneath the surface.

"Excuse me?"

His regard remained on Cal for a moment longer before he turned toward my ride. His knuckles rapped against the passenger's window, waiting for it to lower, and when it did, he spoke to the driver, who nodded and then proceeded to leave.

"Hey, wait, what the hell?"

"You can go now, Calvetti. She's in good hands." Kincaid ignored me and spoke to Cal. The crazy thing was that Cal didn't say a damn word when I knew he wanted to. The muscles in his jaw twitched, but he just walked back inside the club without addressing the fact that the man had basically dismissed him.

"What the hell was that?" I pointed in the direction that my ride had just gone, and Kincaid's spine straightened, but his eyes never left me, their weight lingering as if it were a physical connection. A thickness grew between us while we maintained a silent standoff.

"What were you discussing with Calvetti?"

My eyes snapped to his. "Nothing."

His teeth raked across his bottom lip, and I visually followed the motion before I moved about his frame from head to toe, taking him in. His body was stiff with tension, which I didn't understand.

"His hand was in your hair, and you seemed guarded and uncomfortable. What did he say to you?"

I frowned slightly. *How the hell did he notice all of that?*

Tugging at the straps of my tote, I focused on my phone, needing something to distract and anchor me. The man was intense, and for some reason, I felt a pull to him that I couldn't understand. As intimidating as he seemed, I wasn't afraid. I felt safe in his presence, but regardless, I needed some space.

"Cal isn't an issue. The fact that you sent my ride away is." I fumbled through my phone, pulling up my rideshare app, but my fingers froze when he spoke again.

"I'll take you." He paused briefly before continuing, and I assumed it was because he wanted my full attention. The minute my eyes fastened to his, he finished his thought. "Wherever you need to go."

My eyes squinted, tracing the features of his face. "I don't know you."

"But you want to." His hands moved out of his pockets, a slow grin making its way onto his face while his arms folded across his solid chest. "And you trust me, regardless of what you don't know."

"No, actually, I don't." It was a lie. I did trust him, and that bothered me. How could I trust someone I didn't know a damn thing about? Something was going on between us that I couldn't make sense of. I felt like I'd known that man my entire life. I could feel him, and he could feel me, and not in a physical sense. It was our energy. Something between us that I couldn't ignore. Apparently, he couldn't either.

"You're hungry. We can eat before I take you home." His demand flowed with ease. He wasn't leaving room for me to reject the offer, and like an insane person, I stepped off the curb, nearing him.

"I have mace."

He chuckled, motioning to a corner of the parking lot. It was too dark to see what he was identifying, but I assumed it was his car. "Of course you do. I'm over there."

His motion didn't start until I took my first two steps. That placed him slightly behind me until we reached a black sports car, and Kincaid stepped around me to open the door, motioning for me to get in. While he shut my door and rounded the rear of the vehicle, my body instantly relaxed into the soft leather seats. I wouldn't bother asking what kind, but I didn't have to ask to know the vehicle was expensive. It wasn't until that moment that I was reminded of how exhausted I truly was.

"Where would you like to go?"

My brow arched as I watched him start the vehicle with one of his long fingers. When I didn't respond, his eyes traveled my way.

"I assumed you had that all mapped out."

Again, he chuckled before backing out of the space he was in. "No, actually, none of this was planned. I just showed up."

"Why?" I frowned, and another question popped into my head. "And how the hell do you know my name? My *full* name?"

"I'm a resourceful man. I wanted your name, and it was provided to me."

"So then we're back to why."

"Which one?"

"Excuse me?"

His eyes met mine. "Why I showed up, or why I wanted your name?"

My eyes rolled, and a smile tugged at his lips. It was sinful and tempting. "Both."

"Do you want the truth?"

"Yes." My response was firm.

"That night a week ago, something felt different when you looked at me. I couldn't wrap my mind around it, so I decided to try again to see if it was simply a moment or something more."

"Was it?"

"I don't know. You tell me," he spoke low, his voice filled with force. I chose not to admit what he already knew. It wasn't just a moment. I felt it now, and so did he.

"It's late. Where are we going? There's not much open."

"I know a place."

I nodded and turned toward the window; however, I could feel his eyes on me. I refused to meet them and, instead, focused on the city that seemed to pass by in a blur. We were silent for the rest of the drive, but I was content with the silence. We drove for under an hour, and he spoke after pulling up to a stand-alone building in an area I wasn't familiar with.

"They have breakfast. I figured that would work." I looked through the windshield and then around the parking lot. There were a few other vehicles, and the building was bright from the inside. I could see the faces of those who occupied a few tables and booths.

"Yep, this works."

With a nod, he stepped out of the car and approached me. I had the door open before he could open it, but he extended a hand and kept his eyes on my face while he helped me stand. I was grateful he wasn't a creep checking me out because my dress was so short and had eased up a little too high.

We walked in, and all eyes were on us, or rather him, I was sure. The staff smiled and ushered us to a booth in the back. Seconds later, a young woman was in place taking our drink orders. I had orange juice; Kincaid requested water. He suggested items for me to choose from, and when I asked what he was having, he stated he wasn't hungry. I didn't want to eat alone, so he agreed on a single stack and cheese eggs after I insisted he eat with me. I could tell he didn't want to, but I didn't care.

Not long after our food arrived, I immediately went to work. The waffles were thick and fluffy, the maple syrup was sweet, and my eggs were cooked to perfection. Kincaid had barely touched his food by the time I finished half of mine, but I didn't mind because it didn't feel as awkward with him having food in front of him while I enjoyed my meal.

"How long have you worked at Salacious?"

My eyes lifted from my plate, reaching his. "You don't already know?"

He was amused because I was blessed with a smile. Those things should've come with a warning label. *Caution: these smiles can totally disarm you.*

"No, I don't. I've seen you there a few times. The first being about a month ago."

"Two months."

He nodded as if processing my answer.

"And before then, what did you do?"

"Nothing worth talking about; basically, whatever paid the bills."

Something flickered in his eyes before he nodded again. "How old are you, Nari?"

"How old are you?" I fired back.

"Thirty-one," he answered confidently, so I returned the favor.

"Twenty-four." I examined him a little more.

"You're always in a suit, and they're expensive. What do you do?"

He hesitated for a minute, and I could see him thinking. I had already picked up on that being his thing. Each word he spoke was well thought out and even calculated.

"I invest in failing businesses, mostly hotels, restaurants, and a few clubs. I have my hands in a few other things as well."

"So you're rich?"

"I'm comfortable."

I snorted, lowering my eyes just a bit. "Why am I here? Clearly, we're mismatched. I've seen the type of women who approach you at the club. Not that you ever really give them the time of day, but one thing's for certain . . . They're not me."

"No, they're definitely not you. You're making the comparison as if to say they're somehow a better option."

I laughed lightly, shoving a forkful of eggs in my mouth. I was far from insecure. That wasn't my issue. I was intelligent, beautiful, and had a world of potential; however, I lacked the opportunities that would allow me to blossom. I simply knew that this man sitting across from me could easily attract the finished product, so why would he waste his time with a work in progress? That was basically what I was.

"Something funny, Nari?"

"Yeah, actually, a lot is amusing about this situation. You and I don't fit."

"You sure about that?"

"Positive."

"I'd have to disagree." His voice took on a new tone, lowering an octave while expressing an affinity to what he expressed.

"I'm not for sale," I blurted out. I wasn't sure why, but it seemed to be the only thing that made sense. I was working at the club, and he was snooping around, asking about me. Maybe he wanted to broker a side deal and assumed I would be down.

His cheeks hiked, and his eyes flickered with amusement. "You might not be for sale, but everyone has a price, Ms. Collette. It's something I learned early in life and one of the reasons why I'm so successful."

"Wow." My fork dropped to my plate, the metal clanging hard against the cheap china. "You can go now. I'll find my way home."

His eyes turned serious and dark. "Did I offend you?"

I snorted, tilting my head to the side. "You just basically said that you could buy me. What the hell is with you assholes who have deep pockets? Not every woman will open her legs for money. I damn sure won't."

"That's not what I meant, and I apologize if that's what you understood my words to mean."

"You just said that everyone has a price."

"I didn't, however, say that in reference to a price for sexual favors. I don't have to pay for sex."

"But you do. You have a membership to Salacious." It was something I couldn't understand. That man could have all types of sex with all types of women. I was sure of it, and anyone who was blessed enough to lay eyes on him would agree.

"I don't *have* to pay for sex. I choose to. Sometimes, I need a release without attachment. The women at Salacious understand their role, and even if they somehow allow their feelings to get involved, they understand what happens between us is a transaction. That's all it will ever be. I pay; they service."

"Your business, not mine."

He smiled again, but it was subtle. "Agreed."

"So we're back to the main point. Why am I here?"

"I would like to offer you a job."

"A job? Me? Why?"

"It's one that requires a huge commitment, loyalty, and discretion. I sense that you'd be a good fit."

"You don't know me, so how can you assume those things apply?"

"I trust my gut."

"And your gut says that I'll be loyal?" My brows lifted, and he stared intently before answering.

"Yes."

Bullshit, but I'll bite.

"So, what's the job? And how much does it pay?"

"I can't give you the details yet, but it pays far more than you'd make at Salacious. You also won't be around men who offer to buy you or feel inclined to put their hands on you."

He was referencing the night Asshole hit me. "How do you expect me to entertain an offer, but you refuse to provide details?"

"I will when it's time, but one thing I can promise is that it won't require an exchange of sexual favors for money." His smile surfaced again, and I rolled my eyes.

"Good, because that's a definite no."

"I assumed it would be. Now, finish your food, and I'll get you home. It's late, and I have a few things I need to take care of."

"At three in the morning?"

"My businesses are international, Nari. I have to be accessible twenty-four hours a day sometimes to get things done."

"Oh, so you're big time. *Mr. International.*" A cheesy grin eased onto my face, which caused him to chuckle.

"Something like that."

"Well, I'm on eastern standard time, so just be mindful about my business hours. I need my beauty rest."

"Noted."

I had no idea what the hell that man was about or what he was offering, but I had a feeling that whatever it was would change my life in ways I could never imagine. The lingering question was whether those changes would be worth the demand.

CHAPTER 4

KINCAID.

"I'm not sure I understand what you're asking me."

The perplexed expression on Nathan Calhoun's face almost amused me. He was and had been my lead attorney for the past ten years. My father assigned him to me after my twenty-first birthday. I had been legal since I turned eighteen, but as a young man transitioning to adulthood, my father insisted that I have my own legal team and come from under his. Nathan was extremely intelligent and, over the years, had proven to be a great asset. Even with the slipup of missing the loophole in the contract with Kaber, I still fully trusted his guidance and had complete faith in his legal abilities.

"What's confusing, Nate?"

"You're asking me to take these terms and draft them into a legally binding agreement between you and a woman named . . ." He adjusted his overpriced frames and looked down at the document I'd handed him. ". . . Nari Collette."

"Yes, that's what I'm asking."

"But this says marriage. You're arranging a marriage with this woman when you currently already have a standing arrangement with Aila."

I unbuttoned my suit jacket and lifted my leg, allowing my left ankle to rest on my right thigh while I leaned back for comfort. "I won't be marrying Aila. That contract is no longer valid."

"It's valid, Kincaid. I assure you this agreement will hold up in the highest-ranking court of law, but more than anything, it will certainly make an impact on The Families. You understand what's on the line here, don't you?"

Nathan had full disclosure about my personal dealings—both legal and illegal. That was how much I trusted him. He knew I could ruin him if he decided to try to fuck me over, but he'd proved himself over the years. Nathan was solid and made enough money off me never to want to fuck that up.

"I absolutely understand what's on the line. I also know that there's an out. You missed it." His face showed the irritation from me insinuating that he'd somehow messed up.

"Missed what? I thoroughly evaluated that damn contract to be sure you were protected."

"You did, but that's not the issue. I'm more concerned with the fact that I no longer wish to follow through with the arrangement and need an out. I have one, and you missed it."

"I'm listening." He was pissed.

"Kaber was trying to cover his ass, and in doing so, he left off Aila's *name* where it states that I have to be married within the year. It only says that a marriage has to take place; however, it doesn't clarify to whom. That part was understood between the three of us: myself, my father, and Kaber. I'm sure his snake ass was doing it to be sure Aila would never find out that he'd basically auctioned her off. *That's* my out."

I could see Nathan's mind working. He remained quiet before his fingers began pecking away at his laptop. I was sure that he was pulling up to view the agreement. After a few minutes, I had his attention again.

"Well, I'll be damned. You're right." He had no issue admitting his error. I didn't blame him because, technically, it wasn't an error, just an oversight, considering some things were understood, such as who I was marrying.

"So why are you backing out?" was his next concern.

"The merger would be more of a liability than a benefit. I've recently discovered some things that have changed the direction of my willingness to partner with Kaber."

"Such as?"

"He's in debt and at risk of losing everything. He's also in bad standing with The Families. I'll fill you in on the rest when it's time, but I need you to work on that and have a draft ready by this evening. I also want to schedule you to meet with Ms. Collette and me to negotiate the terms so we can have a final draft in place by the close of business tomorrow. I want to be married by the end of the week."

Nathan didn't like what I was proposing, and the look he delivered was proof. "Why so soon? You have six months before you reach the expiration date."

"I don't trust Kaber, and I need this handled immediately. The more time he has to maneuver with the intent that our families will merge, the more damage he can do."

"I don't like the sound of that, nor do I feel comfortable with this, Kincaid. Who is this woman?"

"The specifics of her identity aren't important. You'll meet her this evening. Just know that my mind is made up regardless of how you feel. As long as she agrees and we can negotiate fair terms, I'm marrying Ms. Collette."

"So, you haven't asked her yet? What makes you so sure she'll say yes?"

My smile slipped in place as thoughts of Nari eased into my mind. My response was simple but confident.

"Because she trusts me."

I lowered my foot to the floor and stood. Nathan did the same, and I offered him a hand across his desk, which he accepted and shook firmly.

"What time should I expect you?"

"Seven."

He nodded, and I left. Now, all I had to do was figure out how the hell I was going to get her there. Once I left Nathan's office, I traveled across town to meet Cast. He and I had a few things to review regarding a few shipments that were being rerouted. My business dealings were all carefully managed; however, with Kaber's recent activities, I didn't want to chance anything.

We met at a restaurant near the hotel where Nari was temporarily staying because she would be my next stop. By the time I'd arrived, Cast was already seated with food spread across the table. His big ass never missed a meal or an opportunity for one. I sat across from him after removing my jacket, which I folded neatly on the bench next to me. The booth was massive and could accommodate twelve comfortably, six on each side.

"You couldn't wait?"

"Could've but didn't." He shoved a forkful of pasta into his mouth and followed it up with a swig from the beer he was working on. After it landed on the table, he tossed his hand in the air, motioning for the server patiently standing by. It was one of my places, so Cast received VIP treatment, which he took full advantage of.

"Good afternoon, Mr. Akel. Will you be ordering?"

"No, just a drink. Cognac, and bring the bottle."

"Yes, sir." She smiled softly and hurried away.

"That's why I didn't wait." Cast shot me a smug look before his fork was buried in the pasta again. His mouth was full seconds later, but he spoke anyway. "You make the call yet?"

"Yeah, they're coming tonight. The first one at midnight, and the other three will follow two hours apart. I need you to be there."

"Got it. But why the change?" I hadn't told Cast what was happening, only that I was making some "adjustments."

"Kaber's moving funny. I'm not sure how much he's been paying attention to things, and I need to be sure we receive these shipments without any issues."

"What type of shit is he on that has you switching up?"

"He's brokered deals with the wrong people. I recently found out that he's in debt."

"In debt?" Cast frowned. As far as anyone was concerned before now, Kaber's net worth mirrored my family's, but over the past few years, he had gotten into bed with the wrong people and made a lot of bad investments. He also made promises to people that he couldn't deliver on, which meant he had to cover the loss personally.

"Kaber tried to bypass The Families and got screwed in the process."

"Damn, so you still marrying Aila?"

"No."

"So how does that work? You had a lot on the line with that deal."

He didn't know all the details, but he had a general idea of how it should work.

"I'm covered. I just have to marry someone to hold up my end of the deal."

"Someone, like it could be *anybody*?" He frowned before shoving another forkful of pasta into his mouth.

"Yeah. Kaber's fuckup. As long as I get married, then I'm good."

Cast grinned. He was amused, which led to his next thought. "So you're going to marry the girl."

"What girl?"

Nari. I already knew who he was referring to.

"You know who the funk I mean, Caid. There's a reason behind everything you do."

I shrugged and lifted my eyes to the server, who approached with a glass and a bottle, which she placed in front of me. "Is that all, sir?"

I nodded, and she hurried away, posting up near the bar in case we needed her again. I covered the bottom of my glass with liquor and then lifted it to my lips, enjoying the smooth blend on my tongue before it glided down my throat.

"There was nothing intentional when I asked you to keep an eye on her. That has since changed."

"Hell yeah, it changed if you're planning on marrying her. Who said she was the one?"

"You just did."

I lifted my glass again and drained the contents before refilling it. Cast reached for one of the garlic knots, ripping into it. "What's your deal with her?"

"There isn't one. When I asked you to keep an eye on her, it wasn't for any specific reason. There was no plan."

"But there is now?"

I nodded. "I'm going to marry her. My out with Kaber is to marry within the year. She's who I choose."

"Why?"

I shrugged. I wasn't sure if I had a legit answer other than I wanted a reason to keep her close so I could control who was allowed to be near her.

Men, specifically. At least until I was sure of what the hell was going on between us. It didn't make any sense, but something was there. It might be nothing, or it could possibly be everything.

Until I had a clear understanding of why I felt so connected to a stranger, I wanted exclusive access to her.

"So, you don't know?"

"Not a damn clue."

"But you're going to marry her?"

"You have a better idea?" I lifted my glass, staring at Cast. That time, he lifted one shoulder in a shrug.

"I know plenty who wouldn't mind being attached to you, but your picky ass would find something to complain about." His cheeks fluffed from the smile on his face, and I chuckled.

"I like what I like."

"What you like doesn't exist. You want perfection."

"I'm not looking for perfection."

"Close enough."

I tossed back the rest of my drink. "I'm particular about what I want, as we all should be."

"Agreed, but if you're marrying this woman, what happens when she doesn't measure up?"

"This is an arrangement. The only things she needs to measure up to are the agreed-upon terms. That has to do with specifics, not her as a person. This is more or less a business deal."

Cast lifted his eyes to me with a smug grin on his face. He didn't believe me, but I didn't care.

"I'm out. Make sure you handle the shipments, and hit me up if you encounter any issues."

"Got it, boss." He chucked his chin my way, that damn grin still in place. Instead of responding, I left with the question he asked heavy on my mind. What if she didn't measure up? Why the hell did it matter? It was indeed a business deal, not a real marriage, so what would she have to measure up to? Nari would only be my wife on paper.

I decided to drop in on my mother since I had a few hours to kill before pulling up on Nari. She ran a nonprofit for runaways. It was established to help keep them off the streets by offering safe housing for those in the system who were not old enough to be on their own. She worked with private funding to place them in foster homes of loving families. Most of the ones connected to the city were people looking to get a check. My mother was a foster kid who ended up on the streets after running when she wasn't being treated fairly. That cause was near and dear to her heart. It was what she called her passion project and purpose.

As soon as I entered the building, the receptionist, Lori, was grinning from ear to ear. She had a little crush. Most of the women who worked for my mother did, but I never entertained them. I kept things respectful because my mother would have my ass if I didn't, and most of the women on her payroll were barely legal.

"Hey, Kincaid. You here to see your mother?"

"Yeah. She busy?"

"I don't think so. She just finished a meeting about ten minutes ago, but she's alone in her office now."

"Okay. Thanks."

"You're welcome." Her eyes remained on me as I moved past her desk and hit the hallway that led to the back. I spoke to whoever I passed along the way and knocked on my mother's open door, entering simultaneously. She lifted her head from the desktop she was sitting behind and smiled.

"Hey, baby. What are you doing here?"

I entered, rounding her desk to plant a kiss on her cheek before I found a seat in front of it.

"I need a reason to come check you out, old lady?"

"Old?" she scoffed. "I'm still in my prime, little boy." Her eyes narrowed my way, and I chilled at the nonverbal threat she issued for me to tread lightly. "I spoke to Aila today."

"Oh yeah?"

"Yes. She received the sample of the invitations and wanted me to see them before they were mailed out."

My mother's smile was soft. She was more excited about the wedding than the marriage. She knew it was an arrangement, but that didn't lessen the thrill of knowing that her only son was getting married. She had asked me several times if it was what I truly wanted to do, and I assured her I was fine with the decision. She also asked if I had feelings for Aila, which placed me at an impasse. I wouldn't lie to my Earth, but I also didn't want to diminish the joy of her only son's marriage. I kept my answer neutral by expressing that I cared about Aila and that she was a beautiful woman with a generous heart. My mother took that to mean that she needed to be at peace with my upcoming nuptials.

"I need you to hold off on any further plans for the wedding."

"Why? Is something wrong? Are you and Aila having problems?"

"No. We're fine. I just need a minute to work through some things. I also need you to keep this request to yourself."

"Meaning away from Aila?"

"And Pop."

A line formed between her brows, and her eyes reflected the questions I wouldn't answer. "Kincaid, what's going on? If you've changed your mind, we should discuss this as a family."

I have, but we won't discuss my decision to do so as a family.

I exhaled a short breath before standing and rounding my mother's desk. I kneeled, taking both her hands in mine. After I kissed her fingers, she placed a hand on my face.

"Sweetheart, what's wrong? You can talk to me, always."

"I know, but what I need right now from you is trust. You can't ask questions, and you have to do as I'm requesting. Everything will make sense in a few days. Just give me that. It's all I ask."

The concern I was witnessing bothered me. I never wanted my mother to stress or worry, especially behind me. The life we were connected to had placed enough weight on her shoulders, where my father and I were concerned.

"Okay."

I flashed a smile, and she delivered one as well while her eyes rolled up to the ceiling briefly before making their way back to mine. "You know I can't resist that smile. You'd get your way every time as a child because of it. You learned early to use charm as a weapon." Her voice was light, which settled my spirit.

Standing to my full height, I nodded to agree. "I did, but it's what you taught me. Charm your way into the hearts of those who fight against your will. Those were your words."

"I won't deny that; however, I didn't realize that same tactic would apply to me with snack and bedtime negotiations."

I chuckled lightly, bending again to kiss my mother on the cheek. "You were always in charge, old lady. I just occasionally bent the rules."

She sucked her teeth and stood beside me, looping an arm through mine. "You're my favorite son. I would give you the world. The problem seemed to be that you learned that too quickly."

"I have to go, but I'll be in touch. Keep Friday open. I have something important planned, and I need you and Pop to be there."

"Care to share?"

"No. Just be available when I call."

She pushed out a short breath with a puff from her lips. "I don't know what's going on with you, Kincaid, but I trust you know what you're doing . . ." She paused, delivering a firm look, "for now."

"Good enough. Love you. I have to go."

My mother detached from my side and nodded, watching me leave her office. There was no helping the heaviness I felt in me because my mother was my first love, and disappointing her seemed to be the worst form of torture. I had no idea how she would respond once she found out that I was no longer marrying Aila and, instead, taking a bride that just dropped into my life and hers without any past association. Unfortunately, I couldn't worry about that thought. I had bigger issues. I was on to my next task, which would prove to be a bit more of a challenge. I had a feeling my smile wouldn't be enough to gain the advantage required to make it go smoothly; however, I was certainly going to use all the arsenal I had at my disposal to get what I wanted.

CHAPTER 5

NARI.

It was just after six, and I was starving. I'd spent most of the day asleep, considering that I worked until two. That was the downside to my job. It felt as if all I did was sleep and work. I had to get rest during the day to survive the night, and weekends were when we received the best tips, so I volunteered for those hours. That meant I barely had free time to do anything besides catch up on my rest.

After sliding my feet into my Nikes, I raked my fingers through my hair, creating a half-assed ponytail, wrapping it into a bun that rested at the nape of my neck before I lifted my room key and cell phone to head downstairs. The good thing about being at a hotel was the café and restaurant on-site and room service when those were closed. Not having a car complicated my life, which was why a decent used vehicle was the first thing on my list after finding a place to stay.

Just before I left my room, my line buzzed with a call. I frowned and almost ignored the distraction, considering no one knew I was here. I didn't have friends or family who checked on me, so there shouldn't be a need for anyone to reach out. I only answered because I felt it might be the hotel confirming my extended stay. I paid by the week, and it was nearing the time for my next payment, so I crossed the room and lifted the receiver.

"Good evening, Ms. Collette. You have a visitor in the lobby."

"A visitor?" *Who the hell could be here to see me?* My first thought was Joey, but I hadn't told him what hotel I was staying at.

"Yes, ma'am. A Mr. Kincaid Akel."

Him!

He had my nerves on edge. I hadn't seen or heard from him since the night, or rather morning, we shared a meal. Afterward, he took me to my hotel without me giving directions to where I was staying. He waited for me to walk through the glass doors of the lobby and then left. I knew that because I crept back to the entrance, peeking out, and watched his car travel through the parking lot to be sure he left.

"Oh, uhh, okay."

"He's requested that you come down. If you'd prefer, I can send him up."

"No, it's fine. I'm on my way."

There was no way in hell I wanted that man in my room. I didn't trust myself with him and not because he felt like a threat . . . well, in a sense, he did, but not in a way that he would harm me. Kincaid was simply a threat because I felt an odd pull between us, which made me bend to his will. I had no idea why and had been struggling to make sense of it, but Kincaid was a mystery. A dark, brooding mystery who had the ability to snatch my soul with one look accompanied by that damn smile of his.

I was anxious going to the lobby, and when I stepped off the elevator, my pulse quickened at the sight of him. There he stood in all his glory, eyes fastened to me as if he'd been counting down the seconds until they pinned to mine. Like always, he was well-dressed in a custom, tailored suit. It hugged his tall frame in the best of ways by tapering at the waist and outlining his broad shoulders. When I finished my greedy inspection of his person, my eyes lifted to meet his. Those dark, intense browns were eager for my attention. My heart thumped rapidly in my chest.

I'd never been drawn to a man of his stature, but something wicked and intriguing about Kincaid had me anticipating each moment with him. He was handsome and stunning, but the core of him was dark and sometimes dangerous, which set off warning signals that I ignored. I was already mildly addicted to even the simplest things about him, which was surely going to land me in trouble of the worst kind.

"To what do I owe the honor, Mr. International?" I attempted humor to simmer the tension I felt rising.

He didn't speak immediately, but I'd learned not to expect him to. Kincaid was staring introspectively, his eyes moving from my face down my body. I was dressed casually in athletic wear— leggings and a hoodie. I hadn't expected company, and since my job required heels and dresses, I enjoyed the opportunity to dress down whenever possible.

"You're nervous," was the first thing out of his mouth. His posture was relaxed, but his presence still felt powerful . . . commanding. It was as if the space he occupied always seemed too small for his energy.

"I'm not. Why would I be?"

The corner of his mouth reflected a hint of a smile that transitioned into a grin, which was charming and cocky.

"You shouldn't be. I'm harmless."

I was sure there was a list a mile long full of names who would testify that was a lie. Kincaid was anything *but* harmless.

"I choose to disagree. Why are you here?"

He chuckled and nodded, moving closer, leaving about a foot's distance between us. Even still, his cologne attacked my senses, threatening to take me down because it was so alluring.

"The job."

"Job?"

"Yes. Did you forget?" His teeth raked his bottom lip, and for some reason, my muscles clenched from the motion. It was dangerously sexy. *Harmless, my ass.*

"No. I just didn't take you seriously."

"Why not?"

"Why so? You don't know me, so why would I assume you'd seriously offer me a job? One that you refused to give me details about."

He smiled again.

Damn it!

"Well, I'm here now to discuss the terms, but I need you to ride with me."

"Sorry, can't. I have to work tonight. I was just about to grab dinner to fuel up to survive my shift."

"I have a feeling that once I explain the terms of the job I'm offering, you'll not think twice about quitting."

"I have bills. I need to be finding a place to stay and—"

"Nari, I need you to trust me. Just this once. Can you do that?"

"This will be the second time. The first was when you sent my ride away and demanded I go with you."

Amusement danced in his eyes. I could see he was somehow entertained, but I wasn't sure why.

"You are correct, so I need you to trust me for a second time. You escaped the first unharmed, agreed?"

Says who? You've done damage to my heart already, and I barely know you.

"Where?"

"Excuse me?"

"You said take a ride with you ... Where are we going?"

"To my lawyer's office."

I frowned, trying to understand why he would want me to go to his lawyer's office to discuss a job. *It might be some freaky shit.*

"That sounds suspect."

"It's not. Just a simple precaution so that if we agree on terms, he can make things binding and official in a contractual manner. I'm an important man, and I need to keep my affairs as private and protected as possible. You're not obligated to do anything. It will simply be a conversation, and if you agree to negotiate terms, we move forward."

Now, I was intrigued. *What the hell could this possibly be?*

"Shall we?" He extended a hand, and my teeth sank into my lip while I considered the offer, eventually giving in.

"What the hell? Why not?"

We ended up in an office downtown. The building was fancy, but the office was even fancier. That time, Kincaid drove us in a matte-black Range Rover. He was loaded, which made sense considering the amount of money he likely had to pay for this lawyer, whoever he was. The man definitely wasn't an ambulance chaser. He had his own practice, and I was sure his clients were exclusive and matched the wealth Kincaid possessed.

As soon as we arrived, we were ushered into a conference room, which housed a massive table. The wood looked expensive, and fourteen chairs surrounded the custom piece—six on each side and one at each end. Kincaid pulled out one chair on the end of one side, where I sat, and he filled the spot next to me. There was a stainless-steel tray within reach of us, which housed a matching pitcher. It was misted on the exterior, which meant it was filled with a cold substance. There were four tall crystal glasses shaped like cylinders and spotless. Not a smudge in sight. *Interesting.* The room smelled clean, and a light scent of something citrusy hung in the air. The entire setup was fancy and had me sitting stiffly in my chair, which Kincaid obviously noticed.

"You can relax. I promise this will be painless." His voice was smooth and easy, a little more welcoming than I was used to. He was comfortable here. But that made sense. It was *his* lawyer.

"My apologies. A call I couldn't postpone ran over by a few minutes." A crisp voice drew my attention to the door. Kincaid stood to greet a handsome pecan-completed man with sandy-brown hair, freckles, and green eyes. He was dressed in a suit similar to the one Kincaid wore, but he was shorter and broader, so it didn't give the same impression. He approached, shaking Kincaid's hand firmly, offering me a smile before rounding the table and taking a seat directly across from us. Placing a thick stack of papers in front of him, he cleared his throat, removed a pen from his jacket, and straightened his spine.

"I assume this is Ms. Collette," he spoke to Kincaid, and after a short nod, he addressed me. "Nice to meet you, Ms. Collette. I'm Nathan Calhoun, Mr. Kincaid's head attorney. Shall we get started?"

Kincaid offered another nod, and Nathan began.

"Do you know why you're here, Ms. Collette?"

"Nari, please, and yes. It's about a job."

The way he addressed me by my last name felt too formal and intimidating.

Nathan's eyes shot over to Kincaid before they landed on me again. "A job of sorts, yes, but I'm assuming it hasn't been completely explained to you what type of job."

"No. I was told that's why we had to come here." I glanced at Kincaid, whose expression was neutral, but I could sense that he had shifted to what I assumed was his business persona. That had me confused.

"Are you going to tell her, or shall I?" Something passed between the two men. There was a bit of tension that let on that Nathan wasn't happy, but Kincaid didn't seem to care. Kincaid was the boss of the two, so it was happening.

"Nari, I've found myself in a bit of a predicament. One that requires me to make some adjustments in my personal life. The job that I'm offering is an arranged marriage."

I frowned hard, tilting my head to the side as I looked at him first and then at Nathan.

"Arranged marriage to whom?"

"Me." He frowned as if my question didn't make sense, but shit, I was confused.

"You're kidding, right?"

"Unfortunately, not," Nathan mumbled, which had Kincaid shooting him a look that caused Nathan to tighten up and adjust his attitude.

"Wait, you're *serious*? You want *me* to marry *you*?"

"Yes."

"Why? That doesn't make sense. A man like you surely has droves of women who would break their necks to fill that role."

"Possibly, but this isn't about love or even companionship. It's more of a business deal. The woman I choose to fill this role has to have a clear understanding of what that means. I'm not looking for a traditional commitment. This will only be a marriage on paper."

"Wait, so 'just on paper' means what exactly?"

"As far as the world knows, you are indeed my wife in every sense of the meaning. We will have a wedding, live together, date each other, and make appearances together; however, we have an understanding that we're both playing roles."

"That's crazy. I don't get it."

"I don't expect you to. I only ask that you consider the opportunity. The job I'm offering is for you to be my wife."

"How does that even work?"

Is this man crazy? Shit, is he . . .

"Wait, are you gay?"

Nathan laughed loudly, clearly amused, while Kincaid's face twisted into a scowl. "Hell no. I assure you that's the furthest thing from the truth."

I grinned at how annoyed he seemed by the accusation. I was certain that had we been alone, he would have offered to prove his point. The way Nathan laughed, Kincaid might've offered so that he could watch and gain the proof as well.

"So then, why the arranged marriage thing?"

"It's associated with family business. Something I choose not to discuss now but nothing that will affect you."

"If I'm marrying you, then it affects me, buddy." I shrugged, and he lifted a hand, working his palm down his face. It rested on the table when he continued, and as he made a fist, I heard his knuckles crack. I assumed that it was his way of controlling his emotions.

"Will you consider the offer?" He got right back to business.

"Depends. How much does it pay?"

Nathan attempted to answer that. "One million dollars—"

I cut him off.

"Holy shit! You're kidding, *right?*"

"Unfortunately, not." There was old Nate again with that damn sarcasm. "Mr. Akel will deposit half up front once you agree to terms, sign off on the deal, and are officially married. You'll receive the other half at the completion of your union."

"Wait, so we're getting divorced?"

Why do I care? It was an arrangement. Not real, but still, in my mind, marriage would be forever. One and done, but I was considering marrying a man I didn't know or love.

"Unless you decide you like the job and want to stay in it for the long haul." Kincaid smiled, and his words were teasing.

Jerk!

"Doubtful," I sneered, and Nathan chuckled. "So what are the terms?"

"That's what we're here to discuss, but to move forward, you must agree to negotiate. Shall we begin negotiations, Nari?" Kincaid spoke in a businesslike manner. I felt outnumbered for some reason. I didn't know shit about negotiating terms.

"He represents you. Who will represent me?"

"I will. This matter has to be discreet so no one outside of this room can be privy to the arrangement."

"How is that fair? You're *his* lawyer."

"I am, but I assure you, Ms. Col—"

"Nari," I interrupted, a bit firmer than intended.

"I assure you, Nari, I will be neutral in this negotiation. Whatever questions you have, I will answer. Whatever you don't understand, I will explain. If I feel you're not getting the best deal with certain terms, I will advise you on how to position yourself and will offer the same discretion for Kincaid."

"He's likely going to make sure you come out with the advantage. Old Nate here is a little annoyed with me right now," Kincaid stated and chuckled.

"Trouble in paradise?" I questioned with an arched brow.

"Nari, stay on topic. Are we negotiating or not?" Kincaid's demeanor shifted to something a little more dominant.

"Why not?" I shrugged.

"Good." I watched as he removed his phone and made a call. "Calvetti, how are you? Great. No, not at all, at least not for me. I'm calling to inform you that Ms. Collette is putting in an official notice. Watch your tone, Calvetti. Let's not forget who you're talking to. As I said, she's giving official notice of her last day. She won't be at work this evening. Will that be a problem? I thought not. You are not to contact her moving forward. Any belongings she has at the club will be retrieved by one of my people, along with her final check. Understood?"

He looked at me and winked.

"Great. I'm glad to know this won't be an issue. Have a good evening."

After ending the call, he placed his phone on the table, removed his jacket, and then turned to me. "Now, shall we get started?"

Who the hell is this man, and what the hell am I getting myself into? The question continuously played on repeat in my mind, but it didn't stop me from making a deal with the devil.

When I returned to my room, it was just after eleven. We spent hours going over terms, and then I signed off on all the legal documents, which would make me *Mrs. Nari Akel* in two days. It was Wednesday, and my wedding was scheduled for Friday. I wasn't sure what the rush was or how he'd pull it off, but Kincaid asked me to leave everything to him. I was also informed that someone would reach out first thing in the morning to take me to the fitting for the dress I would wear on Friday. I was instructed to choose whatever I wanted; the cost wasn't an issue. Kincaid mentioned that it would be an informal affair and that we'd have a traditional wedding a few months down the line, which I could personally plan, or he would hire someone to assist. Whereas this one would be just the two of us and a witness, the one we plan in a few months would be an entire affair with a guest list of family and friends. All from his side, obviously. I didn't have anyone. He also made clear that I could invite anyone I wanted, as long as I kept to the terms of keeping the arrangement between the two of us.

As far as the world knew, we met, fell in love, and married instantly. That happens in real life, so it wouldn't be a far stretch for others to believe. Kincaid also didn't want me to lie, so he planned on painting a picture of events between us that I could use to detail our time together. Either way, our marriage was still a lie, but for what I was being compensated, I decided to roll with it.

He was meticulous about mapping out the details of our agreement. We discussed everything from living arrangements down to date nights or how many times a week I was expected to cook meals. *Real wife shit!* It was optional but preferred. When I chose not to, he would supply a staff, including a chef, to handle meals. There was a provision written in for how we managed our personal lives, and as of now, neither he nor I was allowed to see other people intimately. It didn't mean we had to be intimate with each other, only that there would be no outside relationships.

I wasn't sure how truthful he was being with that part, but Kincaid provided his initials next to the clause, the same as I had, so that for the next three years, which was the term of our agreement, he would remain faithful. If, at any point, he and I decided to become intimate, we could either work out the terms on our own or meet with Nathan to have him mediate the agreement. There was even a line item for future discussion about having children if we chose to add kids as a term. No way in hell was I discussing how many times—if any—I planned on having sex with my fake husband or how many kids would come from the act. *Screw that!*

The entire ordeal was weird, but Kincaid was adamant about me not entertaining other men during our union. I then became adamant about him following the same practice. It didn't sit right with me that my husband would be allowed to see or be physical with other women, even if he was my *fake* husband.

If nothing else, he and I would forge a friendship. We had to spend time together, live in the same house, and emulate a real marriage. I was excited and nervous at the same time. I found myself wildly attracted to Kincaid, but the agreement challenged any thoughts I had of exploring those feelings. Technically, he was now my "boss," in a sense. I worked for him as his fake wife. If I didn't hold up my end, I would have a lot to lose; however, Kincaid agreed to the terms of my keeping the initial payout as long as I remained in the union for the first year. After that, I had the right to renegotiate or end our arrangement, but I kept the five hundred thousand. It seemed fair, so as of 10:23 that evening, I was officially engaged to Kincaid Akel when I signed on the dotted line. I had no idea what I was getting myself into, but I was for certain getting married in two days.

CHAPTER 6

KINCAID.

How's it going?

I sent the text to Nari and then took in my appearance as I admired the fit of my suit. I decided to skip the tux since the marriage wasn't formal. The minute I slipped my jacket on and stared in the mirror, I thought of her, which prompted my text. She had been picked up that morning by the service I provided and chauffeured to the dress shop where she would pick her gown for Friday, but there was a stop before that, which I hadn't informed my future wife about.

Better than this morning when you sent me to be poked and prodded by strangers.

As one of our terms, she was to receive a complete physical. I had several reasons. The one I provided Nari was that in the event we choose to become intimate, we both have a verified clean bill of health. I tested twice a year with my doctor. I was in prime health and clear of any STDs. I needed to know that Nari was as well. I had scheduled an appointment with Dr. Chandler, who just so happened to be the wife of my physician and a very highly sought-after gynecologist. Her clientele was exclusive, and she had a mile-long waiting list, considering she also specialized in fertility. She took on Nari as a favor to me by way of urging from her husband.

> I appreciate your cooperation. I hope it wasn't as abrasive as you're presenting.

> 😑 Okay, so maybe it wasn't that bad, but I still didn't like it. She was extremely friendly, however, and I know for certain she's one of the best.

> How so?

> Her damn office screams rich and famous. The exam rooms were fancier than most hotel suites I've experienced.

I chuckled at the thought. I was sure it was very over the top and upscale.

> Glad you approved, but back to the dress. How's that going?

> Good, but weird. I'm picking my wedding dress, and, well, ya know. But anyway, it's kinda fun. These people are super nice. How much did you pay them?

I grinned at her response. She was indeed a handful and was a good sport. I half expected her to turn me down, and at some point, I felt she would back out, specifically during the discussion about intimacy. I pried about her personal affairs, wondering if she was seeing anyone, and she made clear she had *no suitors to speak of*, her words, which she used as a dig against me. Nari liked to tease me about my formality, but she had only been exposed to one side of me as of yet—my professional one. I was a man of many layers, which she would soon discover. As my wife, fake or not, she'd get all of me.

It was why I was adamant about no outside relationships. I presented it under the guise of protecting our arrangement, but truthfully, she would be my wife. Even if, by contractual terms, she was still mine. The odd thing was that in my agreement with Aila, she would be allowed to see other men intimately as I would be allowed to bed other women. Aila was unaware of that, but her father knew and agreed to my request to add that to the terms. I wouldn't have cared if Aila entertained other men at any point. I didn't see her that way. She was a beautiful woman with an amazing body, but the attraction wasn't there on my end. I had fully planned on maintaining my sexual relationships with other women while married to her, but with Nari, fuck that. No one was touching my wife but me, and I would commit to reserving myself exclusively for her. She might not have known, but I planned for us to take on *all* facets of a real marriage. I would give her time, but she was indeed attracted to me the same as I was immensely attracted to her.

Don't worry yourself about irrelevant details. Focus on making this experience one that creates memories. I'll be disappointed if you don't.

"How's it going in there?" Jennifer, who was handling my fitting, called from outside my dressing room. She was eager to assist, which irritated me because she knew I was engaged. She was the one who helped me pick my tux for the wedding planned for Aila. I skipped the details on the reason behind my fitting that day, but still, she knew I was committed to another woman and was still dedicated to throwing herself at me.

"Good, I'll take this one. I'll only need minor adjustments. Andres should be able to handle that, right?"

"Yes, sir. We can have it done today and ready first thing in the morning. Would you like for me to mark any specifics?"

She wanted me to model the suit so she could put her hands on me—not happening.

"Not necessary. He knows my build and can handle it."

"Oh, okay, well, you can leave the suit hanging, and I'll take care of getting it to Andres."

I felt her standing there, and I didn't respond. After a long moment, she got the message and left me be, so my focus returned to my phone.

> Such a rich-guy thing to say. Money is always relevant. And disappointed? Is that part of our deal? I must've missed that line item.

I chuckled at her response and sent mine.

> As your future husband, I aim to ensure your happiness—total satisfaction. If I don't accomplish that goal, I disappoint not only you but myself as well. No price line can be placed on making my future wife happy.

Those dots started and stopped several times before her message came through.

> You talk a good game, Kincaid. We'll see if your actions back it up!

> Challenge accepted. Dinner tonight. I'll pick you up at 8.

> Hmmm, maybe I have plans. You're not my husband yet . . .

> Agreed, but you are my fiancée, and I'd hate for someone to suffer the consequences of your poor decisions. Be ready by 8.

> 😕 requested attire, please?

Not too dressy, but no jeans.

Got it, boss.

I smirked at her referencing me as boss. I fully planned on being in charge where Nari was concerned, but not in the way she was hinting toward. We had time. I tossed my phone on the satin bench that lined one of the walls and proceeded to undress so that I could leave. I had a few stops to prepare for my date with Nari.

Date!

The thought felt foreign, but I would eventually get used to it. She would soon carry my last name and the privileges attached to it. Nari had no idea how drastically her life would change, and I hoped she was tough enough to survive what would be expected of a woman who was marrying an Akel. Time was of the essence, so I left the tailor and headed to my next location.

I stared at the diamonds that all seemed to be a perfect choice. I had requested anything they carried from the Monelli Collection. Gian Monelli was a good friend, and his family was well known for their one-of-a-kind pieces. Had there been more time, I would've had the ring custom made by Gian personally. Unfortunately, the last-minute decision had my hands tied.

"Any of these catch your eye?" The woman helping me was pleasant and attentive. After leaving my fitting, I ended up at the jewelry store, where Heather was now assisting me in picking a ring for Nari. I appreciated the fact that she hadn't tried flirting while I was viewing rings for another woman. She was attracted but remained professional. "Truthfully, you can't go wrong with the Monelli Collection," she added with a bright smile.

"I'm stuck between these two." I pushed the two choices forward. I had narrowed it down to six rings laid out on the black velvet canvas. They were all extremely nice, the best quality, and massive singular stones set in platinum bands. Some were also surrounded by smaller stones. The shapes varied between oval, square, and round. All exquisite choices when considering quality; however, it was more than that. I wanted Nari to like her ring. For some reason, it mattered that I selected one which fit her style. A style I didn't have a damn clue about. I would've asked, but I wanted the official proposal to be a surprise. She didn't seem the type to lie easily about something so serious as a wedding, so my goal was to create memories that were as close to the real thing as possible. That surprised me as well because why the hell did I even care?

"Aww, both excellent choices. Tell me, is she a flashy woman or more reserved?"

I considered what little I knew of Nari before answering.

"Reserved."

"Then this one. It's simple, elegant, and not overwhelming. Well, as underwhelming as you can be in this price line. Your selections are far above average; however, this one is expensive and exquisite in a way that anyone who sees it will know that the man who gave it to her put a lot of thought and money into the choice, but it's not flashy."

I snorted. "She won't give a damn how much it cost. She'll more than likely be angry if she discovers how much it cost."

"Then definitely this one." She smiled wide. I watched her slide one of the two on her thin finger and tried to imagine it on Nari's delicate hand while Heather modeled it for me.

"What do you think?"

"Let's go with that one." I nodded, and she returned one, collecting all six and moving to a different area to prepare my purchase. While she was away, a call came through from Aila, which had my jaw flexing. I needed to avoid her until Friday but couldn't completely cut her off without creating suspicion, so I answered.

"Kincaid." I issued my formal greeting. I knew she wouldn't like it but would assume I was handling business.

"Are you working?"

"Yes."

I was buying a ring for the woman I'd just recently entered into a business arrangement with. That, technically, is classified as "working."

"Oh, well, will you be free tonight? I was thinking we could do dinner. You've been so busy I've barely seen you."

We had just recently had dinner with her friends, but I didn't bring that up.

"Not possible. I have a business thing that I can't reschedule."

"Well, how late will you be? Maybe we can have drinks after. I don't mind meeting you."

"Not tonight, Aila."

She was quiet. The saleslady approached, and I removed my wallet and handed over my card, which she was waiting for to complete my purchase.

"Kincaid, are we okay? You've been . . ." She paused. "I don't know . . . different."

"We're fine, Aila." It wasn't a lie. We were. However, things had shifted between her father and me, which would change the course of things with us. When she found out, it would be a *huge* issue. That part I hated, but it couldn't be helped. I could not, under any terms, marry Aila and connect myself or my family to her father's bullshit.

"Oh, okay. Well, when you have time, reach out. I miss you."

"I will. I have to go."

After ending the call, I accepted the ring, which was packed nicely in a small gift bag with gold ribbon and black and gold tissue peeking out of it.

"I appreciate your help."

"No problem. Congratulations and good luck."

I chuckled. "Thanks, I need it. She's kinda unpredictable."

"Regardless, I don't think you'll need it. She'd be a fool to turn you down." She winked and then walked off to assist another customer. I left the store, shifting my mind to business. I had a few things to handle before my dinner with Nari, and I welcomed the distraction.

"What's up, brother?" my boy Darius greeted me as he welcomed me into his office. We slapped hands before I made myself comfortable on the sofa in the sitting area off in the corner while he moved in the opposite direction.

"Drink?" He held up a bottle of Gautier Eden, knowing it was my preference, and I answered with a nod.

He crossed the room, sitting across from me in one of the matching armchairs near my end. After filling my glass, he handed it over and proceeded to fill his, leaning back once he was done.

I unbuttoned my jacket and relaxed a little.

"Where you coming from?"

"You wouldn't believe me if I told you." I lifted the glass to my lips and enjoyed the flavor before it trickled down my throat.

"Try me."

"I just purchased an engagement ring."

I watched his face, trying to gauge his reaction. Outside of Cast, Darius was the only other person close enough for me to consider a friend. His family, like mine, was affiliated with The Families, but he and I were close because we came up in the same private schools and circles. Darius was also the one I worked in the trenches with when it came to the product we pushed. Much of what we sold flowed through his clubs, two of which we owned together. He was my friend—but more than that, my brother.

"Aila already has one. I was there at the engagement party. What'd I miss?"

I glanced at the door, which he instantly understood. After standing to cross the room, he closed us off from spying ears and returned to his seat. That time, he remained on the edge as he leaned forward and waited.

"I'm marrying someone else on Friday."

"As in *two days from now*, Friday?"

I tossed back the rest of my drink, then leaned forward to grab the bottle to pour a refill.

"Yeah."

"What about Aila?"

"Not happening."

"What changed?"

"Kaber has been lying about his status. If I follow through, I'm fucked."

"If you don't, you're fucked. I read the contract," he warned with concern. I'd presented it to him while I was contemplating the decision. I trusted him above any other.

"I have an out."

"How?"

"By marrying someone else. Trust me, it's solid, or I wouldn't be considering the option."

"So, who is she?"

"You don't know her; shit, *I* don't know her." I chuckled. "Just someone I crossed paths with."

"And you trust the woman enough to bring her in that close to you? She must be something because, hell, that's not you on *any* level."

"Yes and no."

"Come on, Caid. Either you trust her, or you don't. What we do and how we live require a different kind of commitment and loyalty. That's not for the meek or those born into a world that functions off loyalty."

"I know. She'll give me that. Even if not by choice, she'll do it because she agreed to the terms of playing her role as my wife."

"So what about Kaber? Shit, Aila—does *she* know?"

"Fuck Kaber. I'm sure it will create problems, but he's smart enough to keep his distance, or at least he better be. Aila, that's the only part I don't like. I don't love her. This was never real for me, but I didn't want to hurt her either. It just can't be avoided. I'm going to be the bad guy regardless."

"Shit, man." He brushed his hand over his head.

"Yeah, my sentiments exactly."

He shook his head, laughing lightly before he relaxed in the chair again. "Leave it to your ass to be stuck in a love triangle."

"It's not love."

"Maybe not with Aila, but with this other woman, there has to be more. Especially if you just met her. Your ass is calculated, Caid. There's *no way* you're legally attaching yourself to this woman unless there's something deeper attached. There's no gain businesswise, so it has to be something else. Aila, I understood, but *this*? Nah. There's something with this one."

There was *definitely* something with her. At that point, I just didn't know what the hell it was.

"Time will tell," was all I gave.

"So, Friday?"

"Yeah, and I need a favor."

"As good as done. What do you need?"

"She doesn't have family and no friends that she claims. She's alone, and I don't like that. I would appreciate it if you and Alisha would be there. Maybe Alisha can connect with her so she'll have somebody. Even after the wedding, she'll need someone in her corner. An ally to help navigate my life. Alisha is good at shit like that. You know, making people feel welcome in our circle."

Darius smiled at the mention of his wife. Their union was an arrangement as well, but for different reasons. After five years in, they'd fallen in love and made it real. Alisha was the outsider for all the other couples because everyone knew that she and Darius had initially been married under different circumstances. He broke another deal because he had to have her. Some often gave her a hard time, but she didn't care. She was a tough one with a good heart.

"Yeah, we can do that. She'll love that shit too. You know she was totally against the Aila thing. Said it wasn't a good fit, even if it was just business."

I smiled at the thought. "She made that point several times. Just ask her not to mention Aila just yet. Nari doesn't know."

"A'ight, will do. Hit me with the details, and we're there. What about your parents?"

"They don't know and won't until Friday."

"This ought to be interesting." He was amused, which annoyed me because he was right. It was damn sure going to be interesting, and *not* in a good way.

"Look, just have your ass there, and I need Alisha that morning. I want someone with Nari so she doesn't have to get ready alone. Shit like that is important, right?"

"Hell if I know. Alisha had her mother, so yeah, maybe. It seemed like a big deal." He shrugged.

"I'll send you the details."

"And I'll be there. Now, let's get down to business. We need to discuss the distribution of the last shipments."

Just that quickly, I switched gears. It was time to work, which meant my personal life was temporarily placed on hold.

CHAPTER 7

NARI.

I wasn't sure how I felt after accepting the packages waiting for me at the front desk when I returned from dress shopping. I was fully aware that Kincaid had money. He offered me a million dollars to be his pretend wife, but it was a bit much. I was still adjusting, and a part of me felt he was attempting to purchase me, that he *could* buy me, which left me feeling unsettled.

It was why I chose not to wear the attire he'd gifted me. I didn't want anyone to feel as if I were for sale. But wasn't I? My mind drifted to the agreement I'd signed to be his wife. He was paying me a handsome figure to play the role. But that was work. I accepted a position, and that money was compensation for my time. That was it.

I pushed out a short sigh and finished straightening my hair. I wasn't sure why, but when he mentioned dressy, no jeans, I felt like my natural coils needed to be tamed, so I spent an hour washing and straightening my natural tresses. After another fifteen minutes, I could run my fingers through my fresh silk press that fell just past my shoulders. I'd settled on a center part, which allowed my hair to frame my face. Since I'd showered before, I dug through the tiny closet and found a dress I already owned. Most of what I had was black because of work, but there was one red silk dress I hadn't worn yet. It wasn't form-fitting, would hang loosely over my body, and was held in place by spaghetti straps. It kind of resembled a silk camisole but was long enough to be a dress. The front scooped low enough to allow a peek at my breasts while the back dipped lower, exposing a good bit of skin. I considered it sexy yet classy.

Once dressed, I stood in the mirror, turning from side to side, wondering if Kincaid would approve. The selection he'd sent over was a beautiful silver designer number with strappy heels, with crystals hanging from them, and a clutch that matched. All three likely cost more than I cared to imagine. I was tempted to look them up but didn't want to overwhelm myself. After sliding on two gold bangles and hoop earrings, I sprayed the only perfume I owned. Then I inhaled a cleansing breath, checking the time.

7:50.

For some reason, my stomach was in knots. I was anxious and didn't understand why. Our deal was set. Kincaid would be my husband. Nights like tonight would be a regular occurrence, but still . . .

I was nervous.

So much so that I almost jumped out of my skin when someone knocked on my door. I briefly closed my eyes as I crossed the room and placed my hand on the knob.

"Who's there?"

"Kincaid."

I smiled. Even from that one word, I could sense his irritation and see his expression in my head. He was likely thinking, who the hell else could it be?

Once I pulled the door open, his eyes began to roam. They traveled across my body slowly. It felt like he took in every inch of me, and I held my breath while he did.

"Did you get what I sent?"

"I did."

"You didn't like it?" He frowned as if that concerned him more than it should have.

"No, that's not it. I just . . ." I fidgeted, raking my hands through my hair. His dark eyes were intense while he waited.

"Then what?"

"Those things are expensive, and it feels like . . ."

"Like what?"

"Like you're trying to buy me. You're paying me for this deal, so let's stick to that. You don't have to buy me things, Kincaid."

The muscles in his jaw twitched while his teeth raked over his lip. Shit, he's annoyed. But hell, I didn't care.

"Nari . . ." He paused as if contemplating his words. "You're going to be my wife—"

"On paper."

"Agreed, and don't cut me off." That time, I was the one frowning. "On paper or not, you *will* be my wife. That gives you access to me in every form, including my wealth and status. If I want to purchase things for my wife, it's not with an expectation— just a nice gesture. I need you to wrap your mind around what carrying the title of my wife means. I will treat you with the same respect and privilege that I would had we married under different circumstances. Understood?" His tone was relaxed but laced with dominance.

"Gotcha, boss. Should I change?"

His eyes traveled once more before he offered me a hint of a smile. There was something in his eyes that I could only translate as . . .

Approval.

He was pleased with my appearance.

"No. You look nice. We should go."

"One second." I stepped inside to get my purse and phone before joining him in the hallway. His hand moved to the small of my back, and the contact caused me to flinch a little. It was unexpected. When I glanced at him over my shoulder, his eyes were waiting.

"Same respect and privilege," he said lowly but formally, and I offered a short nod.

The restaurant he'd chosen was nice. I wasn't surprised. We were taken in a private elevator to the rooftop, where a table awaited. A few other tables were occupied, but no one seemed to pay us any mind. I appreciated that. I didn't know how to behave with or around a man like Kincaid. He was comfortable in this environment and exuded wealth. I was ...

Adjusting.

Kincaid ordered a steak, and I had salmon with asparagus. He requested wine for me while he sipped some brown liquor. We chatted about our days until he focused on the details of how I'd faired with dress shopping.

"I assume you found something you like?"

I watched him from across the table. His head was low while he cut through his steak. I admired his features. I could never get tired of staring at that man. He was universally appealing in so many ways. Tall, muscular build, magazine cover-type face, flawless skin, mysterious eyes, and full lips. His lashes were thick and longer than most men, but they didn't look feminine, and he always smelled enticing.

"I did. I have pictures. Do you want to see?"

He shook his head softly, and I watched as a piece of steak left his fork and slipped between those full lips. He chewed and, after swallowing, added, "No, surprise me. I'm looking forward to seeing you in it in person."

"What if you don't like it?"

"If you like it, it's perfect, and I'm easy to please." I didn't know what it mattered, but deep down inside, I wanted him to like my dress. He had been a big part of my consideration when I decided on the one I'd selected.

"And you, did you find a suit?"

"I did. It's just a suit, though. Nothing to brag about. I'm positive you'll outshine me." He winked, which landed a blow right between my thighs. That man . . .

"Maybe, maybe not. You wear those things very well. I can't imagine you in anything else."

He cracked a smile. It was subtle but still charming. "I don't always wear suits."

"It's all I've ever seen you in."

"Is that a problem?"

"No, not at all. I'm not complaining. It's a good look on you. Sophisticated, businesslike. I just never thought I'd find myself attracted to a man who wore suits."

He froze, his fork midair, and his eyes quickly fastened to mine, a grin teasing at his lips.

"Are you admitting that you're *attracted* to me, Nari?"

Shit. Freudian slip.

"No, I mean, yes, but not like that. You're easy on the eyes. I'd be lying if I said otherwise. I'm just generally stating that a man in suits wouldn't normally be my thing. That's all."

He nodded, lifting his drink, but those eyes never left me after he sipped and returned it to the table. I lifted mine. Kincaid made me nervous. I wasn't sure of the exact reason yet, but I identified with random feelings concerning him. He sent my emotions on a roller-coaster type of ride.

"It's not a big deal or anything to be embarrassed about, you know?"

"What?" My eyes shot up to his, and, of course, they were already on me.

"Being attracted to your husband."

"*Fiancé*. Well, not even that since, I mean, well, I guess in a sense you are, but technically, you haven't formally asked me. But what I mean is, I didn't say that I was attracted to you, not like *that* kind of attracted."

His smile irked my nerves. He knew that I was indeed attracted and was calling me out on my lie but without words, simply by how he looked at me.

"How about we do something about that? I can't have my future wife confused about any details concerning the two of us."

"I don't follow."

He pushed his chair back and reached inside his jacket pocket. My eyes grew when I realized what ended up in his hand. Kincaid's expression shifted as he neared me, and I'd be damned if this man didn't lower to one knee, extending the box.

"Ms. Nari Collette, will you do me the honor of agreeing to take my last name and become my wife?"

My eyes dropped to the small burgundy leather box back up to Kincaid's face. I reached for it after carefully tugging at the lid. My eyes went wild again when I examined what was inside. It was beautiful. *Breathtaking* and so perfect.

"Shit," I whispered. "This is mine?"

He chuckled, nodding. "But you have to answer first. Will you marry me, Nari?"

My smile eased in place slowly as I nodded.

"Say it. You have to *say* yes."

I gently rolled my eyes and responded. "Yes, Kincaid. I'll marry you. I mean, since you're begging and everything."

He laughed, shaking his head, standing to his full height. After removing the ring box from my hand and the ring itself from its resting place, he reached for me, helping me stand as well. Kincaid slipped the ring on my finger like he'd been practicing all his life. He kissed the spot just above it before pulling me to him. The closeness had my body anxious while his chin dipped, and he lifted mine. One soft kiss was pressed on my lips. It wasn't anything intense or overwhelming, but it could be classified as everything at the same time. Currents flowed through me in such a soothing rhythm that I felt like I was floating. After he backed away, I could tell he was studying my face for a reaction. When I didn't speak, he did.

"Just practice. We'll have to make this look official on Friday. I hope you don't mind."

Mind? Hell no. I want more!

"No, not at all," I agreed.

I did. That was also one of the contractual line items. So that we looked official when we married, one of the terms was that we sealed the deal with a kiss. It would be expected.

"For the marriage. Not the proposal," he corrected.

My cheeks hiked. "I didn't know there would be a proposal, so . . ." I shrugged, and he nodded, releasing me.

"I told you I would help craft a story as true to reality as we can make it. This part is important. People will ask."

"And now I can tell the truth. You proposed to me at a romantic rooftop dinner under the stars on a Wednesday night."

We both sat again, and I admired my ring. He watched for a moment before asking my thoughts.

"So, how did I do?"

"A-plus, boss. It's perfect. I almost forgot that it wasn't real."

When I looked across the table, his expression transitioned. He seemed angry in a sense. "It's real, Nari. As real as we want it to be. As real as *you* want it to be."

I had no idea what the hell that meant, but I didn't ask. Instead, I finished my dinner and enjoyed the rest of my evening with my fake fiancé, who would soon be my fake husband.

The following two days flew by. I didn't see Kincaid, but I talked to him often, either through texts or calls. After dinner on Wednesday night, he informed me that he had to catch a flight to New York to handle business. It made me wonder how often he would travel when we were married and if I would travel with him. My mind then drifted to how frequently I would see him. One of our terms was that we lived under one roof. Separate rooms would be acceptable, but separate residences weren't up for negotiation. I was okay with whatever he decided, considering I didn't currently have a residence to claim. I also assumed that a man like Kincaid had to have properties large enough to allow us both space. The odd thing was that I didn't necessarily want that. He had called it correctly when challenging whether I was attracted to him. I was, more than I needed to be, and I was sure he felt the same. He flirted every time we were around each other. It was always subtle, but his intentions were clearly stated . . .

I want you!

I simply didn't feel it was smart to confuse what it was. *An arrangement. Business deal.* It was possible that Kincaid approached our deal as having his cake and eating it too. Sure, I would be his wife, so why not take that for what it's worth? It didn't mean he intended to develop feelings, just using a good situation. I refused to travel down that road or get lost in that rabbit hole. At some point, he would no longer have a use for me, and I'd be on my own. But with enough money to live the way I wanted to live.

That was another thing that confused me. He seemed extremely interested in my goals, plans, and what I would do since I had the world at my fingertips. His interest seemed genuine. When I told him that I hadn't considered any of that, he promised to help me figure it out. I loved how he casually suggested that maybe I could start a business of sorts. I laughed at the idea, and he visually scolded me before stressing that he was serious. I tightened up and agreed to let him help me map out my future. It was a promise from Kincaid to invest in me. No one had ever done that. I never had family and barely any friends, so life was always survival of the fittest. His benevolence touched me in ways I was embarrassed to express, and I was marrying him that day. The first man or person really ever to offer a genuine interest to invest in me. The reality made me emotional, but . . .

This was business!

Lifting my hand, I stared at my ring. I hadn't removed it since he'd placed it on my finger. Wearing it made this ordeal feel less contractual. Especially since it seemed like a big deal that I actually liked the ring he'd chosen. His smile was organic, and it reflected in his eyes. That made me smile while I sat, staring at the exquisite piece . . . until I heard someone knocking at my door. It was just after one, and my ride wasn't scheduled to arrive until four.

I tugged at my robe and crossed the room, leaning in to ask who was on the other side.

A female voice responded. "Alisha. I'm a friend of Kincaid's. He sent me." I frowned but opened the door, curious to see who the hell *Alisha* was.

She was a pretty, petite woman with cinnamon-brown skin, a head full of spiral curls, and soft-brown eyes that seemed to accompany the smile on her face. A smile that presented too big for her features.

"Kincaid sent you? Why?"

"You're getting married today. He didn't want you to do this alone, so you won't. You have me."

"He told you?"

She nodded, and those spirals bounced. "Yes. My husband and Kincaid are like brothers, so I'm his sister by default. May I come in?"

"Yeah, sure." I stepped out of the way, and she entered, looking around. I immediately felt self-conscious.

"Temporary residence."

"Girl, don't worry about this. We all have a story. I'd knock you on your ass with mine."

I wondered what she knew about me. What Kincaid had told her about us.

"So, let's see this dress. I have your glam squad on the way. I hope you don't mind using my people. They're good. I've had them for years. You'll need to get a team too. We do a lot of events in this circle." Her mouth moved a mile a minute.

"Circle?"

"Oh, you have no idea what you're marrying into." Her eyes sparkled with that confession. "But we'll get to that later. Today is about you. It's *your* day, and it should be special. That's all we're going to focus on."

"I don't know how much he's told you, but today is not a big deal. Just a few *I dos* and some paperwork."

I wouldn't reveal that it was a fake marriage because it was a part of what I agreed to—the most important part.

"Oh, honey, it's a *big* deal." She placed her hands on her hips, tilting her head to the side. "No matter the circumstances, this is *your* wedding day, which is something to be remembered." She paused again. "I'll let you in on a little secret."

"What's that?" I asked, removing my dress from the tiny closet.

"Oh my God! This is adorable and sexy. You're going to look amazing in it," she all but yelled, a little too excited. My dress was strapless, fitted, and covered in tiny crystals. It was *wedding-ish* but not over the top. "I wish I had your height. I'm too mousy to pull that off, but on you, wow . . . Kincaid is going to lose his mind."

Inwardly, I smiled. It was impossible not to be affected by her enthusiasm. She might have been petite, but she housed big, explosive energy. I quickly shook my head. "I don't think it will matter."

Her face frowned a little. "Oh . . ." she chirped, ". . . back to my secret. I totally understand how you're feeling right now. I've been there."

"Doubtful," I mumbled, laying my dress on the bed.

"Don't be so sure." She sat on the small chaise near my bed, looking prim and proper, her ankles crossed, her spine straight, and her hands resting in her lap. "My marriage was arranged too."

My eyes went wild with surprise. "You know?"

"I do. Like I said, my husband and yours are like brothers. They know everything about each other. They're friends and business partners. Outside of Caid, Darius is the only one you trust—well, other than me, but the point is, I understand what today feels like for you. I'm here to make it not so lonely, and from the perspective of someone who understands what you're going through, I can't express how important it is for you to think of today as special. Either way, arranged or not, this is *your* wedding. Don't view it as anything other than that. Fuck those contracts, girl. You're a bride-to-be," she insisted with sass, making me laugh.

"I guess."

"No, ma'am. That's what you *are* and how you approach today. Regardless of your agreement, it's not *only* business; otherwise, I wouldn't be here. Caid wanted this to be a good day, and he wanted to make sure you had support. This would be a transaction if he didn't care outside of whatever you signed. But he wants it to feel like family. I'm his family, and he's extending me to you so you have family with you today. And listen, my husband don't play about me, so if he agreed on me being a part of this, he knows it's important to Caid."

I wasn't sure why, but that made me a little more settled. I was still nervous about making this thing with us legal, but Alisha being there made it a little less of a formality. She could've been lying through her teeth but presented as sincere, so I accepted the offer of support and friendship.

Another knock was at the door, and she quickly checked her phone. "Oh, that's your glam team. You relax, and I'll get them. We're about to make you fabulous. I mean, not that you're not already beautiful because, shit, girl, I see why he picked you. But they'll work their magic and have Kincaid's knees buckling when you walk through the door. Trust me."

She crossed the room, and I considered what she was saying. Would he be impressed? And did I care? Who was I fooling? That was what had me so anxious. I wanted my husband, fake or not, to see me and be blown away. Hopefully, I delivered.

CHAPTER 8

KINCAID.

"**Y**ou nervous?" Darius asked from beside me. I stood, looking down at the city, fully dressed, minus my jacket.

"No. Why?" I glanced at him before I returned to staring at the movement below.

"Because you've been standing here for damn near thirty minutes just staring at nothing. There's not a damn thing going on down there." When I glanced at him again, he had a grin in place. I couldn't help but laugh at the observation. Maybe I was nervous, but not about marrying Nari. That was the least of my worries. She said yes. Alisha checked in, letting me know that things were going well and that she really liked Nari a lot.

The one piece that I was uncertain of was my parents.

"My folks are walking in blind. I just invited them over, but they have no idea why."

"Your pops still doesn't know about Kaber?"

"No. I couldn't tell him and risk a reaction before I married Nari. I wouldn't have been able to stop him from going after Kaber, and I needed this binding before anyone found out."

"Well, as soon as he knows why you did things this way, he'll be cool."

"Maybe. I made the decision without him. He won't like that; he and my mother know Aila. They like her. She's been around them under the guise of being family. My mother's been planning a wedding with her. Nari is . . ."

"An outsider." He finished my sentence. "You know I get that shit. Hell, my parents still don't really like Alisha. She's my wife, so they accept her, but deep down inside, they still hate that I married her. It's more about what we lost than me being happy, and the shit's fucked up, but I get it. I love my wife, and nothing matters but what's between us."

"Shit, man. It's been five years. You're not giving me hope."

"Hey, it's life. That shit is complicated. Our lives are different than most, and yours is much worse than mine. There are a lot of factors to consider. Marriages are business deals that create power. In their eyes, Alisha didn't bring anything to the table, and we lost as a family."

"And in yours?"

"You already know. I love that girl more than I can even make sense of. So much so that if I had to choose, it would be her over my family. They know that, which is why they learned to live with it."

"That's not where we are."

"But do you think it's where you could be or even want to be?"

My eyes remained pinned to what was going on below. The simple answer was yes. It was why I chose Nari. I assumed that being around her would prove what I felt the first night we crossed paths at the club would lessen or disappear, but it had only grown since then. My connection intensified each time I was around her. I couldn't define what it was, but I knew I wanted her, and not just in terms of an agreement. I wanted Nari as my wife.

"Time will tell," was my answer.

Darius nodded. He was my brother; he knew me. He understood my thoughts sometimes without me having to express them.

"Boss, they're here." Cast's voice caused both Darius and me to turn around.

"Gary is with them," Darius made clear. His wife didn't always travel with security, but it wasn't uncommon. That day was one of those days.

"I'll still meet them in the lobby," Cast tossed out before heading to the elevator.

"You ready for this?"

"As ready as I can be."

My eyes moved about the penthouse. I paid a decorator who arrived that morning for simple decorations, but she had outdone herself. There were vases of flowers throughout the open space with exotic floral arrangements. I wasn't sure if red was Nari's color, but the way it looked against her skin the night I proposed officially made it my new favorite color.

It was the only detail I provided to the decorator when I brought her on. She'd done an amazing job of incorporating the color throughout. I had no idea what she used but recalled her rattling off variations such as amaryllis, anemone, poppy, and calla lilies. I told her any flower arrangement was approved but roses. Roses were typical and cliché, and that wasn't Nari. She was anything *but* cliché.

After one last inspection, I walked over and lifted my jacket from the sofa, slipping into it. Once I smoothed my hands down the front, I turned to Darius.

"Rings?"

He patted his chest to say they were here in his pocket. A photographer and an officiant were on hand and were both waiting in my guest room. I checked the time, noticing that my parents should also be arriving at any moment. I wanted everyone in place, hoping my parents would cause less of a scene. My mother was the type to force decorum. She might not have liked being ambushed at this wedding, but she would behave respectfully and force my father to as well. Once Nari and I were married, I would hash things out with them.

"Oh, wow. This is absolutely gorgeous." That was Alisha. I was aware of her presence, but all my attention was trained on the woman by her side. I had no words, none at all, because she had rendered me completely speechless.

Nari's dress was some form-fitting number, which sparkled because of the tiny crystals affixed to it. The material hugged her body, exposing curves I knew she had, but damn if they weren't amplified in that damn dress. I seriously regretted my decision to choose slim-fitting pants.

She seemed nervous. Her eyes brushed around, giving me time to fully take her in. She was wearing makeup, but it was light and barely noticeable. I was well acquainted with her fresh face; both were equally pleasing. She was a beautiful woman, with or without. Her hair was styled on one side with a cascade of curls that brushed her bare shoulder. The dress she chose was strapless, adding to its appeal. I approved. When her eyes finally made it to me, she smiled. It was soft and anxious. *Ahhh, she's nervous.*

Nari followed Alisha as she moved from the elevator into the living room. Alisha tucked herself against Darius's side while Nari approached me.

"Perfect, right?" Alisha said as Nari and I stared at each other.

"Better than," I responded, but my eyes never left my future bride.

"Told you, girl. Buckling at the knees."

I chuckled, shooting my eyes over to Alisha, who winked. I inched closer to Nari, leaning a bit to speak privately. Not only did she look like perfection, but she also smelled like heaven, which contradicted my sinful thoughts at that moment.

"You're beautiful." My lips brushed her ear when I spoke, and I noticed her body shiver. It was subtle, but I caught it.

"Thank you."

I gave her some space, but it was more for me. If I remained that close, we'd both be in trouble.

"You don't look so bad yourself."

"Glad you approve. You ready for this?"

"Are you?"

"Yes."

"Then I am too."

"Good." I pressed a kiss to her cheek and stepped away, returning with our officiant and photographer. Once everyone was in place, she began capturing photos. Nari and I posed for some, and others were candid. The combinations varied from Nari and me to Nari and Alisha and then the four of us. I wasn't sure what else they'd captured and didn't care. The day would forever be ingrained in my memory.

"Kincaid, what's going on?" My mother's voice brought all eyes to her. She was dressed as I'd asked, in red, the same as Alisha. My father was in a black suit, but his face was tight.

"My wedding."

"Your wedding?" My mother looked confused. Her eyes bounced around the room and eventually landed on Nari at my side. My hand rested protectively on her hip, holding her close.

"Wedding? To whom?" My father was next to speak as they both neared us. I lowered my eyes to Nari before addressing my father.

"Mom, Dad, this is Nari Collette. Nari, these are my parents."

"Kincaid, I'm confused. What's going on?" my mother asked once more.

"Again, my wedding. I'm marrying Nari."

My father's face went tight. "How the hell are you marrying this woman when you're engaged to Aila? Make that make sense to me, son."

I felt Nari's body stiffening next to me, and she attempted to inch away, but I held her in place.

"You're here because it's important to me that you be here. I'm marrying Nari, here, today—with or without you. I hope you stay because it won't feel right to experience this next step in my life without you, but regardless, I'm doing it."

"Kincaid—" My father began, but my mother cut him off.

"We're staying." She shot my father a look that shut him up but didn't fix the scowl on his face. She then smiled at Nari, extending her hand.

"Pleased to meet you, Nari. You're absolutely stunning."

"Thank you. Pleased to meet you as well." She offered my mother a genuine smile, which I appreciated.

My father mumbled a half-assed greeting after my mother shot him another look, which issued a silent warning, and instead of harping on the tension, I decided to move on with the ceremony. After we had some space, Nari hissed at me with an evil look.

"You're engaged to another woman?"

"It's not what you think. I'll explain later."

"Why not now?"

I leaned down and kissed her cheek before whispering, "Because we're getting married, agreed?"

Her face showed every bit of annoyance she felt, but she forced a smile and nodded. "Agreed."

I didn't care if she was angry; she was about to be my wife, which trumped everything else. We'd figure out the rest later.

The ceremony flowed effortlessly. Nari wasn't happy with me, but she still seemed pleasant through it all. I also half expected my father to object at some point, but he didn't. He was, however, pissed with me. I could see it all over his face and feel it in his energy. It was why once we sealed the deal with our first kiss as Mr. and Mrs. Kincaid Akel, I was grateful for my mother and Alisha bombarding Nari with well-wishing because I could speak with my father privately.

"What the hell just happened, Kincaid?"

"Me protecting our family."

"How? You marrying that woman, whoever the hell she is, just put us in a bind. I pray you have a plan for how we will deal with what comes next."

"Marrying Nari is my plan."

"How?"

"Kaber has been lying. I don't want to get into all the details. Regardless of how you feel, today is still my wedding day. It's not ideal, but it's important to me, and more importantly, I refuse to ruin this for my wife."

"Your wife?" He snorted, shooting daggers at Nari.

"Yes, my wife. Please don't be disrespectful because I am a man first. Your son second. You will not be unkind to the woman I just promised my life to."

My father realized I wasn't budging on the issue and moved on.

"At the very least, tell me what changed. He's been lying about what, Kincaid?"

"He's broke, his businesses are failing, and he's in bad standing with The Families. There's more to it, but again, I'd prefer to discuss this at another time." My regard moved to my wife.

"I don't understand. If that's the case, why wouldn't you come to me? We—"

"No, not we—*me*. The deciding factor was on me. *I* was the one who was supposed to marry into that family. Doing so would've been a liability—"

"And now? You had a valid contract with Kaber."

"It's handled."

"And Aila?"

"Casualty. I'll personally tell her, but I couldn't until I was officially married to Nari."

"I don't like this, son."

"I don't either, but this is where we are. I just need you to trust me, and more than that, I need you to accept my wife. She was thrown into this like you were, but she's not the enemy. I won't stand for her feeling as if she is."

My father stared at me, wanting to say more, but he trusted me. I'd proven over time that he could, so that day, that was what he relied on. After a long moment, he hugged me.

"Congratulations, son. I hope you know what you're doing."

"I do," I assured him.

He offered a nod, finally granting me a smile. "So, this Nari?"

"A story for a different day."

He chuckled and nodded. "Understood. Let me go meet my daughter-in-law."

My father hugged me once more before we rejoined everyone else. The next few hours, we enjoyed drinks and catered food with my parents and the closest people to me—Darius, Alisha, and Cast. Nari seemed to be in a much better mood, and I attributed that to my father welcoming her to the family with open arms, as well as my mother's and Alisha's complete acceptance. Alisha and my mother were close because Darius and I had been friends for so long. They were on several committees together and mentioned bringing Nari in as well. She seemed completely open, but I could tell my life would be new and a bit of a challenge for her. I'd fully support whatever would make her feel welcome, but I had to feel her out to know how to make that happen. Before my mother left, she shared with me her displeasure with how I'd handled the situation and made me promise to find a way to make things right with Aila.

I promised to speak to Aila face-to-face, but there was no making things right. She would be devastated and wouldn't understand. No matter how closed off I'd been during our time together, she had crafted some love story in her mind that would be ours. I owned my part because I led her to believe we would indeed be married and have a good life together. We would've . . . had it not been for her father. That was out of her control, but she would pay the price. I wasn't happy, but that was how things worked in our world.

My parents were the first to leave, followed by Cast, who had a date waiting, making Darius and Alisha the last to linger. While Alisha and Nari were tucked away in the living room, Darius and I burned one on the balcony. I didn't smoke often, but when I did, it was usually with him.

"How you feel?"

"The same. Ask me tomorrow," I chuckled, glancing at Nari, who just happened to be laughing at something Alisha said. She seemed free and unguarded, a side I hadn't been blessed with just yet. I was happy that she accepted Alisha as a friend because her intent was genuine. She approached the situation because I asked her to, but they instantly clicked, and I could tell Alisha truly liked Nari. She'd told me several times throughout the night, but I could see it in how she embraced my new wife.

"Dog, you're in trouble." Darius chuckled and reached for the blunt.

"How so?"

"That woman in there is going be your greatest weakness. I just pray she's also your greatest strength."

I glanced at Nari and nodded. "Me too."

"We're about to be out. When will you be back?"

"Next weekend, but I'll be in touch before then."

"I'm good. Do ya thing. Enjoy your time with your new bride." He smirked, mocking me.

"I plan to. If she doesn't try to have this shit annulled before then." I thought about how pissed Nari was after my father's outburst filled her in that I had been engaged to another woman.

"Nah, she in this with you."

"What makes you so sure?"

"The way she looks at you. You can't fake that shit. She might not have it all figured out, but she's in this with you. The question is, are you in this with her?"

"This is an arrangement."

"That's how it started, but that's not how it has to end."

"For now, it is what it is."

Darius nodded and ashed the blunt against the side of the building before we dapped and embraced in a brotherly hug.

"Be intent, Caid."

"Always."

After saying our goodbyes to Darius and Alisha, Nari and I were alone for the first time that night. The first thing she did was step out of her shoes and sigh in relief.

"You could've done that before now. No one would've minded."

"Possibly, but it didn't feel right. Thank you for today. You didn't have to do all this. I really expected something a lot less—"

"Real."

"Yeah, I guess so, but it was nice."

"And I've told you several times, this is as real as you want it to be."

"You sure about that?"

I leaned against one wall in the kitchen while she stood over the counter, picking at the icing on our wedding cake. Even that intrigued me. The way she dipped her finger in the pearl-colored cream and sucked it off had my dick swelling.

"One thing I'll never do is lie to you."

"Okay, so who's Aila?"

"The daughter of a business associate."

"Who you're engaged to?"

"Yes, but it's not what you think."

"So explain because what I think is that you married me while you were promised to another woman. How does that work?"

I studied her face, gauging her mood. If I wasn't mistaken, she was either hurt or disappointed. Neither pleased me.

"She and I were engaged."

"*Are.* Your father made it seem as if this situation is current."

I brushed my hand down my face and nodded. "It is, but my situation with Aila was in some ways similar to ours."

"How?"

Our eyes remained fastened to each other until the moment she understood.

"An arrangement," I clarified.

"Then I really don't understand. Why would you marry me when you were supposed to marry her?"

"Because the terms changed. It was no longer beneficial, and the only out I had was to marry someone else. I chose you."

"Wow." She leaned on the counter, facing me. Her face twisted while she processed the obvious. "So that's why you rushed this?"

"Yes."

"Did you love her?"

"No."

"But you would've married her?"

"I would've."

She brushed her palms down her thighs and nodded. "Well, I guess we should figure out what's next. Are we staying here?"

"No. We have a flight to catch. The jet is fueled and waiting."

"A flight? Where are we going?" The way her eyes squinted and her lips pursed was cute.

"Honeymoon."

"Oh, I just assumed . . ."

"I promised to make this as close to reality as you allow me to. After the marriage comes the honeymoon, if I'm not mistaken. But I'm new to this too, so . . ."

"That is the natural order of things, but this isn't exactly a normal marriage."

"It can be. So are we catching that flight or what?"

"Free trip? I'm down." She smiled softly, attempting to hide that she was actually excited about the possibility. I wouldn't push. I would give her space to process everything that was between us. She was officially my wife, so, like it or not, she was stuck with me.

CHAPTER 9

NARI.

I woke up in paradise. There was no other way to explain it other than one simple word . . .

Paradise!

After we left what I learned was Kincaid's penthouse apartment, things moved kinda fast. We cleared out my hotel room, and I packed in a luggage set that Kincaid gifted me. It was expensive and matched the set he owned. Of my belongings, what I didn't need for my trip was sent somewhere. I wasn't sure where, and I didn't ask. Kincaid had also purchased items for me to travel with. We would be gone for seven days, and based on the swimwear, dresses, shorts, tees, and coverups in one of the luggage pieces I'd been gifted, I assumed it was somewhere warm.

Kincaid spent the three-hour flight working. He sat across from me on a jet he owned, with a laptop and two phones, navigating between the three devices. Glasses sat on his face while he worked, which I found adorably sexy. He was also dressed down after having changed out of his suit. My husband, a term that still felt foreign on the tongue, was dressed in gray athletic pants and a black T-shirt. He wore a pair of expensive sneakers, but even his casual clothes seemed to capture his professionalism. The man had

CEO embedded in his DNA. While he worked, I found myself stealing peeks at him. He seemed intent and focused on whatever he was doing but was still very aware of my presence. I knew that because the slightest adjustment of my body gained his attention. I eventually drifted off to sleep, but I heard him on the phone during my half-lucid states. I couldn't recall any specifics of what was being said, but I remember his voice being very assertive and businesslike.

I was awakened at some point by a kiss on my forehead. It was nice and felt natural, as if it were a normal exchange between us. Once I was awake and functioning, Kincaid informed me that we'd arrived at our destination. We stepped off the jet, and a car was waiting, everything moving like a well-oiled machine. I briefly glanced at the men loading our his-and-hers luggage into the trunk of our vehicle while we slid into the rear seat. Kincaid sat on one side while I occupied the other, watching the city pass as we whizzed through the darkness.

We eventually ended up in a resort of some kind. It was dark, but I could still tell that it was exquisite. It felt airy, and my body immediately relaxed. The staff was overly nice as they hurried through the check-in process. We were then taken on a golf cart down a long, winding trail to a private area. I didn't explore much. I simply showered and climbed into bed. I was, however, informed that our villa had five bedrooms and to choose one. That was how I ended up in such a comfy space. That place was indeed too much space for only two people, but it was telling of my husband's taste.

Kincaid's quarters were across the hall from mine, but he set up in the living room, mentioning that he had more work to do. After asking if I needed anything, to which I said no, he was gone, and I was buried under the softest bedding I'd ever experienced in my life and was out in minutes. And then . . .

Paradise.

"I hope it suits your expectations."

That voice. It was a little gruffer than usual, which I assumed was because he'd just woken up.

"Are you kidding? This is heaven on earth. We're on the beach, like actually on the beach. And I received a notification that I am half a million dollars richer than I was before I went to sleep."

"A deal is a deal. I'm a man of my word," he returned with a hint of humor on his tongue.

"It seems you are."

I grinned, glancing over my shoulder to find my husband standing in the doorway. His upper body was tilted toward the frame, resting on one of those solid shoulders while he watched me. His chest was bare, and he wore gray sleep pants that sat low on his waist. His shoulders were broad, his chest and stomach were carved with defined lines, and indentions on either side of his hips formed that forbidden V. His pants sat so low that they exposed a patch of black hair, which barely peeked from beneath them, but it was visible.

I could sense his intensity even before my eyes began to roam. I was dressed in a silk gown that stopped midthigh. Another gift selection from my husband. It was packed away in my travel bag. Kincaid was always watching me in a way that made me feel that he assumed if he didn't, I'd disappear.

Odd!

"It was last minute, but I wanted to ensure you were pleased and enjoyed our honeymoon."

"I'm more than pleased, so another A-plus, but where are we?"

"Tulum."

I frowned but was too embarrassed to let on that I had no clue where the hell Tulum was. The extent of my travel was the city I'd been raised in.

"Mexico." His features relaxed, and I was offered that barely-there smile. It traveled up to his eyes, and they left me briefly and transitioned to the ocean view. It was breathtaking and my new favorite thing.

"I think your view is better than mine." His voice was throaty, as if he had to force the words out.

"We can switch if you want."

Those dark, serious eyes landed on me in a matter of seconds. "Or we could share this one."

My lips parted, and he broke the tension by offering a charming smile.

"The chef is preparing breakfast. I put in a request for you, but if you would prefer, you can change it."

"No. I'm sure it will be fine. I would be willing to bet that even the grass here tastes good."

He laughed, his gaze pinned to me as if he were in no rush, like he had all the time in the world, but those mysterious eyes exposed his thoughts and made my heart race. Something about them delivered the words that threatened to leave his lips but wouldn't.

"Quite possibly, but I assure you, your breakfast will be more than just grass."

"Well, either way, I'm game."

"Good. Meet me downstairs when you're ready."

I nodded, and as he turned to leave, my thoughts spilled out before I could control them.

"Was this for her?"

He paused, turning to face me again, his brows inching in, his eyes lowered in my direction.

"Her?"

"Aila . . . Was this where you were taking her?"

"No." His answer came quickly, but I didn't physically relax until he continued. "She and my mother were planning the wedding. I didn't care about the details. She'd casually mentioned a few places for our honeymoon, but Tulum was never on the list. I chose this, specifically for you, with you in mind."

We remained in a stare down before he spoke again. "I'll be waiting for you downstairs. Take your time."

And then he was gone. Kincaid didn't seem upset, but I couldn't say he was happy either. I didn't care. I had the right to know. He married me while engaged to another woman. A part of me didn't want to be inserted into a plan that was put in place with thoughts of another woman. I might've agreed to this as a business deal, but that didn't mean my feelings shouldn't be considered.

When I finally made it downstairs after a quick shower, I found Kincaid standing just outside the open space with a phone to his ear. He noticed me entering the room and followed my path to the table with his eyes. He smiled before addressing his caller.

"Aye, D, let me call you back. We're about to have breakfast." He paused, and when I looked up, I caught him smiling hard, amusement in his eyes. Whoever "D" was had said something funny. "We'll see how it goes. A'ight, later."

He ended the call and moved toward me, now dressed in shorts that looked like trunks and a gray T-shirt. The material was thin, giving it a lightweight appearance. Once Kincaid was close enough, he pulled out my chair. I sat, and he kissed my temple and filled the space across from me. I lifted the lid to my dish and smiled at my meal: Belgium waffles, cheese eggs, and freely sliced fruit.

"You approve?" Like always, he'd been watching, waiting.

"I do. Thank you." With a nod, his lid was removed, exposing an omelet, which looked full of diced vegetables and sausage links paired with fresh fruit identical to mine.

A tin of coffee was in the center of the table, with sugar and cream in separate tins. Next to that was a glass pitcher of orange juice and a glass cylinder of what I assumed was maple syrup.

"So . . ." I began after saying a quick blessing over my meal, immediately cutting into my waffles. "What's on the agenda?"

"Whatever you want. Our villa is on the private section of the beach."

"So, it's just us?" I questioned after shoving a forkful of waffles into my mouth, moaning as it melted on my tongue. I hadn't used the maple syrup, and the flavor was still perfect.

"Be careful with those sounds, Nari. My patience is thinning."

My eyes shot up to his, and he smiled seductively with no shame. Was he saying . . .

Yep, flirting.

"Yes, just us. We can schedule activities, but I'll have to call and arrange them. They have scuba diving, parasailing, boat excursions to explore, and likely anything else you can imagine. The list is a mile long, but if that's not your thing, we can just hang out here."

"Is that your thing?"

"I travel a lot, so I've done most of those, but I can't say they're necessarily my thing. Just something I've experienced."

"With business, you travel a lot?"

"Yes, and pleasure as well."

"With women?"

His hands lowered to the table, resting there while he took me in.

"Yes. Occasionally, in the past, women have accompanied me."

"Has *she*?" My eyes narrowed on his. We engaged in a visual battle before one hand lifted and a palm brushed down his face. He then balled a fist, and his knuckles cracked while he lowered them to the table.

"Let's get this over with."

"What?"

"Your questions about Aila. I'm here with *you*. I only want to be here with you, but until you let that go, she'll be right here, between us. Ask what you want, but once we get this out of the way, we're not wasting our time on the topic again. Not here, not at home, not ever. Understood?"

I shrugged with one shoulder. "Fine."

"Okay, go."

"Does she know about me?"

"No, but she will."

"And then what?"

"Then nothing. I've made my decision. You are my wife. Nothing changes that. No one's opinions but yours matter."

"What kind of relationship did you have with her if it's that easy to cut her off?"

"We didn't have one, at least not on my end. It was more of a friendship. We spent time together, had dinners with friends, and went out occasionally, but truthfully, I spent so much time working that we were hardly ever together. That was done on purpose. I like Aila but wasn't attracted to her like I am to you." His words were confident, leaving no room for argument.

"So you weren't in a relationship with her, but she was in one with you?"

"Yes, which will make it hard to wrap her mind around me marrying someone else. She won't like it. She'll be hurt by it, but it won't change how I feel."

"So, all business for you, huh?"

His eyes grew serious. "With *her*, yes."

Message received.

"Let me be clear, Nari. My world is not always pleasant. Deals are brokered daily, and people lose their life's work because of poor business decisions. The terms are never favorable to all parties involved. Someone always loses. In this situation, it's Aila. I hate that it's come to this, but the matter can't be helped. I can't protect her feelings and yours at the same time. I had to choose, and I chose you."

The intensity of his stare had my chest tight. I wasn't sure of all the layers to what I'd gotten myself into, but it felt . . .

Complicated.

"Your parents were upset. Whatever deal you had that included Aila affected them?"

"Yes."

"Is that why they don't like me?"

"They don't dislike you. The wedding was tossed at them without warning. I take full responsibility for how they reacted, but they both apologized and welcome you to our family."

I felt they were open to the possibility but couldn't guarantee that they actually liked me. I suppose I'd find out soon enough. So I chose to move on.

"Is what you do dangerous or illegal?"

"Some of it, yes."

I frowned at the thought.

"Why wouldn't you tell me that?"

"You didn't ask."

"That's not fair, Kincaid. How would I have known to ask?"

"You wouldn't."

"Wow! So me being with you is dangerous?"

"To a degree, yes, but nothing will touch you—ever. That's my word."

"How can you—"

"Because I can. You're my wife, Nari. Nothing touches you."

"On paper," I shot back. He snorted and lifted his fork.

"Eat." Those eyes were on me again. "And no more discussion about Aila, agreed?"

"Agreed."

I didn't miss that Kincaid didn't respond to my rebuttal of simply being his wife on paper. Deep down inside, I already knew that we'd crossed that line and were traveling into something more. I simply wasn't sure how open I'd be to any of it; however, I was here in paradise with my fake husband and fully intended to make the most of it.

Our first day was a lazy one. We both agreed to spend our time at the villa, but even that was eventful. I spent the morning through early afternoon relaxing in a knitted hammock. Kincaid busied himself making calls and working on his laptop, but he did so from a lounge chair beside my hammock. In between acquisitions and mergers, he checked in to make sure I was okay, but oddly, the sound of his voice was enough to bring me peace. His business persona turned me on. Listening to him boss people around while managing and brokering deals that I was sure were valued in millions was a complete turn-on. Combined with the visual I was blessed with of him as well as my surroundings, I'd sworn I'd died and gone to heaven.

After lunch, Kincaid packed away his devices and shared a meal with me—fresh fish, salad, and the most tantalizing tropical drinks I'd ever experienced. I was a little buzzed because they were strong, and I wasn't much of a drinker. He seemed to be faring much better than me but was enjoying my inebriated state. His eyes were always exploring, taking me in like I was a work of art; he made me feel as if I were. I was falling for my husband but felt that it was forbidden . . .

How insane is that?

"What's on your mind, Nari?"

"You." Somehow, I had diarrhea of the mouth, and my thoughts were no longer filtered. I didn't care because, well, shit . . .

He was my husband.

"What about me?" We were now sharing a hammock, my body tangled with his, which was below me. Another side effect of the multiple drinks I had. When he climbed in with me, I didn't object.

"Everything about you. Shouldn't I know my husband?"

"You should."

"Well, I don't." My head tilted back, and I stared at Kincaid. His eyes were no longer on me. He focused on the ocean, and he seemed to be at peace. We'd been there less than a day, and I was already experiencing a different side of him. Even when working, he was at ease, relaxed to the point of seeming happy.

"Then let's fix that. I can't have my wife feeling inadequate where I'm concerned. You, of all people, should know me best." He lowered his chin, pressing a kiss to my forehead. One of his large hands moved down my side to my thigh. His fingers danced across my skin, creating electric currents that moved through me at lightning speed.

"What's your favorite color?"

He chuckled but answered. "Red if I had to choose, but I can't say I've ever claimed one."

"Red?"

"If it feels odd, blame yourself. It became my obsession after I saw you in that dress."

"The night you proposed?" I grinned, lifting my eyes, but his were on the ocean again.

"Yes."

"Favorite food?"

"Don't have one."

"There has to be one. Don't be difficult." I frowned, and he lowered his eyes to meet mine.

"Seafood."

"I suppose that works. Did you want to be married?"

That time, my eyes remained pinned to the ocean view, but I felt his on me.

"Why do you ask?"

"Both situations were arranged." *Mine and hers.* "It's not like you proposed because you found a woman you loved and wanted to spend the rest of your life with."

I could feel him thinking. The time that passed made me anxious.

"How can you be so sure I hadn't?"

"Hadn't what?"

"Found a woman I wanted to spend my life with?"

"Because if you had, you would have married her instead of me."

His fingers paused briefly but slowly began dancing across my skin again. It was rhythmical, soothing in a sense.

"I knew that I would be married one day. So, to answer your question in the simplest way, yes. And you?"

"Marriage? I guess, but when you're struggling to make ends meet, you don't invest much time in fairy tales."

"Marriages don't have to be a fairy tale. In my opinion, they're far from it. Fairy tales aren't real, and that's not how I view marriage."

But ours isn't real?

I spoke the words in my mind but decided to leave things there. No sense in ruining a perfect moment, and there, right then with him, felt just that . . .

Perfect!

CHAPTER 10

KINCAID.

We were on day three of our honeymoon, and I had no complaints. My time with Nari had been better than I could have imagined. She was awkward in an adorable way. She wasn't used to my lifestyle. There was no limit to my access. When she mentioned something, I made it happen. Each time, she seemed thrilled with the enthusiasm of a child but reserved, as if she shouldn't be enjoying the privilege. She was also tough and guarded at times. We'd be deep in conversation under the guise of getting to know each other, and at times, she would shy away or back down. It was mainly when our life experiences didn't align because of the differences in our backgrounds. I was raised with wealth; she was raised being bounced around foster care. I had no expectations for my wife. I knew her background or what little there was to know. I'd done my research and was well versed in her humble beginnings. I didn't want or need anything *except* her, but I believed she felt she had to match my ambitions to provide.

It was exposed in little things like the fact that we had a full staff, but she kept our villa immaculate. When I made clear that she was on her honeymoon and her only responsibility was to relax and enjoy, she waved me off, promising it wasn't a big deal to clean up after us. I often had to pull her away or keep her distracted so she wouldn't waste time completing the staff's duties.

For the most part, I had no complaints until now. I sat, staring at my phone, face tight from the photos I was scrolling through. They were of our villa, the beach, or selfies of Nari looking stunning in the items I had hand selected for our time in Tulum. The visuals were perfect, but one thing was missing . . .

Me!

I wasn't in one damn photo on her page, and that sent fire through my veins. It was why I sat inside my room brooding while she enjoyed a peaceful afternoon in one of the hammocks that had become our go-to spots.

That woman had me infuriated and pouting like a spoiled child at the same time. I tried to convince myself that it wasn't a big deal, but internally, it was. Regardless of how we started, she was my wife.

Mine!

Mine to possess, to show off, to appreciate. The pictures she posted over the past few days presented a different story. Nari might've assumed it was all business, but I'd long since demolished that idea. I wanted her and everything that came with her. So much so that when she asked about marriage, I was close to expressing that I had never considered a lifetime with anyone until the night I crossed paths with her at Salacious. I couldn't define it, but I felt things that weren't normal. I felt her and wanted more. My proposition of marriage was indeed a way to end my arrangement with Kaber, but it was also a way to allow Nari time to catch up. To share the same space that I was in. She was getting there. I could feel her falling, moving closer to the idea of us as a real connection and not just being bound by terms and agreements.

Expelling a breath in an attempt to calm my annoyance, I rose from the bed and traveled through the villa until I was standing over the hammock she rested in. That day, her beautiful skin seemed to glow even more due to days of being under the Mexican sun. She was in one of the suits I'd gifted. A black two-piece that fit to perfection but exposed her body. Nari was beautiful, and her body was a work of art. It was naturally composed of thick, toned thighs, toned arms, and a waist that dipped in just right to expose the curve of her hips. Her stomach wasn't completely flat, and no defined abs existed, but she was fit. She was tall for a woman but still aligned nicely when I held her close. She was not so tall that she didn't have to look up at me. She was my new obsession. Everything about my wife was appealing, and the fact that she had no clue just how beautiful and sexy she truly was enhanced my growing attraction.

"You've been working? You were gone for a while."

My eyes barely connected to hers because she tented them with her hand. The sun was shifting, so it reflected on her face.

"No. I promised to give you my full attention for the rest of the trip."

She'd casually mentioned at dinner our second night that I'd been busy since we arrived. I had; our trip was last minute, which meant I was working remotely. However, I delegated a few things and only worked while she was asleep, slipping out of bed to do so. After the first night, she ended up in my room. We shared a bed, wrapped in each other, but hadn't been intimate. It was driving me crazy, but I wanted it to be Nari's decision to move forward, not mine. I didn't push, but I flirted often, and then again, so did she.

"Then what were you doing?" She frowned, and I lifted my phone, which was in my hand. She peered at the screen and then back to me.

"That's my page?"

"It is."

"You're following me?"

"No, but I will."

"Then how?"

"You commented on one of Alisha's photos. It came across my timeline."

"Oh, if you don't want me to post, I won't. We haven't really discussed the rules on that."

"I don't care what you post. I do, however, care what you *don't* post."

"I don't . . . What do you mean?"

"If I didn't know better, I'd think you were here alone. It seems as if you're having an amazing time. *My wife* is enjoying her time in Tulum, but there's no mention of me. And not one of these photos shows your left hand. It's always hidden."

Her frown grew deeper. "Are you upset because I didn't post you or us or that we're married?"

"I'm not upset."

She squinted a little before sitting up. I offered a hand to help, and she eventually managed to sit upright with her legs hanging over the edge.

"It seems like you are. I'm still struggling with what's approved and what's not. No one knows about us—"

"But they will. You're not a secret, Nari."

"But our terms are—"

My teeth raked across my bottom lip. I couldn't dispute that. "As far as the world knows, you are my wife. You behave as such, which means that on our honeymoon, you're allowed to let the world know that your smile is partially due to me, or at least I hope it is."

I studied her face, and she studied mine. Seconds later, she pushed out a huff of air. "I didn't think it would matter. I assumed I was following the rules."

"You didn't *think* of me."

"And you thought of me?" she challenged.

"Always." I lifted my phone and navigated from her page to mine. I didn't post much, but I had a following as if I did. Social media wasn't something I placed much value on because my time was extremely limited. I was sure most of my followers were women with specific intentions who wouldn't be pleased with the visual I presented, but not even that deterred me from what I'd done our second night here. Nari was asleep in my bed. *Our bed*, and I caught a photo of her on her stomach, hair layered across the pillow. The covers were at her waist, but she wore a silk gown. One arm was folded beneath the pillow, and the other was at her chest with her hand balled into a loose fist under her chin. Perfection. The caption was simple. *Mrs. Akel. It's official.* Aila followed my page, stalking it even, which was why I blocked her number after making the post. I would have to deal with her eventually, but not while I was with Nari. I wouldn't ruin my wife's time here with Aila's tears and tantrums.

When I handed over my phone, Nari stared at the photo, face relaxed, her eyes slowly lifting to mine after she made sense of what was on the screen. Those pretty browns revealed her thoughts and expressed her confusion. She didn't know what to make of the act. Instead of having a discussion, I leaned close to her face, our eyes leveled, before I gently gripped her chin. "You're my wife, not my secret, and I don't want to be yours."

She opened her mouth to respond, but our lips met before she could. My mouth clashed against hers, initiating a kiss. It was our third. The first was the night I proposed; our second, after our wedding was final, and that one. That time, I extended all of myself. My tongue tangled with hers. I was starved for a closeness that only she could provide. Like always, her energy leaped onto me, feeling like it was in me. She was so consuming without trying, and I welcomed the gift. When I backed away, standing to my full height, she stared with lazy eyes, lips parted, which she eventually reached to touch with trembling fingers. My eye focused on the diamond, which caught the light of the sun, and a cocky grin tugged at my lips.

"I'm your husband, Nari, not your secret. Agreed?"

"Agreed." She almost whispered the response, but I heard her.

"Good. Let's get cleaned up for dinner. We're eating on the beach tonight."

I walked away, not waiting for her movement or response. I had proved my point, for now, but I was sure I would have to reinforce my intent until it was natural for her to think of us as a union. That mattered little because I fully intended to convince my wife that this was more than just signatures on paper.

"You're almost pretty."

"Pretty?"

"Yes, pretty, but not in a feminine way. There's something rugged about you in a way that lacks perfection, but at first glance, you're insanely gorgeous." She flashed me a smile while I chuckled behind my glass as it met my lips. We'd finished dinner, and she enjoyed what was left of her wine while I enjoyed tequila. My preference was brown liquor, but it wasn't as common here. The Jose Cuervo 250 Aniversario I was drinking was exclusive and smooth, so I enjoyed it as a viable substitute.

"I'm sure you meant that as a compliment, but I can't say that's how it was received."

Her cheeks hiked, causing her eyes to thin out. "It most certainly was a compliment. My husband is extremely handsome. That might not be a good thing. I'm not much of a fighter." She frowned, her lips puffing into a pout.

"You don't have to be. You'll never fight over me. I wouldn't allow it. I'm all yours, Nari. No one can challenge that."

"No one?"

"Not one soul. That I can promise you."

"Hmmm, that sounds very exclusive."

"That sounds like marriage," I stated bluntly.

Her eyes lowered a little. She was tipsy. I'd quickly learned that tipsy Nari revealed secrets she would otherwise protect with her life.

"I like you."

"Good."

"Do you like me?" Her eyes fastened to mine, and she leaned forward on her elbows, chin resting on intertwined fingers.

"What do you think?"

"I think that you make me nervous because you're always watching me. And it's not just that you're watching me, but how you do it."

"Which is?"

"Intensely, like you're sometimes afraid that I'll disappear. And other times, you stare like you're trying to remember every detail about me."

"You're correct about both."

She frowned a little.

"You're rare in ways I can't even explain. You're beautiful, sexy, and addictive, and it's hard for me to process sometimes. Hard for me to believe that you're real."

"You think I'm rare?" She snorted. "You're the rare one, buddy. The wealthy, pretty boy with the world at his fingertips but never makes me feel as if I don't belong in his world. Do you know that you're the only one who's ever genuinely seemed invested in me?"

"I doubt that."

Her head shook softly. "It's true. My mother wanted me, but her parents made her give me away. Then she got depressed and left. She disappeared. My cousin told me that. It might not be true, but then again, why would she lie? The families I stayed with weren't all bad; some were. Most were nice. They took care of me but never in a way that made me feel like they loved me or I belonged. People always think that foster care is either good or bad. Sometimes it's in between. Not good or bad, just kinda okay, but even *okay* leaves you feeling lonely. They took care of me but never invested in me. You said you would help me figure out my life." She smiled softly; it was also innocent, unfiltered. I simply remained still, not saying a word, allowing her to speak. "You're the only person who's ever cared enough to do that, so thank you."

She turned her head away from me, staring out at the ocean. It was dark, but we could still see it, and even if we couldn't, we knew it was there from the smell of the water hanging in the air and the sound of the waves reaching the sand.

"Nari?"

"Hmmm?"

"You're my wife. It's my job to pour into you and ensure you're the best version of yourself. I pledged to do just that when I gave you my last name. You never have to thank me. It's my duty and my promise to you."

Her eyes shot over to mine, and she stared intently for a long moment before she smiled again. "Gotcha, boss."

I laughed lightly because I was learning my wife. That response was her awkward way of accepting my promise. She was still uncomfortable with my commitment as her husband, and I was okay with that as long as she accepted it on her terms.

"We done here?"

"Yep. Now what?"

"It's late, so that's up to you."

We'd been out there for hours. It had to be close to midnight. I was relaxed but not necessarily tired. Something about being there provided the right amount of everything. That was due, in part, to my companion.

"How about I surprise you?" She lifted her chin to look up at me while we traveled down the bamboo path leading us back to the villa. She was tucked under my arm at my side because I had an affinity for having her close. Nari never seemed to mind, leading me to believe the sentiment was shared.

"Should I be worried?"

"Possibly, but you have to agree."

"Says who?"

"Me . . . your wife. If you get to pull the husband card, I'm allowed to use my powers as well, agreed?"

"As much as it worries me to say this, agreed."

"Good."

By then, we had reached the villa. It was an open space, so we stopped on the deck that led to the living room, and she slipped away from my side, stepping in front of me. Nari's small hands rested on my chest briefly before she lifted onto her toes and kissed me. It was timid and innocent but still had my pulse quickening. She could totally control everything about me, but I was sure she had no idea of the power she possessed or how dangerous that could be if she abused the privilege.

"Go shower and meet me back out here."

"Outside?"

"Yes. We'll end our evening here, if that's okay with you." She bit down on her lip, and I nodded to agree. I wasn't sure what she had in mind, but I was with it. She could have or do anything she wanted as long as she included me. Instead of asking more questions, I headed inside to shower and change, anxious to find out what Nari had in store for me.

CHAPTER 11

NARI.

I was anxious. The more I thought about what I was about to do, the more my stomach knotted, and my nerves consumed me.

He's your husband, Nari. You've been with men before who were barely your boyfriends.

That was different. What I felt for Kincaid was undoubtedly different. He was nothing like I expected, but then again, I hadn't expected much. The money was my original reason for accepting his offer. I'd be lying if I said it didn't play a huge role in my agreeing to marry Kincaid, but that wasn't the only reason. Each time I was near him, I felt a pull somewhere deep within. It frightened me but excited me at the same time. I couldn't figure him out, and that angered me at times. His words and actions aligned, so I couldn't call bullshit when I began to feel things that he was orchestrating.

One thing I did know about the man whose name I now carried was that he got what he wanted, and his current acquisition was me. I didn't mind because I was on the chase as well. I simply wasn't as confident in my pursuit as he was. Even then, when I decided to consummate our marriage, a part of me was still anxious and unsure. Kincaid was physically attractive, and there was no doubt in my mind alluding to his desire for me, but once we crossed that line, what would be next? Would it be a temporary agreement? Sex didn't guarantee anything. Our deal was for three years. He still had the right to walk away when the time came. I was no longer confident that was what I wanted.

Inhaling deeply, I closed my eyes, taking a last look at myself in the mirror. My hair was damp from the shower, framing my face in damp ringlets. I wore a red silk kimono that stopped midthigh. My body was moisturized with a cucumber melon lotion, and I'd sprayed a mist of perfume and stepped through it.

Kincaid had already left his room. I'd timed things perfectly. I wanted him there first, waiting. I wondered if he knew what my plan was. If he did, he hadn't let on. Either way, it was happening, so I left my room and traveled through the house, peering into the darkness until I located two long, toned legs. They were bare, which meant he was in shorts. I stepped down into the sand, padding over to the cabana, where I found Kincaid stretched out on his back, his arms folded behind his head. His eyes were closed, but he smiled when I stepped between his legs.

"I smell you. It's become something I look forward to."

"I was thinking I'd give you something else to look forward to."

My eyes remained on his face when his opened and slowly lifted to mine. They were low, and his breathing slowed. I could tell from the rise and fall of his chest.

"You're wearing my favorite color." It was a joke, so I smiled. He'd informed me he didn't have one, but after our first date, red won by default.

"I am, but I didn't really have a choice. It seems my husband selected most of my attire for the trip."

"Did he do a good job?"

"I'd say he did whatever is classified as better than good."

Kincaid chuckled and sat up, his hands resting beside him, but I could tell he wanted to touch me. "I thought you were giving me something."

"Oh, right. I am . . ."

I tugged at the belt that kept my kimono tied, and my robe slipped open, exposing a sliver of skin starting at my chest and traveling down my body. I watched him watching me before I continued with one word that would change everything between us.

"Me."

His face shifted through several emotions and ended on one . . . *Need.*

He remained still for a moment or two before he was on his feet, his body colliding with mine. The impact would have sent me tumbling to my ass had he not held me steady. His kiss was rough, his pace aggressive, but I didn't mind. His actions mirrored my thoughts. I was starved for him and had no clue what it felt like to be full of Kincaid. I did, however, sense that I was about to find out.

My feet left the sand, and my legs opened wide when his body pushed between them. He started toward the house, his mouth never leaving mine until I pulled away. "No, out here."

Kincaid frowned a little, staring at me as if I'd spoken in a foreign tongue. "I . . . uh, out here under the stars. I've been thinking about it a lot."

His expression turned placid before I heard his raspy voice. "Just in general or with me?"

"With you, only with you."

My husband had a bit of a jealous streak. I'd recently learned about it after he reprimanded me for posting pictures of my stay that excluded him. It was cute and not characteristic of what I expected from a man like Kincaid.

"Good."

We turned, moving back toward the cabana. He sat with me in his lap, and one of his hands worked me out of my kimono while the other fisted my hair from the back. His lips clashed against mine again, and I felt him rising beneath me. I'd experienced his arousal before, several times, but this night was different. He was solid and firm beneath me, and the friction of my hips grinding against him while his tongue explored my mouth was . . .

Unnerving.

His mouth and hands were greedy on my skin once it was fully exposed. His lips and teeth grazed different areas, altering between piercing my skin and soft kisses. His fingers dug into my flesh, moving me closer as he explored my body, but abruptly, everything stopped. When my eyes found his, I saw the heat burning behind them.

"This is what you want?"

I nodded, but his features tightened.

"Use your words. I need to hear you say it."

"This is what I want." My voice was strained because I was in heat. I missed his mouth and hands on me.

A slow smile eased onto his face. It was alluring . . . and dangerous, telling of what he'd had planned for me. In a matter of seconds, I was on my back, and he was covering me. His body pressed between my thighs, his erection hard and solid against my center, and it made my pulse race.

His mouth traveled from my neck down the center of my chest. His lips pillow soft while his tongue applied pressure in each place he showed attention. When he reached my nipples, I moaned from the sensation that shot through me when his teeth bit down on it.

"What I tell you about those sounds, Nari?"

I swallowed hard while he lifted his head just enough to lock eyes with mine. It only lasted for a brief moment before he was exploring again. My back arched as Kincaid traveled down my body until his head found its way between my thighs. They trembled from the expectation, and he made a point of torturing me. Soft kisses traveled down my thigh, but not the spot that ached the most. He inched close to it but didn't touch it. His beard brushed against my skin, intensifying the electric pulses that flowed through my body.

He pushed my thighs apart, and when his lips finally landed *there*, making contact, my world began to spin out of control. A tortured sound traveled from my throat, barely escaping my lips. Kincaid responded with a low growl that vibrated against my skin.

I was losing the battle between control and chaos. I bucked against his mouth, attempting to receive more of what I was feeling. The feeling was initially contained in one area, but it was now traveling at lightning speed through every nerve in my body. My arms and legs felt heavy, and my spine began to spasm. My groin rolled, pulsing and vibrating, warning me of what was to come.

My breathing picked up, causing alarm. I panicked because my breath rushed through me too fast. I was spiraling out of control, and then it happened . . .

I took flight.

My body betrayed me, handing over complete control, and Kincaid refused to let up. He carried me through my high, never removing his mouth from me. When my body finally gave up, completely depleted of every ounce of energy I had, his face appeared above mine, his lips brushing lightly against my mouth.

I felt him moving below me but wasn't sure what he was doing until my legs spread wider from the pressure of him between them. I sucked in a deep breath when I felt the tip of him at my opening, and I held onto it until he pushed farther, introducing himself to me inch by inch. My God, that man was an anomaly, blessed in every way. The stretch I felt immediately erased anyone who came before him. There was no way in hell anyone could come after him. I was instantly ruined.

His face was close to mine. I lifted my head, sending my tongue into his mouth. He responded, offering his. At the same time, he rocked into me with such precision that I lost track of the number of times my body quivered from his skillful thrusts. His tempo matched the melody of his tongue until he withdrew so that he could see my face. The way he stared with that smug grin intensified the experience. His arrogance was such a huge turn-on, but it ignited mine. I lifted my hips against his thrust, and my nails pierced the skin of his lower back, bringing him closer. The look in his eyes grew more intense, as did the grin he held on to. I felt him pulse against my walls, somehow growing harder.

"I wasn't prepared," he muttered, lowering his head and pushing deeper, which caused me to gasp from the pressure. "I couldn't have crafted a dream that compares to my current reality."

He licked, sucked, and kissed my neck, shoulders, and breasts while never disrupting his rhythm.

"Breathe, sweetheart." My eyes peeled open to find his waiting. They were intense and concerned. I was so caught up in the moment that I hadn't realized I'd been holding my breath. When I released the first one following his command, my body opened up a little more, and Kincaid took full advantage. A devilish grin slipped in place as he thrust into me harder, faster, deeper than I was sure he needed to be.

My body was stiff with pleasure. He leaned closer and nipped my neck, intensifying the combination of feelings that were occurring. Something within erupted from my core, traveling through me like a freight train.

"Fuck," he groaned against my neck, pressing into me a little closer. That depleted the last of my willpower. His name danced on my tongue and eventually escaped while my thighs quivered, my stomach rolled, and my mind lifted. I climaxed in such a dangerously intoxicating way that I lost ownership of my body. It was his. He was in control, and the way he continued drilling into me further confirmed the exchange of possession. He knew just how far to push, and when I felt as if I couldn't take anymore, he grunted hard, thrust deep, and emptied himself in me. My walls continued to pulse, extracting his release until I felt the weight of him on my chest.

My eyes remained lazy even after I felt him lift above me. Kincaid pushed his tongue into my mouth, taking away my ability to breathe. "Best fucking gift ever." His tone was teasing, but his eyes were filled with desire. A desire he felt the need to express. Without warning, he was back. That soft, warm tongue glided down my body, and my legs were draped over his shoulders.

"Wait." The request fell on deaf ears. My spine jolted when his lips twisted and sucked my clit. There was no point in objecting. My opinion no longer mattered, but I wasn't interested in putting up much of a fight. Every inch of me was enjoying every inch of him. Kincaid was a master of pleasure, and I was on the verge of losing my mind. *Consider me as good as fucking crazy then.*

I welcomed the experience. It didn't take long for my core to begin to tingle with another round of pleasure. The climax hit me like a wrecking ball, and with no time allowed to recover, he flipped me over onto my stomach and was inside of me again.

"It's going to be a long night, sweetheart," he growled after I felt his lips gently press against my spine.

When I rocked back hard, meeting his thrusts, I made clear, "For both of us."

He chuckled, fingers digging into my skin while he continued to work me over. It was the beginning of a dangerous addiction.

The following day, I woke, feeling the effects of Kincaid on my body, but I wasn't able to focus on the damage he'd done because I felt abandoned when I realized I was in bed alone. I quickly swept my legs to the side of the bed, straightening my back before I stood to give my body a complete stretch. I felt Kincaid in every inch and every muscle, but it was the best kind of pain. A smile encased my lips as I crossed the room to put my hands on something to cover me. I chose one of his shirts, pulled it over my head, and lifted the collar to inhale his scent.

Needing to freshen up, I crossed the hall, entering what was technically my room to clean my face and brush my teeth. Once I finished my morning routine, I moved around the house, searching for my husband. His voice alerted me to his presence first, but it was harsh and angry. I paused, frowning while I listened.

"That's bullshit, and I'm not standing for it. They know better than to cross those lines. We have rules for a reason. If they refuse to follow, we're shedding blood. Maybe then they'll understand the severity of their poor choices. As soon as I land, we'll meet once I get my wife settled. I'm not to be played with, but obviously, someone needs to be reminded."

When Kincaid finished his call, I was at the edge of the living room; however, his back was to me. I could physically see the tension in his body. The muscles in his shoulders and back flexed as he gripped the phone, which was still in one hand, while the other lifted to massage his chin. He was angry.

"Hey, everything okay?"

The sound of my voice had him turning toward me. His face was as hard as stone, and so were his eyes. They were dark, but the muscles around them loosened at the sight of me. Kincaid waved me over by extending an invitation with an open arm. I accepted, finding my way into his personal space, quickly engulfed by his strong arms. The firmness of his body should've been an issue, but

I fit perfectly. After a kiss on the top of my head and then my temple, I felt him relax.

"Good morning, sleepyhead."

"Doesn't sound that way. Is there a problem?" Kincaid leaned back, searching my face. He always studied my features as if using subtle hints to gauge how to respond to me.

"Business. Nothing for you to worry about. You hungry?" My chin was between his fingers, and his lips met mine. "Chef made breakfast. I was about to come get you."

"Starved. I had a productive night."

He chuckled, nodding. "Me too." His arms closed around me again. And I noticed he smelled clean, freshly showered. We'd both shared one before climbing into bed last night, but he'd also had one this morning. That time when he kissed me, I was blessed with that skillful tongue. Memories of what he'd done with it the night before flooded my mind while I enjoyed the hint of mint that coated his mouth.

"We need to talk. Let's eat." That serious persona eased in. Kincaid switched gears within the blink of an eye. It fascinated me and also sometimes irritated me as well. Occasionally, it was hard to keep up.

I wondered if he would discuss what I possibly heard. The man mentioned that blood would be shed for someone's poor decisions. That should've terrified me and had me running away at full speed, but I felt totally protected by the man issuing the threat. He would never harm me and had pledged to protect me with his life. I believed him. The two of us sat across from each other.

I lifted the lid of my dish, but Kincaid didn't touch his. He simply stared. After I smiled at my selection, a fruit salad and an omelet with spinach and cheese, I blessed my food and took my first bite. My husband had been watching and learning me. He knew my habits and my preferences; I appreciated the effort.

My breakfast had been intentional. After sharing his omelet, I mentioned I wouldn't mind one with spinach and cheese. There it was, the next morning, and my request was provided.

"You're making me nervous. Is something wrong?" I mumbled before swallowing and lifting my glass of juice. He hadn't said one word as of yet.

"I'm not sure, which is what we need to discuss."

That had my eyes on his quick and a frown in place. "I don't follow."

He massaged his chin for a moment. His words were carefully selected. "Last night—"

"Was my decision, and I have no regrets," I made clear.

"Good. Neither do I, but it shifts things. We never discussed the specifics of being intimate other than we wouldn't engage in entertaining others. We don't have terms in place."

"Good. I don't want any terms. I'm good with winging it with this one." I shrugged, digging into my omelet, allowing a forkful to enter my mouth while I stared at my husband. It was hard to embrace the thoughts of what we'd done the night before while negotiating terms of how it would happen moving forward. Who the hell wanted to ruin the moment with that shit? Damn sure not me.

"No discussion?"

"No! Look, I understand if things change. I'm okay with that, but I don't want some outline of when and how you get to do what you did to me last night."

His smile surfaced quickly. It was cocky and smug. "I don't either, and as for things changing, they've not changed for me, possibly for you. I was intentional from the time I presented you with the offer, Nari. I've been intentional since you agreed. I've even expressed that intent multiple times."

"Do you always have to talk so damn formal?"

He chuckled before allowing his teeth to graze his bottom lip. That simple motion had my groin rolling. "I married you because I wanted you as my wife. When I said this could be as real as you want it to be, I meant that in every definition of the word *real*."

"Real as in we're a *for real* husband and wife?"

"We are indeed committed to each other, regardless of how you define it. The marriage is binding and legal. I'm referencing how you view the commitment moving forward."

"Kincaid—"

"I'm not expecting a response right now . . ." he started, cutting me off before lifting the lid from his dish. "I'm simply making clear where I stand. I am your husband, and you are my wife. When you're ready, you decide what that means to you. We can stick to the terms that are in place, or we say fuck it and just let things play out however the hell they play out. My choice is the latter of the two, but I won't push. I'll allow you time to decide."

He gave me that look, the amused one, which let me know that he, in no way, was allowing me not to be in it on *his* terms.

"Eat," Kincaid demanded, but not in an intrusive manner. "It's our last day, and I'm sure you want to take full advantage of every moment." He winked and then returned to his food as if he hadn't just thrown the whole fake wife and husband concept out the window. Unfortunately, I needed time to make sense of the declaration, so I did as he asked and finished my food so that we could tackle our last day in paradise.

CHAPTER 12

KINCAID.

On the way to Tulum, Nari slept, and I worked. That was the same on the way home. Our flight was early—six a.m. We'd only gotten a few hours of sleep because after she dragged me around the resort while she spent the day exploring, our night was spent with me exploring . . .

Her.

There was no way in hell I could return to a simple arrangement. I had tasted the forbidden fruit, and just as I expected, it now controlled me. She controlled me. When I lay between her thighs, we became one, and that filtered over into other experiences. The pull on me was stronger, more powerful. I feared the moment she realized what that truly meant. Darius's words were on repeat in my head. *My greatest weakness and my greatest strength.* Nari had taken on the role of both, but it was time for me to return to my reality.

Aila and her father now knew that the plans had changed. Their reactions were different. She was likely confused by the fact that another woman had stepped into a role she had claimed to be hers. Kaber felt anger and betrayal. I was sure he assumed I'd found out he'd been lying, but maybe he hadn't. I would deal with them both once I introduced Nari to her new world. Part of our terms was that we lived together. There were no specifics about anything other than us residing under one roof. I fully planned on purchasing a new home—one of her choosing. My penthouse was nice but not where a family should be raised.

Kids.

That posed another issue I would have to work around. Nari was on birth control. I had the full report of her visit with Dr. Chandler, but my goal was for us to have our first child as soon as possible. Within the year would please me. I simply had to ease into that. She was still processing my affirmation that our marriage was more than an arrangement. It was possible that she would still want to stick to the terms, but I felt in my heart that she would fall in line with my plan. I could feel her heart the same as I was sure she could feel mine. She was, however, still young and, from what I'd gathered, had little to no experience with love. I couldn't say that I had been in love before. Still, my experiences allowed me to recognize its existence, and my maturity would allow me to be open to embracing the prospect.

My wife felt things but wasn't quite able to make sense of them. She was inadequate in that department due to a lack of experiencing love in any form, which created a fear of being open to the idea. I'd give her time. I'd give her whatever the hell she wanted without hesitation, as long as it didn't include leaving me. That wasn't happening. One word came to mind when I thought of her: *Mine.* In its simplest form, the idea seemed barbaric in a sense. In a way, it was, but I didn't want to possess and control Nari. I want to love, protect, and encourage her growth. I wanted to provide the security she wanted but lacked all her life. I would die for mine, and she was . . .

Mine.

After our flight landed, Nari chatted about our time in Tulum just to make a casual conversation. Her mood was light, and she seemed happy, which made me happy. She had already learned to go with the flow where I was concerned. My wife allowed me to lead, which I appreciated. I would never steer her wrong, ever. The fact that she trusted my leadership as well and trusted me with her well-being was a good start. Nari was positioning herself well in the role of being my wife.

Once we reached the penthouse, she looked around as if it were her first time there. Even though it was where we sealed the deal with our union, she hadn't been given a chance to explore and find her place.

"So this is home, huh?" She smiled, moving around the space, allowing her fingers to explore the texture of the furnishing. I had my place professionally decorated, and the décor could be described as lavish; however, I realized there was a lot missing at that moment. It wasn't until I took in the space with Nari present that I realized *she* added value to the high-end décor. However, her energy was colorful and raw, which clashed with the black and gray that made up the backdrop. She seemed out of place—all the more reason for us to find a home that fit us both.

"For now."

"Oh, we're moving? When?" She frowned at me briefly before walking over to the balcony and pressing the button that opened the blinds. She remembered from watching me the night we were married.

"That depends on you. Check your phone."

"Why?"

"I sent you a list of properties."

She reached into the crossbody bag and removed the device, finding the email I sent while we were on the plane. Her eyes searched with curiosity. Annalise, my realtor, had sent a list of potential properties as requested. I received her suggestions while we were in Tulum, but I wanted to wait until we were home to task

Nari with finding our home. I watched her scroll through the list and chuckled at how her eyes expanded and then squinted.

"You're kidding, right?"

"About?"

"These are multimillion-dollar properties. You want me to pick from this list?"

"If you find one you like, yes. If not, reach out to Annalise and give her specifics on what you're looking for, and she'll prepare another list."

"I don't know how to pick a house. Especially one that you will like. No . . ." She was shaking her head. "You can decide."

"Whatever you like, I will love. Just stick with Annalise's recommendations. She'll search based on your preference, but she'll select properties with the best value."

"I just—"

"Nari, this is your life now. It's an adjustment, but it's one I have faith that you can handle."

"How much are you worth? I might need to rethink our agreement." She arched an eyebrow while a grin teased at her lips.

"*We* are worth a lot. You're my wife, remember? What's mine is yours, and what's yours is mine," I teased, knowing she would follow my comment with a snide remark.

"I'm worth half a million, but technically, that's yours too, so I'm kind of a dud. More debt than anything, which means you, buddy, got the short end of this deal."

Not hardly.

"I would disagree."

"Of course you would." She playfully rolled her eyes. Those moments were my favorite when she seemed unguarded. It was when she was the most exposed, which meant I got to experience Nari without the filters she liked to put in place.

"I have to head out for a while. I'll be gone for most of the day but should be home in time for a late dinner if you wish to wait up."

She seemed disappointed. That pleased me in a sense because, after a week of having her by my side 24/7, I had gotten used to her presence. It would fucking blow me if she didn't feel the same.

"I guess I'll figure out something."

"Start with finding us a house. If you want to head out, use the concierge's line and let them know. I have a service in place to take you wherever you want to go."

"I don't need that. I can—"

"Nari, it's a precaution. A lot of things shifted with you taking my last name. We'll discuss that in full detail at some point, but for now, please use the service I have provided if you go out."

Our eyes were at war. She wanted to protest and had questions, but instead of doing so at that moment, she nodded.

"Got it, boss."

I smiled, closing the space between us. "You're my responsibility. That's a task I don't take lightly."

My hand slipped into her hair. It was in its natural state, loose coils, which I loved. It was my favorite look. I stole a kiss, and she moaned in my mouth, melting into me.

"Careful. I'm short on time, but don't mind making people wait if it means time with you."

She blushed. "No. I've had you all week, and besides, someone has to pay for the million-dollar house I've been tasked with selecting. I've already established it won't be me."

I nodded. "Make yourself at home. I left everything you need on the nightstand by the bed on your side."

There was an access card to the penthouse elevator, passwords to the security system, and cash. Cards to my accounts were ordered and on the way. She would object once I handed them over because that was who she was, but in time, Nari would understand and accept the privileges attached to being my wife.

"My side? I wasn't aware I had one."

"Cute, but I'm sure you know better. Text me if you need me. Call if it's an emergency." I kissed her forehead and headed to the elevator. She watched, giving me a goofy wave just as the doors closed.

My sweet Nari.

With Cast by my side, I stepped onto the block, feeling a rage slowly building. It was one of my neighborhoods. I had several. They all contained affordable housing, community centers, and shopping plazas. My investment allowed these things to be available to those who called the communities home. It was my way of maintaining balance. My properties were all over the city. Some in better neighborhoods than others. They were like an oasis in the middle of chaos. Often, I wished I could do more. I was working on it, but anything was a start. Balance . . . good for the bad.

For me, I was born into a lifestyle of privilege. It was attached to the sins of those who came before me, my father included. I wasn't offered a choice. The legacy continued being passed down through each generation, and it was my turn. The good thing about the syndicate was that they wanted their members to maintain balance. Have families, grow legal businesses, and give back. It was like their penance for the blood on their hands. The Families were selective about who they allowed to get close. Once you were deemed worthy, it was a lifetime commitment—a duty in a sense. If a family were infertile and couldn't produce an heir, one was placed in their care, a private adoption, or a son-in-law was provided through an arranged marriage. It was understood how things worked. When you crossed The Families or were found to be a resource with no value, you were cut off, your family ties severed, and your spot was replaced.

I was often at war because my conscience struggled with the things I was a part of, such as the underworld I was connected to, so I made sure to provide balance.

Yet another reason why I was on the block. It was a protected territory. When we approached, I stood silently, waiting to be acknowledged. He knew I would show up eventually, and it was that day. It was why his first response was somewhat disrespectful. His ego was larger than it needed to be.

"Can I help you?"

Knotty was what they called him. He was a local dealer who had grown in popularity over the past few years because of his Haitian roots. I knew about him and was aware of how he moved. I didn't like what he represented, but there was a part of me that felt like a hypocrite in a sense. We did the same things, just on different levels. I moved weight by truckloads, and it ended up on the streets, but I never put men on corners to introduce it where a need didn't already exist. A junkie was going to be a junkie. It couldn't be helped or controlled, but it could be contained and kept from those genuinely trying to live a decent life. I sold in bulk, which ended up in the hands of men like Knotty, who didn't live by rules driven by morals. I was just as guilty as he was in a sense, but at least I attempted to maintain balance. I did what I could to make up for my sins. He raped and pillaged, taking advantage, pocketing the money for his selfish needs. He didn't understand balance.

"Yeah, actually, you can. Get off my fucking blocks."

"Your blocks?" He looked me up and down with a blunt dangling from his lips. I hated for people to question me—one of my pet peeves.

"Are you familiar with the zones?" I was giving him the benefit of the doubt. He was well aware. I supplied his supplier, Toussaint, who was also Knotty's blood relative somewhere down the line. Toussaint agreed to work under my terms in order to reap the benefit of the purity and price of my product. Our agreement was the only reason why Knotty would receive a warning over immediate action.

"Yeah, I heard about that shit. And?"

"And this one is off-limits. Get your men off my fucking blocks. This is your first and only warning."

After I made my point, I walked away, not bothering to wait for a response. His thoughts didn't matter. Knotty would either make the conscious decision to preserve his life, or I would personally handle the outcome. My rules were not negotiable. The only issue was that I would have to go through the proper channels or risk reprimand from the syndicate. I was, however, fully prepared to take matters into my own hands and deal with the consequences.

"See you around, Kincaid," was spoken at my back. Neither I nor Cast turned to respond. I slipped into the driver's side of my McLaren Roadster 722. That day, I craved power, and it was always my go-to. Cast eased into the passenger's seat, not happy that I was driving. I tended to be reckless when I was in my Roadster. When I made it down the block and passed Knotty, his team of minions were around him, watching as if their visual threats mattered. He smirked, and we shared one last look before I was far enough down the block for him to care any longer.

"He's got an ego. Too fucking big for his own good." Cast was the first to speak.

"Agreed, and that's going to cost him."

"How long are you giving him?"

"We'll see how he moves. If nothing changes, we make an example."

Cast nodded. Men like Knotty rubbed me the wrong way. We did our best to allow children to feel safe playing in the streets of their neighborhoods and create jobs, programs, and partnerships that provided services and income for their parents to keep food on their tables and roofs over their heads. It was the dark and the light. I understood that what I had a hand in wasn't always good, so I did my best to give back. Men like Knotty didn't give a damn. Power and greed were far more important than balancing the evil in which we sometimes played a role. It was all about money for him, which would be his downfall. I would simply be the one responsible for putting an end to his ill ways.

"How was the honeymoon?"

When my eyes shot over to Cast, he grinned like a fucking child. I hated that shit.

"None of your gotdamn business."

"I thought we were boys, Caid. Maybe I just want to make sure you have the right one."

"Fuck you," I chuckled. "She's *definitely* the right one."

"Ah, hell. She put that shit on you. It was already bad, but now it's out of control."

"I'm always in control. Nothing has changed."

"Nah, Caid. That might've been the case before, possibly with Aila, but this one's different. She's got you by the balls." He chuckled, digging his phone out of his pocket.

"She does. But I'm still in control."

"Seriously, though, I like her. She's a good look for you, but is she a good fit for you? It takes a lot to be in this world. Can she handle the responsibility? Does she even know?"

"To a degree, yes, and she'll be fine."

He lifted his eyes to me once more before shaking his head and shifting gears. "Kaber's been quiet. Too fucking quiet. I've been on him, but it's not adding up."

"What's not adding up?"

"His moves are too programmed. It's like he knows you're watching."

"I'm sure he does. Aila knows that I married Nari. She would've gone straight to him after she couldn't get to me."

"What do you think he told her?"

"Fuck if I know, and I don't care. I told my mother not to say shit and that Aila was to speak directly with me. Kaber would be trying to cover his ass. He will take her side and promise to handle me, but that's not his priority right now. He's panicking, trying to figure out his next move. He was counting on carrying my family's name in his pocket. I didn't give him time to find an alternative plan. Right now, he's lost and sweating bullets. That's why his moves are programmed. He needs to present the appearance that things are normal so that I don't come for his neck."

"But you are."

"In time."

I pulled up in the parking lot next to Cast's vehicle. "I have to be in New York for a few days, and then I need time to make sure Nari is getting adjusted. If you need me—"

Cast chuckled, tugging at the handle. "By the balls, Caid. She's got you by the balls."

I shrugged, not ashamed that my wife's well-being was now a factor in how I moved. Cast also knew me. Regardless of the jokes, he would bet his life that business would be handled. I compartmentalized my life. It was necessary to keep from fucking up. Once he was on his feet and out of my car, he leaned in with a smug grin.

"Send my regards to the wife," he tossed out, his tone laced with amusement, shutting the door before I could respond. I had one more task to complete, and that one wouldn't be pleasant. It caused me grief that I had to confirm what she already knew, but I owed her a face-to-face.

The minute she opened the door, I felt her wrath. Aila's hand landed across my face so hard I had to stop myself from reacting. I turned to the left, absorbing the impact, but when my eyes met with hers, I issued a warning. She didn't care, which was understandable because she tried again, but I caught her wrist that time before her hand could make contact. My grip was firm, and I stepped forward, entering her apartment, leaving Aila no choice but to move with me. Once inside, I used my foot to shut the door and then let her go.

"Once. That's all you get."

"Fuck you, Kincaid," she sneered. Her eyes flashed with an energy I'd never seen in her before, but again, I understood and would allow her the open space to express her emotions.

"I look stupid. You've made a fool out of me. All my friends know. They've been calling, asking what happened. And it's not like any of them really care. They just want to rub my nose in it."

"Same as you did by attempting to dangle me in front of them like I was a fucking prize."

"You're far from a prize, Kincaid. I just didn't know it at the time," she made clear, walking away. Releasing a harsh breath, I followed her as she moved through her home toward the kitchen. That wasn't my thing. I didn't explain my decisions to anyone, ever, but I would be accommodating this one time. It was the least I could do.

Aila was uncorking a bottle of wine when I entered. She skipped the glass and held the bottle to her lips, turning it up when she was done.

"You owe me an explanation. I asked your mother, and she told me nothing besides that I had to speak to you. She barely even looked at me."

"That was my request."

"For her to treat me like a fucking stranger? Like we hadn't been planning a wedding—*our* wedding?"

"No. For her to let me explain. She was just as surprised as you and didn't play a role in my decision. You're right. I do owe you an explanation."

"Then let's hear it. Humor me because I'm sure nothing you say will matter. You embarrassed the shit out of me. How am I supposed to show my face after what you've done?"

Her tone was sharp, and her words were consistent with one theme, which prompted my next question. I prided myself in being good and seeing people for who they really were, but somehow, I'd missed so much with Aila. We both had an investment. Hers was just hidden better than mine.

"Do you love me?"

She looked at me as if I had grown three heads. "Why the hell would you ask me that? What does it matter? You're married and putting it out there for the world to see."

"You said humor you. How about you humor me? Aila, do you love me?"

She lifted the bottle to her lips, turning it up again, but her eyes never left mine, speaking after she lowered it. "Do you love me?"

"No, but you've always known that."

She snorted. "What makes you think that because you barely had time for me, blaming it on work? You hardly ever touched me. A kiss was a privilege. And sex?" She laughed hard.

We'd exchanged oral sex a few times. It was at her insistence, but the only place my dick had been on her body was in her mouth. That was why I spent time at Salacious. Well, one of the reasons. The other was business.

"You're avoiding the question, Aila." I remained on track.

"Yes and no. I cared about you and was falling in love with you, but you wouldn't allow me to. You kept me at arm's length, and that shit hurt. You have no idea how hard it is to be with a man of your stature, Kincaid. You're closed off and don't care how that affects other people."

"I gave you what you accepted and allowed me to give. You never demanded better."

"Why would I? So that you could hurt my feelings when you refused? Who the hell sets themselves up to feel rejection? You did enough of that without me asking."

"Then why marry me?"

Our eyes were at war again. "Why not? You're *Kincaid Akel*. The name alone is worth more than the deepest pockets. Don't think I'm that naïve. I know that my father played a role in your seeking me out. I always felt it deep down inside, but I knew with certainty when I went to him after I found out about *your wife* . . ."

I didn't like the way she referred to Nari. She said the word *wife* as if it were sour on her tongue. She was more or less insinuating that Nari was somehow not good enough. It made my pulse quicken out of sheer instinct alone. It was my duty to protect Nari at all costs from anyone who defiled her worth—*even Aila*.

"He pretended to be just as hurt as I was . . ." *He wasn't pretending. He was just as devastated as you but for different reasons.* ". . . I could see the lies he was keeping. My father was shocked in a way that let me know it shouldn't have happened and that you shouldn't have married *that woman*. He was shocked because I'm sure you two had some sort of agreement. Well, you know what? Fuck you both."

The tears came fast. She might've had a personal agenda, but that didn't cancel the fact that she'd fallen victim to her emotions. Maybe not with love, but she had built a life with me in her heart and mind, and the reality of it not happening was like an arrow to the heart and not from Cupid.

"I apologize for hurting you, Aila. I do. Whether you choose to believe that or not—"

"Then fix it. Get rid of her, and we can still make this work. *Please.*"

"I can't do that. She's my wife. Nothing's going to change that."

She stared blankly at me, blinking back tears. Some escaped, which she wiped, but Aila stood her ground.

"Get out of my house."

I nodded, reaching into my pocket for the keys she had gifted me. I had access to her; she never had access to me. I placed them on the counter and left. The minute I shut the door behind me, something crashed against it, but I didn't turn back because she was no longer my problem. My loyalty was to Nari, and I wouldn't disrespect her by comforting another woman.

CHAPTER 13

NARI.

My day was pretty dull and unproductive, but it felt good not to have any obligations. I missed him. That was a feeling I was struggling with. To keep my mind off the need I felt to text or call my husband, I pulled up the link from Annalise on my laptop instead. It had seen better days but was functional enough for me to get the job done. As I scrolled through the list of houses she'd sent, my mouth dropped and hung open with each one because, my gosh, they were . . .

Gorgeous.

Expensive.

Beyond my expertise.

Never in my wildest dreams had I ever seen my life take shape in the way it had been over the past couple of weeks. Since my first encounter with Kincaid, my circumstances had done a complete one-eighty. I was indeed the cliché rags to riches, but that came with a price. One that plagued my soul with a darkness that I wasn't sure I was prepared for or could shake. Had I made a deal with the devil? It was impossible to know the beauty and depths of the ocean until you dove in to explore. The reality, however, was that you will likely drown before you realize how dangerous it is to try. Kincaid was the ocean, and I was at risk of drowning.

There were several reasons behind my rationale. One was that he branded and claimed me, and I didn't fight one bit. It was pointless. The power surrounding that man couldn't be seen, but it could be felt so much so that I was drawn to him and connected in ways I couldn't even explain. How? He worked his magic on me; that was how. His looks were irresistible, and his charm was silent but deadly. Even then, staring at the TV, watching the faces of men I knew he had crossed paths with and were now identified as missing, I trusted this man. I was still at war about whether I wanted to run away and never look back or stay and accept my fate. *Stay* had won the battle because there I was.

"Gains and Taylor," I mumbled their names, studying their faces. "Missing." I pushed out a harsh breath, shaking my head. Kincaid's cryptic message was repeated in my mind.

I apologize. He will never step foot in here or anywhere else you are ever again.

They'd been missing since the night we shared the same space. The man who assaulted me was missing. The friend who was with him was missing. Both men were presumed dead, but the case was still pending . . .

"Is there something you want to ask me, Nari?"

I dropped the remote, and my head whipped around to find Kincaid standing in the doorway looking incredibly delectable . . . and *dangerous*. The way his eyes fastened to my face was the most unnerving. How long had he been there? My focus had been transfixed on the news which flashed across the screen, so I had no idea.

"What? No." My eyes shot over to the TV and landed on my husband again. The story had changed, but the awareness of what I had seen lingered between us.

"You sure?" His gaze was heavy, his features too beautiful to appear so cold and callous, but in a twisted way, it made him more appealing.

You're already sick for this man . . .

"What happened to them? Those men from the club. They talked about them on the news. They've been missing since that night. Did you—"

"Yes. They're dead. Do you want to know how?"

He spoke casually and unbothered as if he were asking if I wanted wine with dinner. How was he so detached while admitting he'd taken a life . . .

Two lives.

"No, but why?"

His eyes squinted. Not one muscle in his face moved, but I could feel the shift. At that moment, something about him was different. Animalistic, protective. That was my answer.

Me!

I was the reason why he took those men's lives. But what I didn't get was why it happened. I wasn't his wife . . . I wasn't his anything . . .

But he killed for me.

"I'll do it again. Never will I hesitate to make that call, nor will I apologize." Our eyes caught and remained pinned intensely.

How the fuck . . .

"There's only a slim margin between good and evil. No one is perfect. We all struggle with what the world classifies as right and wrong. A thin line separates the two. When it comes to those I hold close, I'm judge and jury."

"And where does that leave me . . ." I paused, releasing a breath so that my words came out even, "as your wife?"

"Untouched."

There was no room for even the slightest argument. I nodded. What else could I do? I was married to a man who wore virility like a rare cologne. There wasn't an easy out, but if I were being honest with myself, I wasn't looking for one.

"Now, are we still on for that late dinner?" Just that quickly, he shifted again. His eyes were warm, his energy balanced, and his need for me was telling in the way he took me in. *His!* That was what I felt each time he looked at me, and not in a controlling manner, but it was still sensual and intense. I was his to love, cherish—and *protect*.

"Yes, where?"

"I know a place." He winked, and my stomach took a dive. How was it so easy to fall so hard?

"Whose house is this?" As we drove past the front gate, my body began to tense. I was sure of the answer before I asked the question but released it anyway, searching for confirmation.

"My parents'."

"Wait, why wouldn't you tell me that?"

"Because you would've worked yourself into a panic an hour ago instead of two minutes ago."

"That's not fair. At least I would've had time to prepare." My voice elevated as he slowed to a stop in front of a home that looked as if it should've been on the list of the ones I was provided. It was stunning and huge. Even at night, the white stucco was lit by strategically placed lights that made the mini-mansion seem as if it were glowing.

"Prepare for what? These are your parents . . ."

"In-laws. They love you because you're theirs. I'm just the woman who stole you."

He smirked as if my words were amusing, but there wasn't a damn thing funny.

"I thought it was the other way around . . . that I was the thief?" He chuckled, leaning across the seat and planting a kiss on my cheek. "But I suppose it goes both ways. I am indeed yours."

I wanted to be upset, but it was damn near impossible when faced with that man's charm. Losing battle . . . Yep, that was precisely what it was.

Once he opened my door and extended a hand to help me, I brushed my hands down the front of my jeans and tugged at my T-shirt. Nervous tension flooded my body, which had my fingers raking through my hair immediately after, but Kincaid put a stop to my fidgeting by forcing me against him.

His cologne was the first thing that put me at ease, and then his arms closed me into a cocoon. The man was so ruggedly handsome that it was impossible not to feel at ease in his personal space. Kincaid radiated an intensity that could easily suffocate me if I wasn't careful.

"You're perfect, and this is not a test. The only person you have to impress is me, and I'm already under your spell, Mrs. Akel."

"They don't like me."

He pressed a kiss to my forehead and then my lips. "We've already discussed this. It was the surprise wedding they didn't like. That has nothing to do with you and everything to do with me. My parents followed certain rules, and I stepped outside of those without warning. Now, let's go."

Nodding, I released a cleansing breath, taking my husband's hand as we traveled the short distance to the front door. It was metal and glass, allowing me the opportunity to peek inside. I could already see how exquisite things were, which didn't help my anxieties.

"I look like I'm about to go bargain shopping on a Saturday morning," I mumbled.

"You're cute when you're nervous." My eyes shot up to meet his, angled down at me but only briefly because he pressed a code and motioned for me to enter once he had the door open. I did and had a *wow!* moment. The place was wide open, with a massive marble staircase leading to a balcony overlooking the foyer. Above our heads by at least twenty feet was a crystal chandelier that was extended from the ceiling. It resembled those you'd expect to see in fancy high-end hotels. The place was beautiful, but more than anything, it felt warm, cozy, and like home, regardless of how grand everything appeared. Not what I expected.

"Caid, is that you?"

A soft voice traveled through the air, but I couldn't place which direction it came from until she appeared. His mother was dressed in all white: silk blouse and wide-legged trousers from her hips down to her feet. I was sure she wore shoes but I couldn't see them because the pants swept the floor. She smiled, and it was welcoming, so I returned one.

"About time," she muttered, feigning annoyance, but the smile on her face contradicted her act. She stopped at Kincaid, who enclosed her in his arms and issued a kiss on the cheek, but the second she released him, she was on me. A hug so tight surrounded me that I was completely thrown off balance. I almost stumbled and would have had she not had her arms around me.

"Nari, sweetheart. Welcome. Come, we have some catching up to do." Her bare, slender arm was looped through mine, and I was moving beside her. I hadn't been given a choice.

"Love you too, old lady."

She sent a warning glare over her shoulder, followed by a demand. "Your father's in the living room. Go, now."

We traveled through her home, one I assumed Kincaid was raised in. It fit the man I was learning, so I could see him here as a child.

I grinned.

No, I couldn't. He was too much of a force for me to think of as a child.

We ended up in the kitchen, where she motioned for me to sit at the island. She did the same on the opposite side, placing her delicate hands on the marbled surface. I noticed the massive diamonds on her hands and the string of them around her wrist. Each item was elegant but still classy, and none seemed overbearing or out of place. They fit her persona to a T. These people exuded wealth but not in a way that was flashy or overbearing.

"First, let me apologize. I can't imagine how horrible it must've felt to feel attacked on your wedding day." Her tone was soft, and her eyes were sincere.

"It's really okay. You were ambushed, so I understand your reaction," I tried, but she wasn't having it.

"No, there is no excuse. It was a huge error in judgment. One that has plagued me since that day, and I pray you can forgive me. Well, us—my husband as well."

"You already apologized. It's not necessary—"

She smiled, halting my words. "I've seen the way my son looks at you. It *is* necessary. He'd have my head if I didn't make this right, but regardless, I don't want you to feel that he's the driving force behind my apology. You're one of us. You're family, and I need you to know that we stand with you, not against you."

"Thank you."

She relaxed. I could physically see her body unleash the tension pinned in her shoulders.

"Now, let's get down to business." As subtly as I had seen it happen with her son, she shifted. Her cheery spirit was buried somewhere within, and a hardness surfaced, only she seemed more serious than intimidating. Kincaid was both, but the intimidation was more potent.

"You don't have a family." I frowned, and she smiled. "That's not an insult or spoken to hurt you. It's just a fact. Before you married my son, you were alone. You're not anymore. We're your family. There are ties that bind us so deep you will never see them, but you will feel them in time. They're always there. It's happening already with Kincaid." Her eyes remained steady with mine. "If you're as stubborn as I was, you'll kick and claw and go down fighting to deny it, but the Akel men always win the hearts of the women they set their sights on." She laughed lightly, her smile returning. "My point is, you're not alone. You have us. You have me. You'll need support to love my son the right way."

"The right way?" It sounded almost cryptic but, at the very least, like a goal that was impossible to accomplish. Had I been blindly thrown into the ring to fight a battle I would never win?

"I don't know how much you know. If I'm guessing, Kincaid is slowly prepping you for who he is and all that comes with his life—our lives. Only the strong survive without losing themselves in the process. Happiness is a luxury. Loyalty is a requirement. Loyalty will always come first, but love will be the reason you surrender to its demand. You have to be loyal to your husband in ways that challenge you, but . . ." She stood and rounded the island, taking my hands in hers. "I feel your strength. It's going to take a lot to break you. Embrace his leadership, but stand firm, ready to be his compass when he's too blinded by emotions to find his way out of the darkness."

I stared at her for what felt like forever, trying to make sense of whatever the hell that meant, but the moment was broken by the sound of his voice.

"You're not in here trying to convince my wife to run, are you?"

I felt him before he touched me. His hands landed gently in a protective manner on my shoulders, easing down the sides of my arms. That was his mother, but he was still standing guard. My stomach took another dive while I pressed my head against his stomach, lifting my chin to find Kincaid's eyes, waiting, even though he'd spoken directly to her.

"Not likely, son. She's in here feeding the young lady secrets on how to control you. That's far more dangerous."

My father-in-law moved past us, winking at me, pairing the gesture with a warm smile. It was welcoming, the same as his wife's had been. Once he kissed her cheek, he motioned to an adjoining room.

"Now, can we eat before I wither away?"

She waved him off but blushed under his loving stare. I could feel their hearts. They were joined to create one. When my eyes shot up to Kincaid's, I saw his intense expression. It was the kind that let me know he'd read my thoughts.

"As real as you want it to be, Nari."

The declaration that he delivered with all the confidence in the world repeatedly was on his tongue again, daring me to do anything but believe him.

CHAPTER 14

KINCAID.

Seven. That was how many houses we had viewed in the past week. Each time we pulled onto a property or rounded a circular drive, I would study my wife, searching for a reaction. She smiled, was polite, and asked questions of Annalise while we moved from room to room. She listened intently as each feature and amenity was highlighted. Some amused her, and she would laugh, such as when we toured a built-in spa, private elevator, or staff quarters. I was sure the humor lay in the fact that those things seemed over the top and unnecessary, but with the homes carrying price lines such as the ones we were viewing, those amenities were expected.

Nonetheless, not once had she expressed a genuine connection to any of the seven. She was happy and would've moved forward with any I selected, but not one so far made her eyes light up how I needed them to. I had seen that look several times while we were in Tulum, and it was when I could tell that she was truly happy. I could've selected one, but I wanted it to be Nari's decision. It would be our home—something she'd never had before. Not in a way that she could settle her spirit and feel at home, so as we sat in Annalise's office while she stepped out to speak with one of her junior realtors, I decided to pry.

"We've seen seven houses. We have three scheduled for today."

"Mm-hmm." She smiled, lifting her eyes from the phone in her hand. My possessive nature had already prompted me to steal a peek to know who she was communicating with. *Alisha*.

They talked often, and I appreciated their budding friendship. Nari was a loner and was perfectly happy in her own space. I frequently felt like an intruder because of how comfortable she was with solitude. Alisha was good for her. My wife needed family and friends, and it was my job to hand them over, but only from a select stock, which I trusted to protect her the way I would.

"You didn't like any of them?"

Her eyes lifted, slamming into mine hard. Her face warmed with uncertainty. "I liked all of them."

"Maybe *like* isn't the right term. You haven't found one that feels like home?"

She shrugged. "It's hard to do that when they're empty."

I nodded. "But you have to imagine how it feels once you've filled it with your things . . ."

"*Your* things," she corrected.

"*Our* things. We'll furnish our home with whatever you choose. I just want you to find one that feels right to you."

"And what about you?" She arched a brow, waiting.

"If you're happy, I'm happy. That's how this works."

Her eyes rolled quickly from annoyance. I chuckled because she was cute when aggravated. "That's a lot of weight to carry, buddy. It's not fair to put that on me. You might absolutely hate what I choose, but tolerate it because it's what I want."

"It wouldn't matter. If it makes your eyes shine the way I've known them to when you are truly happy, then I don't give a damn. It's just walls, ceilings, and floors. You being there will make it home for me, so what's the problem? Is it the money?"

She snorted, shaking her head. "No, *sweetheart*. You've made clear the sky is the limit." Her words were mocking.

"Then what?" I chose to avoid that rabbit hole. My wealth was still something she was uncomfortable with.

"Your mother said that I don't have family."

"And?"

"How would she know that?"

"Because I told her." My eyes fastened to hers, searching for what was lying beneath those words. It was deeper than my sharing that she didn't have a family.

"Why?"

"There are no secrets between us. Not that I felt as if your bloodline was a secret."

She pushed out an exasperated breath. "I'm well aware of how this started, but we've crossed lines that changed the course of things. It was okay not to know each other then because this wasn't real . . ." She paused from the look I delivered but challenged mine with one of her own. "I don't care what you're pretending, Kincaid. This originally was a business deal. All we were required to know were the terms that bound us. Now you want me to pick a house we'll share, and you're taking me to dinners with your parents. It's a lot. I don't know you, but you know me. *They* know me. Apparently, everything about me. That's a lot."

She's scared.

Overwhelmed.

Feeling exposed.

"I'll tell you anything you want to know. Just ask, Nari. No secrets between us, and I'll never lie."

"Why did your mother tell me I would need her to understand how to love you 'the right way'? What the hell does that even mean?"

Ahhh. Clarity.

"Do you trust me?"

She frowned, her expression uncertain, but her eyes, they handed over the truth. *Yes!*

"I'm not a complicated man, but I do have a complicated life. When you find yourself having to choose and feel stuck in the middle of chaos where I'm concerned, trust your gut. Lean on what feels right. Nothing else matters."

"That doesn't help." She was frustrated.

"Then it's a good thing that it's not time for you to love me yet. You have the luxury of feeling your way through the process." I winked and lifted my eyes, glancing over my shoulder when Annalise joined us again.

"Sorry about that. We're in the middle of a major deal with some commercial properties. Every detail has to be aligned." She stood behind her desk, placing a hand on her hip. "Are we ready? I have three properties to view. I feel good about one especially. I'll save it for last." She smiled at us both, but my eyes remained on my wife.

"Shall we?"

She sucked in a breath, nodding. "Your time, your dime."

I issued a warning look, but Nari was unfazed. Where others cowered from a simple gesture, my wife simply dug her heels in, prepared for battle. *Good.* She will have to be strong to be connected to me.

As promised, we viewed three properties. The first two were nice. I even preferred one over the other, but the minute we stepped into the third, I knew. That was the one. Not because I liked it better than the other two or the seven before it but because Nari's eyes lit up. I could see her shoulders relax seconds after she inhaled the air around us. That was the one. I, however, kept quiet while we toured.

It was an eight-thousand-square-foot home with three levels, two master suites, and a fully furnished basement, which could sub as a separate residence. It had a pool, spa, gym, and theatre room. It was all standard compared to what we had seen so far, but my wife's reaction was priceless. Nari's smile was subtle as we moved from room to room, but her eyes . . . They told me everything I needed to know.

"Well?" Annalise questioned as we circled back to the entrance.

"Give us a minute."

She nodded. "I'll step out to check in with the office."

"Well?" I repeated Annalise's question.

"It's a'ight."

I chuckled, and she grinned.

"Oh, well then, I'll ask her to schedule a few more. Maybe next week."

"Do you like this one?"

"I do."

She was attempting to force me to make the call. I wouldn't. It would have to be her decision. When Nari caught on to what I was doing, she straightened her spine and squared her shoulders.

"This is the one."

"You sure?"

"Yes." Her eyes swept the empty space before they returned to me. "And I don't care if you don't really like it. You had your chance." She shrugged and then turned to walk away, but I caught her by the waist, bringing her soft body against mine. We hadn't been intimate since we returned from Tulum. We slept in the same bed, shared the same space, and her body snuggled against mine while we slept, but no sex. Just a closeness that I appreciated but wanted more of.

She stared, taking me in. I caught the point where she inhaled, a soft smile teasing at her lips. My cologne was one of her favorite things. She'd told me several times while we were on our honeymoon.

"I'm an only child. My mother wanted a daughter, but it never happened. I don't know the specifics, but she carried two babies after me. Neither survived past the first trimester. At a certain point, she refused to try again. I never heard her say the words, but I was a child, so the discussion wouldn't have been presented to me. I did, however, sense it the older I became from how she changed. Her energy shifted to me. She would always talk about the day I gave her a daughter. It would be the woman I married. That's you. You're that daughter. Let them in. They mean you no harm, and neither do I. You want to know me? Let's start there. This is new for you, but I promise you can trust what you're afraid of."

"What am I afraid of?"

"Being loved."

Her lips parted, but I kissed her before she had time to argue or deny. "I'll let Annalise know to finalize the paperwork so we can start preparing to move."

"Wait, that's it?"

"What else is there?" I lifted a brow, and she shook her head.

"Nothing, I suppose when you're Kincaid Akel."

"Or his wife." I winked, taking her hand and bringing her fingers to my lips. I planted a kiss just above the diamond I'd branded her with, but my eyes never left hers.

"So it seems."

"Glad that you're finally on board with how this works."

After I squared things away with Annalise, whose eyes shined while she calculated her commission, I took my wife for a late lunch. It was just after three when we reached our destination. We were dining at one of my restaurants, so I thought nothing of bringing her there. I should've expected the possibility of running into Aila, but a part of me assumed she'd be too embarrassed to be seen there. Not a damn chance. Apparently, my ex-fiancée would continue to use the association until I put a stop to it. Not that her being here mattered to me in the least, but I didn't want Nari to feel ambushed.

We didn't have to wait for a table because my staff knew better; however, I'd have to work around the inconvenience of Aila's being near where they would seat me. Only a few were offered that privilege, and I was sure she'd used her association with me to be granted favor, which landed her in our exclusive section.

My eyes caught hers the minute we entered, and she smiled. I was sure she hadn't intended to, but it couldn't be helped. That quickly changed seconds after she realized I wasn't alone. An expression so evil and deadly that I felt the chill radiating from those icy, brown eyes that landed on Nari, and I was confident she felt it as well. Her words confirmed it.

"That's her . . . Aila." It wasn't a question. She knew.

"Yes, we can leave."

"No." Something flashed behind her eyes when they lifted to mine. "Introduce me."

"To Aila?" I wanted to be sure I understood the request.

"Yes, unless that's a problem for you." She was testing me. It wasn't necessary because I'd made my choice and without hesitation. With a nod, I placed my hand on her back and moved toward Aila's table. She and her guest shared a look before their cold glares landed on Nari.

"Dr. Bowen," I offered with a toss of my chin. "Let me introduce you both to my wife, *Mrs.* Nari Akel." I made a point of stating her entire name. My tone was even because their opinions didn't matter to me.

"Your wife?" Angela began. The good old doctor had drawn a line in the sand. She'd chosen sides over etiquette, and her choice was clear. "I was under the impression that you were engaged to Aila. What did I miss?" She already knew but wanted to make the point of tossing that in Nari's face. It was childish, and she looked stupid because regardless of that truth, I had married someone other than her friend.

I chuckled, refusing to entertain either of them. "Enjoy your food, ladies. I'm sure Aila placed your meal on my tab."

"Not necessary. I can cover our expenses." Dr. Bowen tried her hand at putting me in my place.

"I'm sure you can. How's your *wife*?" She frowned, and I smirked. "My apologies. Slip of the tongue. Your husband? Send my regards."

I nudged Nari gently so that we could leave. That was pointless.

"It was a pleasure, ladies," she tossed out casually with a smile in place.

When we stepped away, Aila spoke. "Kincaid . . ." I glanced over my shoulder, and she continued. "She's not what I expected. I didn't take you for a man that tolerates mediocrity."

Aila's eyes remained on Nari. I was amused because both women were beautiful; however, my wife had that thing about her where she didn't have to try. Aila's comment was a sign of her insecurity. She could see every feature that attracted me to Nari. Her flawless skin, her enticing and feminine curves, and there was no denying how organically attractive she was. Aila might have been hinting at the fact that she was draped in labels and jewels while Nari was in jeans and a racerback tank with Nikes on her feet. Either way, my baby was anything but mediocre. She could be wearing a paper sack and still turn heads.

"I guess we're both at a loss then. I didn't take my husband for the type to be attracted to weak women." The final shot landed right in Aila's heart, but she only had herself to blame.

"Shall we?" Nari's eyes lifted to mine. Without hesitation, my hand rested at the small of her back, and we traveled to our table. The hostess was standing patiently, waiting. The fact that I signed her checks was a guarantee that she wouldn't move until we were seated. Once we were, she placed menus in front of us and then tossed out that our server would arrive shortly.

Nari began studying hers while I watched, waiting for a reaction, any reaction. When there wasn't one, I addressed the situation.

"I told you that you would never fight over me."

She smiled but didn't give me her eyes. "And I won't. That was child's play. You'll know when my claws come out because I won't stop until there's blood."

I wanted to be surprised, but I had known all along that she had it in her. I could feel it. Nari wasn't to be fucked with—by me or anyone else. She was the type that would strike with a deadly blow, which could end you instantly, and you'd never see it coming.

My sweet Nari has a mean streak!

CHAPTER 15

NARI.

Weeks flew by, and before I realized it, I'd been married for a whole month. That last week, I spent away from my husband, who had to travel for business. I hated to admit that I missed him, but I did. Regardless of how often we communicated throughout the day or that he called and FaceTimed at night until I promised I was seconds away from sleep, it wasn't enough. In the little time I'd known Kincaid, I got used to his presence and energy filling my space. Sleeping alone in his bed, in his penthouse, was a conflict. It smelled like my husband, reminding me of what I was missing, and it felt like him, keeping me up until my body lost the battle and finally drifted to sleep. I never told Kincaid that part. He assumed that when we ended our calls at night, I was instantly encased in a peaceful slumber, when in reality, I was up, my mind racing, trying to make sense of why he had a hold on me so quickly.

I did my best to fill my time with tasks to keep me busy. Busy for me meant spending the week ordering furniture, picking paint colors, and deciding on looks and styles for our new home. It was overwhelming to be tasked with such a huge responsibility, but at the very least, it kept my mind occupied. What I did appreciate was having help. I objected a million times, but Kincaid still sent his mother my way to help prepare to move to our new home. She was all too eager to assist, which actually worked in my favor.

I now had unlimited access to my husband's funds by way of the cards that he'd gifted me to his accounts. He made clear that I had the freedom to spend whatever I wanted, which was even more intimidating. Who the hell thought that someone gifting the ability to spend with no limits would create so much stress? Money knew how to spend money. I most certainly was not that. That was where my mother-in-law came in handy. She enlightened me about designers and brands. She also offered to extend her hand-selected interior decorators, whom I agreed to work with. It made the job a lot easier, and by the end of the week, I had line items for just about every room of our new home. Now, I was on to the next complication in my life. My husband was scheduled to land that evening, just in time to dress and drive me to our very first formal event as husband and wife. It was what landed me here in the overpriced boutique with Alisha.

"How the hell am I supposed to choose?" I frowned as my eyes moved about the exclusive formal gowns hand selected for privileged clientele such as myself. Kincaid had called in a favor, scheduling me for a private fitting after throwing the event at me at the last minute. I was grateful that Alisha volunteered to accompany me. As a friend, she had been a lifesaver while I adjusted to my new lifestyle.

"Start with a color. After the color, pick a fit. This is an evening formal, so it should be a gown. Something sexy but conservative at the same time. The benefit is hosted by The Families."

"How the hell do you have sexy and conservative in the same sentence?" I frowned at her, and she flashed me a big smile. We were both dressed casually in athletic wear, which I appreciated because that was another issue for me. I was married to Kincaid Akel, meaning I was expected to look the part. I wasn't sure what the hell that meant, but I felt it was important. Although Kincaid hadn't said a word about my looks or clothes, everyone I came in contact with did. It was always subtle, like statements such as, "*If you would like, we can shop together.*"

"Trust me, it's a whole thing. It took me awhile to figure it out, but after my first few events where I was over- or underdressed, I learned my lesson. Color?"

Alisha had her back to me while her hands glided through the rack of dresses she stood in front of. They looked so expensive that I didn't even want to touch them.

"Uhh, red."

"Oh, sexy. Red. I like that." She glanced over her shoulder with a devious smile.

"It's his favorite color," I spoke my thoughts out loud, and she turned with a smile that expanded.

"Then definitely red." She turned and lifted her hand to the sales associate who was assigned to us. She damn near broke her neck speed walking in her six-inch heels toward Alisha. That was the part I didn't think I would get used to. Money changed everything. Before being labeled as Mrs. Nari Akel, I wouldn't have likely been allowed even to browse a store like this one. Alisha walked in, smiled, and dropped my name, and the entire store lit up with eager eyes while their Botoxed lips curled.

"Yes, ma'am? How can I help you?"

"Not me, her. Mrs. Akel has decided on red. Bring up what you have and make sure they're all one of a kind."

"Absolutely, Mrs. Akel." She turned and landed a perfect smile. "What are you, about a ten?"

"Yes, sometimes twelve pending the cut."

"Got it, and you're tall, so I'll keep that in mind. Please head back, and I'll be right there with some of our newest selections."

I looked at Alisha, and she winked at me and addressed the saleswoman. "Perfect. Thank you, Claudia."

Claudia nodded and hurried away. Alisha looped her arm through mine and guided me to the back. There was an area with a three-way mirror, and across from it was a plush white rug and matching white velvet love seats. It was similar to what I had seen in movies with women trying on wedding dresses. There was no lift for them to stand on—only the three-way mirrors to catch every angle.

"What color is your dress?"

"I don't have one. I'm not going."

"Why not?" I frowned. That was the only thing that settled my nerves. Not only had Alisha become a friend, but she'd also quickly become my personal guide, helping me navigate my new life.

"We weren't invited. Only a select few for tonight, and we didn't make the cut."

I wasn't sure what that meant and didn't ask. I didn't know if it was appropriate to. Again, I was still learning the ins and outs of this crew.

"So what should I expect tonight?" The people in Kincaid's circle were expecting a marriage, just not to me. We showing up together would confirm the rampant whispers behind our backs— *my back*. After crossing paths with Aila, I was positive that she would be leading the pack with hateful thoughts directed at me. No matter how poised she pretended to be, she felt slighted, and I would bet my life that there would be more to come.

"It's a fundraiser. There will be some politicians, celebrities, and deep pockets who will pay for overpriced tables so that the host can donate to a charitable cause. The Sinclairs are responsible for this one. I'm not on their committee."

"Why not?"

"Because I'm the outsider. The spoon I was born with in my mouth was plastic, not silver." Alisha grinned.

"Then I suppose I won't be on their committee either. At least you had a spoon. I've been eating scraps off the floor from birth." I shrugged, and Alisha shook her head, those signature spirals bouncing.

"They will extend an invite, regardless. Even if they don't like you, and trust me, they won't. Those are Aila's people, but Kincaid is the golden child. They treat him differently. He's like the second coming." Alisha raised a hand as if giving a short praise to the man above.

"I don't get it."

"The Families have a certain level of respect for all their members, but some more than others. Everyone knows the hierarchy. It's kinda like the mob. You have the bosses, one from each country considered a powerhouse: Nigerian, Kafi Aku; Italian, Angelo Ricci; Chinese, Jun Li; Colombian, Saulo Perez; and American, Razi Price. Kafi and Saulo are the two head families—the most powerful. The word is that in the next few years, Razi will choose the next in charge. Right now, Kincaid is considered a boss, kind of like a capo, but it's unspoken that the syndicate is looking to make him the head of the American Family, so everyone kisses his ass. They know the type of power the title comes with. It's why they don't have to like you to include you. It will be their way of showing favor in the hopes of receiving it . . ." she paused, "from your husband."

"Great, so I've married into the mob."

Alisha's smile grew. "Damn near close to it, but the mob don't have shit on the type of power The Families have. The mobs run cities and states. The Families run the world, and our husbands are a part of that. It's their decisions that move in the background, which keep balance in the world."

"How do you know so much?" Kincaid hadn't discussed any of this with me. I wondered why.

"Darius. He tells me things."

"And where does he fall in this hierarchy?" I'd witnessed the bond between him and Kincaid. They had to be in similar positions.

"He's kinda like a soldier, but because he and Kincaid are so close, like brothers, he's ranked above the others. They respect him, but rules are still rules, which is why we didn't make the cut for tonight."

"Wow, this is a lot. Kincaid hasn't mentioned any of this."

"He will in time. If he laid it all on you at one time, you'd likely say to hell with this and run." She offered a comforting smile as if attempting to reassure me that my husband wasn't keeping secrets. However, he was, though, but I had to agree. Kincaid was choosing his battles wisely so that I wouldn't run. Unfortunately, that wasn't an option.

There were no outs. It was too late. The man had a hold on me.

"I have five selections for you. If none of these work, I'll bring more." Claudia returned, interrupting our conversation. Alisha was on her feet, taking one from her arms.

"Start with this one." It was a halter that would expose my sides and back. It would gather around the neck with spaghetti straps that did a crisscross down the back until it reached the waist. The bottom was a sea of pleated silk that swept the floor. "I absolutely love this one, and you can pull it off."

"That shows a lot of skin." I frowned. "I thought this was formal."

"It is, but you can still be sexy. Trust me."

"You want me to trust you, but you won't be there when I fail."

While Claudia hung the dresses inside one of the fitting rooms, I peered at the one Alisha was extending to me.

"I would never set you up to fail, Nari." She shoved it into my hands and then followed up with a gentle push toward the dressing room. I groaned but decided to go with the flow.

An hour later, I had modeled eight dresses and decided on the first one. The one that Alisha had chosen. She smiled through the rest, but none met her approval like the first. I had to agree.

The way the expensive fabric flowed around my body, I'd fallen in love.

As we cashed out and my dress was packaged, I handed over the card that Kincaid had provided me. Yet another new layer to my life as a married woman.

"A girl could get used to this kind of lifestyle," I teased until the woman presented me with the leather pad to sign the receipt she'd placed on top.

"This dress is six thousand dollars," I whispered roughly to Alisha, who seemed unfazed.

"That's nothing. You're just getting started." She winked at me, but my stomach knotted. Kincaid was wealthy, but that didn't justify spending that kind of money on a dress that I was sure I would only wear once. That was how things worked in their world. It made me uneasy.

After signing, I was given my purchase. Alisha sensed my anxiety about making such an expensive purchase. "Stop worrying. You're married to a *capo*."

"So it seems," I groaned, and she laughed. I had no idea how I was going to manage in this world. It already felt as if it were suffocating me.

That night, Kincaid called from the car, letting me know that he was on his way up. We were running a bit behind because his jet was held up on the runway, so I was instructed to be ready. His eyes were on his phone when the doors to the elevator opened. When they slowly lifted and attached to mine, I felt my stomach take flight. He took me in slowly, as did I him. The black suit he wore, much like the others, fit like it had been designed and stitched specially for him. He stood shoulders relaxed, stance wide, staring with one hand submerged in his pocket while the other held tight to his phone. I felt the pulse in my neck throbbing from the thrill of being so close. It was a feeling I couldn't curb and hadn't gotten used to yet.

Without words, he commanded I join him by extending an arm, but I noticed how his teeth raked across his bottom lip. When I stepped into the elevator, the first sense that I reacted to was smell. His cologne danced around me like a dangerous memory. Next was touch. My body shivered as his finger moved from my neck, then down my arm, and when he met my waist, I was pulled into his solid frame. A kiss landed on my shoulder and then my neck.

"You want my hands to be the color of your dress this evening, I see."

I smiled, instantly picking up on the hidden message. He would have blood on his hands if anyone crossed a line with me.

"No. I was simply trying to show my husband how much I've missed him all week."

He chuckled, leaning into me, and while his teeth grazed my shoulder, I felt him reach for something behind me. Seconds after, we were closed in together on our way to the lobby.

"I missed you too." He drew back, his eyes fastened to mine. Seconds, possibly minutes, passed before half of his mouth curved into a salacious smile. I still had no idea how he could stop time simply by how his eyes consumed me.

"How long is this thing?" I questioned about the event we were on our way to.

"A few hours, why?"

"I don't know anyone."

"You know me." He was on me again, a kiss pressed to my lips before he stepped away, taking my hand. I noticed two bodies move as soon as we stepped out of the elevator. Usually, Cast was with Kincaid, but neither of the faces belonged to him that night.

Both men were dressed in suits, equally as nice as the one my husband wore, but they didn't wear them as well as he did. That thought made me smile.

Once we reached the front, Kincaid held the door open for me, and we stepped out into the night air. One of the men disappeared in the front seat of an SUV while the other opened the rear door. I entered first, and Kincaid followed, pulling me to his side once he was comfortable. "Stop overthinking. You'll be fine." I was staring out the window, and he was studying me.

"You don't know that."

"I do. Nobody touches you, Nari. Ever."

"That might be true, but that doesn't mean they'll accept me." I felt like a child starting their first day of school. I imagined that was how the people in his circle would function. Either I was one of the cool kids, or I wasn't, and even sometimes being attached to the cool kid didn't guarantee you a pass.

A kiss landed on my cheek. "Tell me about your week. My mother said that the house is coming along nicely."

There it was—that shift. The conversation of my anxieties about tonight was done. He'd made his point. One thing I quickly grasped about my husband was that he didn't argue and barely liked to be questioned. Once his point was made, there was no moving him on it.

"You talk to her?" I lifted my eyes, and his were waiting.

"Of course. She's my direct line to knowing that you're okay while I'm away."

"Shouldn't I be your direct line? No one knows me better than me."

He chuckled, nodding. "You're still adjusting. I never want you to feel obligated to lie on my behalf. She will be honest and tell me if I'm fucking up with my new wife." He winked, and I rolled my eyes.

"So, basically, she's your spy."

"No. I wasn't aware that I needed one. Do I?" His eyes smiled in a teasing manner.

"No, but if she's reporting to you . . ."

"She's not reporting. I asked questions, and she answered."

Same difference. I wasn't sure why, but that kind of rubbed me the wrong way. I inched away, only to be brought right back to his side.

"I trust you, Nari. If I didn't, you wouldn't be wearing this or carrying my last name. It's just a genuine concern. A new husband worried about his new bride. You're honest with my mother. She said that you're relaxed around her. That guard you usually have up with me you don't maintain when she's around."

My eyes shot up to his, searching for the meaning behind that. "I'm not guarded with you."

"You are. But I'm not offended. You're still getting to know me. I don't mind fully gaining your trust. I'm a man who doesn't mind working for things that are important to me . . ." He paused, lifting my hand and kissing my wrist. "You, Nari Akel, are at the top of my list."

And there it was. That feeling that washed over me from a look, the sound of his voice, the acknowledgment of his touch. How the hell could he feel that I had my guard up? Maybe I did, but he obliterated it with a simple kiss.

The event was held at a private estate. There was no way to describe it other than luxurious. Once inside, staff greeted us, and I was offered a glass of champagne. We both declined, but Kincaid requested Cognac. I was too anxious to drink. We traveled through the house to what appeared to be a ballroom. It was beautifully decorated with crystal chandeliers and ivory and gold décor. There were several tall tables throughout the room, but the center was clear, aside from a massive, carved ice structure. It was some type of abstract art design.

"Who the hell has an event space in their home?"

"You'd be surprised."

Kincaid smiled, placing his hand at the small of my back. The feel of the warmth of his fingers as they connected with my skin caused my spine to shiver. I not only missed his presence but also his connection as well. I was also starved for sex. The things Kincaid had done to my body played on repeat in my mind. It was like a sick obsession that I couldn't get enough of.

As soon as the attendees noticed Kincaid had arrived, he began greeting people and introducing me. I could see the looks in their eyes when he used the word *wife*. They were judging . . . harshly. Some even allowed their eyes to sweep the room mindlessly searching for her. *Aila*. Regardless of their thoughts or opinions, they were all polite, even if it was forced. I noticed what Alisha meant about the level of respect they had for my husband. Everyone flocked to him. At one point or another, they found their way into his space, kissing ass and doting over his presence. He didn't seem moved by their doting one way or another. Kincaid didn't need to draw attention to his authority. There was no way for anyone in his presence to overlook his attributes. He wore them like the expensive suits that were tailored to fit his frame. They announced his entrance and lingered in his absence.

However, they weren't so enthralled with me. I could see the women turning up their noses or squinting their eyes with pursed lips. They simply knew better than to express their thoughts around my husband; however, that didn't stop them from whispering when he was out of earshot.

I didn't miss the mixture of guests. All were high-profile, with dollar signs hanging over their heads like conversation bubbles. Some I even recognized from Salacious, and a few recognized me as well because they would briefly drop their eyes or lower them to the women by their sides as if issuing a warning. I didn't care how they spent their time or lived their lives. I had bigger issues than their infidelities, such as the women who were cliqued up with Aila. She was there. I couldn't deny that she was styled to perfection, with flawless makeup, not a hair out of place, and her strapless navy floor-length gown fit her body like a glove. That was a woman who appeared to have it all, but I knew better. I smiled because the one thing she wanted most was at *my* side, clinging to me protectively while he mingled with men who held him in high regard. She watched through thin eyes while the four women who remained close whispered back and forth.

When I looked back at my husband, a man approached. He was older and nice looking, with gray in his hair and beard. He smiled, offering me a courteous nod before he spoke lowly to Kincaid. I didn't hear him, but his look was firm, which caused my husband's posture to straighten before he addressed me.

"Give me a minute. I need to have a private discussion. I won't be gone long." Kincaid's breath beside my ear brought my attention back to him. His eyes were warm, but he questioned me without words, asking if I was okay.

"Sure. Go ahead. I'll be fine." He frowned slightly, his eyes drifting across the room before they were on me again. A kiss met my shoulder before it traveled to the spot just below my earlobe.

"Be nice. She's not relevant."

"I know, and I will as long as she remembers her place."

He chuckled and tossed his chin lightly. "Go get us a drink." He handed me his empty glass and motioned to the corner opposite of where we were. My eyes followed, and I nodded once I located the bar. He watched as I crossed the room, and once I reached my destination, I turned to find him, but he was gone.

"What can I get you, Mrs. Akel?" The voice came from behind the bar. When I turned and my eyes locked onto his, he offered a smile. "You know my name?"

"Your husband's name, yes."

"Oh."

"Wine. Pinot, please, and—"

"Gautier for Mr. Akel. Got it." He turned away from me, and I shook my head. They knew his name, his drink preference, and what else, I wonder? That man was far more important than I imagined. Suddenly, a body strode next to me, but I didn't bother lending my attention until he spoke.

"Lady in red. The color of sin." The voice next to me sounded eerie, far from friendly. The way he spoke wasn't a compliment, which had me turning toward him cautiously. He immediately picked up on my unease and lifted a brow. "No smile for me?"

"I don't know you."

"Ah, but you should. You cost me a lot of money, young lady. I'm not happy about that either. Your husband has created a lot of enemies behind his decision to marry you instead of my daughter."

"Your . . ."

Aila. This is her father.

"Take that up with Kincaid. His decision, not mine."

His eyes reflected something I couldn't decipher, but he followed with a smile. "Marriage should be a mutual agreement, *Mrs. Collette*. I suppose that answers my next question, though. How this thing between the two of you happened. What did he offer to gain access to that pretty little ass of yours? It's nice, but I'm sure he paid far too much."

I frowned at his disrespectful words and the fact that he addressed me by my maiden name. When the bartender returned, sliding both drinks I requested across the table, his eyes bounced between us before they searched the room. I was sure he was looking for my husband.

"Mr. Kaber, can I get something for you?"

"No." His eyes never left me when he answered.

"Are you sure, *sir*? I wasn't made aware that you would be in attendance this evening, but I might have a drink you would accept."

Aila's father's eyes eventually left mine, and he glared hard at the bartender. Something passed between them that I couldn't keep up with, but no words were exchanged.

"Your husband's debt just became yours as well, sweetheart. He's playing a dangerous game. When you challenge an animal, backing it in a corner, they fight for blood and with all they have."

"What's between you and my husband doesn't concern me. I suggest you take that up with him."

A devious, threatening smile inched into place. "I fully plan to, sweetheart. It's now my only focus."

He walked away, and the bartender spoke. "Keep your distance. There's a war between the two, and you're at the center of it," he warned, walking away before I had a chance to ask him what the hell that meant. When I lifted our drinks and searched the room, I didn't find Kincaid, but another pair of eyes were on me. Her grin matched the one her father had just worn. It expressed a small victory.

I quickly looked around just in time to see her father leave the event room. Then, I nearly jumped out of my skin when I felt hands at my waist. I relaxed when I recognized not only his touch but also his scent. I smelled him around me like a pleasant memory. He placed a kiss on my shoulder before he stepped in front of me, coming into view. Kincaid removed his glass from my hand, but those intense orbs were pinned to mine while he lifted the glass to his lips.

"You okay? You seem tense."

"I'm fine. Just feeling out of place." I forced a smile, and he studied me for a minute longer.

"I've made my donation and been seen. How about we head out? We can have a late dinner before you welcome me home the right way."

"The right way?" I arched a brow, and his arm circled my waist, pressing his body to mine. He was hard against my stomach, and when Kincaid's eyes lowered to the space that connected us, his lips curled into a smile, causing my thighs to clench and my stomach to take flight. His intense browns conveyed the words that never left his lips.

Staring into my eyes, he drained the rest of his drink, taking mine from me before I was even allowed to taste it. Both glasses met the surface of the bar behind us before I was escorted through the room. We were leaving, and I had no complaints. I'd much rather Kincaid be in me, where he belonged, than I be in there with those people, where I felt I didn't.

CHAPTER 16

KINCAID.

A shaky breath escaped her lips, and a soft, trembling moan followed it. The way she responded was like handing over permission for me to go deeper, so I did. My hips thrust upward in search of heaven. That was exactly what lay between Nari's thighs, *heaven*. We barely made it off the elevator before I had her against the wall, and her legs wrapped around my waist. The way I needed her was dangerous. I had been challenging my will over the past month, trying to prove the lie I was telling myself. *I was in control.*

That was bullshit. She held all the cards, and that frustrated me. The only bonus was that she had no idea. The minute Nari discovered her superpower, I would be in trouble. *Serious trouble.* She possessed me. I'd often heard how a man classified a woman as his reason for existing while also being the bane of that same existence. That was currently my dilemma.

I moved deeper, my strokes growing in intensity. Our breaths aligned, escaping forcefully in our pants. Hers out was mine in. I needed it all. She was bending to my will, and no matter how deep I explored, her body opened a little wider, but still managed to hug me tight.

My name left her lips in a low, trembling whisper, and I felt her unravel. *Beautiful. Just fucking beautiful.*

When her eyes peeled open and lazily found mine, I smiled just before my mouth clashed with hers. My pace increased because I was close. She pushed against me while sucking me in to pull it from me. Remaining steady but hard, I kept consistent until I was utterly consumed. My heart raced out of control while I spilled myself as deep as I could go, and she came at the same time, tightening around me.

When our breathing slowed enough to be considered regulated, my mouth fastened to hers again, and I spoke into it.

"*Itaque ut accipias benedictionem et maledictionem.*"

She frowned against my lips, pulling back with curious eyes. "What language are you speaking?"

"Latin."

"What does it mean?"

"A blessing and a curse."

That was precisely what my wife had become, and I had no defense against it.

"Me?" Her smile was slow, and I chuckled, stealing one last kiss in place of answering.

After we showered and climbed into bed again, we lay face-to-face. My mouth aligned at her forehead while she draped her leg across my waist, the other pushed against me. I could feel the heat from between her thighs, which had me hard as stone, but I chose to employ control. We needed to talk. I had eyes and ears everywhere—especially where Nari was concerned. When I left my wife alone that night, she wasn't truly alone. When it was reported to me after my meeting with Razi that Kaber had approached her, I had a good mind to hunt him down immediately. He was trying me and testing my resolve.

There was an order of protection over his life, which was the only thing keeping him alive. Had he laid one finger on what belonged to me, not even The Families would have been enough to preserve his life. He was on borrowed time. The call hadn't been made yet to sever his ties, but the second it was passed down, his heart would be in my hands. I would physically rip it from his chest and allow him to live through the pain long enough to take his last breath while he watched the arteries bleed from my palm right before I crushed it with my fingers. Until then, I needed my wife to truly understand how serious I was about *no secrets*.

"What did he say to you?"

Her body tensed briefly, but she relaxed when my lips grazed her skin.

"Who?"

"Nari, what did he say?" My eyes lowered to meet hers. She stood her ground but still gave what I asked.

"That I cost him a lot of money, and your debt is now mine."

My blood heated to a dangerous temperature like fire moving through my veins. He was threatening my wife.

"What else?"

"That was pretty much it. He called me Collette and not Akel." *He's done his research.*

I lowered my chin to the top of her head while my hands glided across her skin. My fingers created a rhythm and pace that soothed my anger.

"This is new, but I need you to understand one thing." I paused, giving her a minute to hand over her complete focus. "The only way nothing touches you is if I know where the threats come from. You tell me everything, agreed?"

It took a minute for her to respond. She inched closer and allowed her forehead to rest against my chest before she delivered one word.

"Agreed."

The next morning, I was up early. I had a few calls to make before I promised the rest of the day to my wife. She was settling into her role nicely, but I still needed Nari to understand that things were different. We would discuss a few things while I made up for the week I had been deprived of her presence. After I finished the call to ensure the home we purchased would be set up with the proper security, my wife toed into the kitchen. She was moving sluggishly, wearing one of my T-shirts. She must've slipped it on after leaving the bed because she wasn't wearing anything when I climbed out a few hours ago.

"Good morning." She paused a few feet away, her eyes still lazy from having just recently opened them. I waved her over, and she stepped between my legs but not close enough, so my hands found her hips, bringing them closer. My body rested against the counter, which now held the weight of both of us.

"Good morning," I returned, pressing a kiss to the top of her head while she rested the side of her face against my bare chest. "I didn't expect you for a few hours."

I sensed her smile and felt it against my skin before her head went back, and I could see it on her pretty face. "Why? Because you tried to take me out last night?"

I laughed, placing a kiss on the corner of her mouth before I actually sampled her lips. Her mouth was minty when my tongue explored.

"I didn't try to take you out."

"Oh . . ." Her nose wrinkled some. "That's right. You were showing me how much you missed me."

"Yeah, something like that. You didn't complain or resist."

"No."

"Then you, Mrs. Akel, were a willing party, agreed?"

"Agreed. You spoke Latin last night. Every day is something new with you."

"I speak several languages. It's necessary. I can teach you any of them if you would like."

"Ahh, that's right, Mr. International, and no, I'll just use the translator on my phone to make sure you're not lying about the meaning." Her cheeks hiked in amusement.

"You hungry?"

"A little. I can cook something for us."

I wasn't sure why that pleased me so much, but it did. My mother always said a woman who never hesitates to take care of your basic needs loves deeper than most. A woman who will fuck you but won't feed you is selfish by nature. She didn't use those exact words, but the meanings were the same.

"No, we have plans. Get dressed."

Her eyes softened a little, but a frown slipped in place. "We can't stay in?"

"We could, but I have a few places I would like to take you."

"Should I be worried?"

I caught the hidden message behind her words. "Just us today." I pressed a kiss to her lips once more, and she nodded. My wife had a sour taste in her mouth after last night. I couldn't blame her. She was adjusting, and my world was very challenging for those who didn't understand.

"Good."

She attempted to step away, but I pulled her back. The separation of the weight and warmth of her didn't sit right with me. I was so fucking obsessed. She lost her breath when her soft landed against my hard. Our contrast somehow blended perfectly.

"You told me to get dressed," she breathed out. The warmth of it tickled my skin, causing me to lean my head closer to hers.

"I did, but then I missed you again."

She cracked a smile. "Then *maybe* you shouldn't allow so much distance between us, Mr. Akel."

"I suppose not." After I kissed her once more, she pulled away, and that time, I allowed the separation. We had a busy day, which meant we needed to get moving. However, before I could leave the kitchen, my phone vibrated on the counter next to me. I lifted it to find a text from Cast. Two words.

Found him.

I cleared the message from my screen. Cast would be in place with eyes on Kaber until I could get to him. He needed to be reminded of what I was capable of. Rules were rules; however, I didn't give a fuck about protocol where Nari was concerned. She was mine to keep safe. That meant protecting her peace as well as her physical. He had disrupted her balance when he crossed the line and approached her last night. I would be crossing a line with him soon enough, and pending his reaction, I might soon find myself meeting with the syndicate while they decided my fate.

"Your family."

Her eyes shot up to mine, thinning some after I used the word "family." I was seated across from my wife and watched as she finished the last of her breakfast. She was quiet, but not in a way that concerned me. I understood it as happiness, and that allowed me to relax.

"I don't have one," she made clear. Her tone was even but icy in a sense.

"You're an Akel. You have family regardless of those who share the same DNA," I made clear in a manner unwavering, which she wouldn't argue. When my mind was set, nothing could change the course of my thoughts or decisions. It was one of the first lessons she was taught. "But I'm speaking about the other. Your parents and their parents."

"I don't know them." She shrugged, lifting her glass. Once she finished the last of her juice, she continued. "I told you that, so they're not mine to claim."

"Would you like for me to find them?"

I already had the details of her grandparents. I knew where they lived and where they worked. Their house was on the South Side, only a few streets from one of my neighborhoods. They had one other grandchild, the cousin Nari had mentioned to me one night while we were in Tulum. From what little she told me, they forged a friendship that ended abruptly the night we met. She didn't give much else, but I could sense that whatever happened between the two hurt my wife. That placed her cousin on a list of people on thin ice with me. She was now near the top.

"Why? They don't care about me."

"Does that include your mother?"

Her eyes squinted. She was thinking. "Can you find her?"

"Possibly, but I won't try unless it's something you want." Our eyes met again and engaged in a war of sorts. She was testing me while she considered the offer.

"She might not want to be found," her voice was soft, unsure, and she hesitated before finishing the thought, "if it's me who's looking."

My eyes were hard on her face. I didn't like the way thoughts of being unwanted dimmed her light. I wanted her. Hell, I fucking *needed* her like air to my lungs. "It's your decision."

"You can try." She smiled softly, but it increased after a few seconds passed. "Thank you."

"Never thank anyone for doing the things required of them."

"It's not your requirement to find my mother."

"It is my requirement to keep a smile on that pretty face of yours by any means necessary. Now, let's go." I stood, extending my hand. The bill had already been covered after our server made her last round. Once on her feet, Nari's eyes moved slowly around the space. It was like something had just occurred.

"Do you own this place too?" Her curious eyes met mine.

"No, I just like the food." She nodded and moved to me as I extended an arm, motioning for her to walk ahead. Once we reached my car and she was in the passenger's seat, she lifted her gaze to mine.

"What all do you own? I guess I should become familiar with those places so I know where to toss your name around to get the royal treatment."

I chuckled and shut the door, getting comfortable in the driver's seat a moment later. "You can toss my name around anywhere you want and receive favor. As for what I own, I'd have to provide a list. It's hard to remember sometimes, but I'll send word to Nathan to draft a list and forward it to you."

"That much, huh?"

"Let's just say I'm in a good place with business."

"And the other things. Will there be a list of those too?" Her tone was sharp, telling of the tension that still lingered from last night.

"No, you'll never get close to that side of my life. Not in a way where you have clarity on how things work." She would soon learn how I compartmentalized things in my life. They were all connected in one way or another but purposely kept separate. She would be aware in a sense but still unknowing of certain aspects, but that was mostly for her safety. We were taught to keep the women we loved out of harm's way by keeping them detached. She would move parallel to my life, my business, and my family but never fully cross those lines. My world rotated around the dark and the light. Nari's role would be to keep me balanced so that I wasn't completely consumed by either side.

"How is that fair? You get all of me, but I don't get all of you?" She stared with an intensity that was unnerving in a sense. She was challenging my loyalty. Something she never had to do. It was hers without question.

"You have all of me. That's proof." My eyes lowered to the ring that she was mindlessly fidgeting with. Hers dropped seconds after mine but shot back up to me, narrowing.

"Then let it be why you trust me enough not to hide. You can't expect what you refuse to give. Alisha knows things."

I snorted at the thought. She didn't know shit. Darius knew better, and like me, he wouldn't place that type of target on his wife's back. Knowledge was dangerous.

"She thinks she does. What she knows won't get her killed, same as what you will be privileged to."

I caught when her breath hitched. It was subtle, but I was trained to see all things.

"You asked me if I trusted you. I do, but do you trust me?"

"With my darkest secrets and my biggest fears. I'll tell you the one that plagues me the most right now."

"I'm listening."

"Failing you. Not keeping you safe or not keeping my promise as your husband and protector. Trust that what you need to know you will and what you don't is so I don't fail you."

She stared for a minute longer before asking, "Are there people who want to hurt you?"

"Yes. Several, I'm sure. Some I know, and others I don't, but they won't come for me unless they have a death wish."

"Will they try to hurt me?"

"Yes, but again, nothing touches you." *Or I touch the heads of everyone they love until there's nothing left but a memory of what used to be.*

"So you *are* like the mob?"

My eyes narrowed a little, and then I laughed. "No. Not even close."

"You have bosses and leaders. You're one of them." She shrugged. "That's similar."

"The blueprint possibly mirrors theirs, but that's about all."

"Your life is a headache," she groaned. "*You're* a headache."

"Of the best kind, though."

"I disagree."

"Then tell me you want an out, and I'll give it to you. I'll give you anything you want, always." That was a half-truth. The one thing I would never offer or allow was an out. Our souls were tied the first time I touched her. She was the one thing I never knew I wanted, but I was now desperate to hold on to.

She kept her eyes fastened to the passenger window. "Not a chance in hell, buddy. You're my only chance at becoming a millionaire, and I only have half now. I'm not going mess that up."

Her eyes landed on me, and a teasing smile tugged at her lips.

"If this is about money, you'll have to try again. What's mine is yours, remember? You surpassed millionaire status the second you said, 'I do.'"

"Then I guess I'll have to hang around just for the hell of it. You're kinda cute in an annoying way. Well, once you get past the brooding and bossiness."

I laughed, focusing on the drive. *My fucking wife.* She was going to bring me to my knees in the worst way, but I welcomed the challenge.

The hour was late, so my surroundings were dark. I could barely see my hand in front of my face if I held it at the tip of my nose. The place was secluded by design. Kaber was hiding. He understood the risk of approaching my wife. The worst consequence was a visit from me. He had seen her and now knew what she meant to me. There was no way to look at Nari and not see her value. There was no way to be around her and not feel the power she could hold over a man. Even if he didn't understand what was between us, he understood me to a certain degree. Not just any woman could earn my loyalty. Aila tried but failed, which had him toeing the line between life and death.

"You're here to talk, ah?" A figure neared me. I knew someone was there but assumed it was Cast. The accent placed and identified one of Kafi's men.

"Why are you watching me?" I asked when his body moved closer to mine. He was at my shoulder briefly before he stepped in front of me. He touched his side but didn't have to. We both understood that weapons, like wallets, keys, and cell phones, were carried.

"It's not you I have eyes on."

He was watching Kaber.

"I'm not going to kill him unless he gives me a reason."

Ekon grinned. His teeth were white against his dark skin. My eyes had adjusted some, but the backdrop around us was still black.

"He gave you one. Your wife."

I shrugged. "He didn't put his hands on her, so this is just a warning."

"You need to let The Families handle this, Kincaid. You have a bigger focus. The decision will be made soon."

"I don't give a shit about that. This . . ." I paused. "This is where my focus is."

"For her?"

"For my family. Some still feel like we owe the debt that Kaber created."

"We have rules for a reason. If you allow exceptions, then the rules no longer apply. Rules maintain order. If there is the understanding that there's a way around them, you ensue chaos. We all lose. It makes the system weak, which makes us weak."

He stared, and so did I.

"Go; have your talk, and then go home to your wife." His hand landed on my shoulder before he stepped away. I had been warned. He wouldn't stop me from taking Kaber's life, but he also wouldn't request favor on my behalf if I pulled the trigger.

It took nothing for me to enter the house. I assumed it was because Kaber didn't expect anyone to connect him to this place. It was old and had belonged to his wife's family. I was sure he assumed he was careful, but you could never be too careful when you played Russian roulette with another man's gun.

I stood over the bed he slept in, my gun in hand. I could easily pull the trigger and end his life, but that would also complicate mine. I needed to be patient. Soon enough, he would no longer be protected. At that point, his life would then be in his own hands.

"Speak your mind, shoot me, or leave," he mumbled, never opening his eyes.

"You shouldn't be so cocky when your life is in the hands of a man who has no fear."

"You might not fear, but where blood flows through most men's veins, the need for power flows through yours. It keeps your heart pumping. Killing me could possibly end your reign, Kincaid. You wouldn't risk it. Not even for her."

I pressed my gun to his forehead, and his breath stilled. "You willing to bet your life on that?"

"Yes," he finally spoke, and I smirked, pulling the trigger seconds later, but I had already moved my gun to his shoulder.

He growled at the pain of the bullet that tore through his flesh. I was so close there wasn't a chance in hell that it wouldn't.

"I understand balance. Power doesn't rule me. Men like you are an embarrassment. You're greedy to the point of not caring who starves to feed your pockets. You fucked over your own daughter simply because she was expendable, and you needed a bargaining tool."

"I'm no different than you. We're one and the same. Does she know who you are? If I had to guess, I'd say no. You're bringing her into a life she hasn't been groomed for. You were smart, though. She doesn't have anyone to miss her when you fuck up, and it costs her—"

Before he could finish, my gun was pressed against his forehead again. "She's the only thing I break the rules for. I won't even think. I'll just act. She is the only thing I'd die for and is my new motivation to kill. If there's a threat to her life, then there's a threat to mine. Don't mistake what you think you know about me with what you've been told will control me."

With that, I left the bedroom that smelled of old wood and now, fear. Kaber only received one warning. Only one.

I stepped past Ekon on my way out. He stood, hands crossed in front of him, stance wide. I didn't have to see his face to feel the question on his tongue.

"I should have, but I didn't. He needs a doctor, but he'll live. Tell him he can go home. I'll always find him, even in the darkness of the shadows." I paused, tucking my gun away against my back before I delivered my last words. "For now."

When I stepped off the elevator, her eyes slammed into mine. She sat in the center of the sofa with her legs crossed at the ankles, her hand resting in the center.

"Why are you up?"

"Why weren't you here?"

"I had something to take care of."

She watched as I crossed the room but headed to the kitchen instead of to her. She was on her feet, following me. After I removed a bottle of water from the refrigerator and turned my back to the counter drinking it, our eyes were in a standoff.

"You don't get to make me worry and walk in here like leaving our bed in the middle of the night is normal."

"It is," I challenged, but she didn't back down. Instead, she closed the space between us, leaving inches. I could smell the coconut on her skin, or maybe it was in her hair. She used it for both. Another thing I was fucking obsessed with.

"For business or pleasure?" Her voice was steady, but her eyes gave her away.

"We have terms, Nari. We agreed. I signed, and so did you."

"Things change."

"That never will."

"Then where were you?"

"Not with another woman," I smirked, and her eyes narrowed. I could see her pulse quicken through the vein in the side of her neck. "Do you want me to prove it?"

"No. I'm going to bed." She was angry for a lot of reasons. Possibly because she worried when she woke up, and I wasn't there. Possibly because she thought the reason was another woman. But mostly, my wife was angry because she cared. She still hadn't fully accepted the thing between us because she didn't understand it. She was battling her emotions as if she could somehow control them. It was pointless. I knew personally. I tried and failed, which was hard for a man like me. I never failed at anything, but this was one loss I would take with grace.

"You sure?"

"Yes, I'm sure. I refuse to drive myself crazy worrying about things I can't control. You don't have to prove anything to me."

She turned to leave, but my arm hooked her waist, and her back slammed against my chest. "I wasn't asking if you were sure about me proving that I hadn't been with another woman. I was asking if you were sure you were going to bed."

My palm moved down her stomach beneath the shirt she wore. It was mine. That was her thing now. Sleeping in my shirts, and if she didn't, it was the first thing she grabbed when she left our bed.

My fingers created a rhythm across her warm skin before they moved between her thighs. There was nothing beneath my shirt. I smiled when I felt her coat my fingers. I bit down on her neck, piercing her skin before kissing the same spot.

"I will never leave our bed for another woman. I gave you my word that the only woman I would be with is you."

She released the breath she'd been holding when my fingers pushed deeper. Her legs spread a little wider, giving me access.

"Men lie."

"I lie, but never to you. Never to my wife," I admitted, undoing my pants with one hand; the other remained busy between her thighs.

She bit down on her lip, and I felt her body giving in. She was close. I pushed deeper, moving my finger in her faster. Five, four, three, two . . .

"Fuck," she hissed, falling hard against my chest. I nudged her forward, pressing hard against her back so that she bent against the island. Before she was allowed to recover, I entered her hard. I reached her depths with the first stroke.

"I would be insane to risk this. Only a stupid man gambles with things that are priceless. I'm not a stupid man, sweetheart."

With each thrust, I buried myself deep, pulling back to return with the same intensity. I was fucking her with control. She would feel every inch but still enjoy it.

"Do you believe me?"

Her head twisted slightly, just enough to give me her eyes. Nari's teeth sank into her lip, but she said nothing. I smirked and began moving faster, harder, leaning over her body while my hand fisted her hair. When I pulled back, she jerked against me just before I shoved my tongue in her mouth.

I spoke against her lips. "I will never lie to you, especially not when you have me this exposed. Consider the heaven between your thighs a haven of truth. Fuck what you think. Rely on what you feel. When I'm here, inside you like this, I couldn't lie even if I wanted to. Just you, Nari. Only you."

"Same," she pushed out in a sharp breath. The way her eyes narrowed on mine triggered something in me. For some reason, I toyed with the idea of anyone else being where I was, that deep in heaven. My grunts aligned with her panting as the sound of our bodies slapping together echoed through the kitchen. She held up until seconds before I gave out. She unraveled just before I spilled myself inside of her. My chest rested against her back, pressing her against the coolness of the marble. Neither of us said a word until I kissed the back of her neck and eased out of her.

"So maybe it was business, but I still don't like waking up, and you're not here." She was at her full height but still had to look up to me. I walked over to her, my chin low so our eyes aligned.

"Noted." I kissed her forehead, the bridge of her nose, and then her lips.

"Good." My smile was slow to surface, but it didn't affect the stern look she gave. It was a warning with many meanings. The two which were the loudest . . .

Always come home and never cheat.

One I could promise, but the other I couldn't, so I chose silence.

CHAPTER 17

NARI.

"**Y**ou look different." Joey had been studying me since I sat down across from him. I was out doing some light shopping when we crossed paths. He asked if we could grab a bite to eat, and I agreed. He wasn't necessarily a friend, but Joey had always been kind to me, and for some reason, I felt as if I needed something to remind me of who I was before Kincaid.

BK, before Kincaid, felt eerily close to the classification of BC, before Christ.

He was all-consuming, with a brilliant mind and power to control and change. He had changed me in a sense, and I felt like I was spinning out of control, struggling to remember who I was. The issue with that seemed to be I never truly had an identity before he shook up my world. Now, I could claim something. Him. *Mrs. Akel.* That name carried so much weight it was unnerving at times. I was learning how much power I held simply by being attached to my husband—my fake husband.

"How?" I already knew the answer. My clothes were expensive, which adjusted my attitude. I couldn't wear the type of labels that filled my closet and not personify a certain level of distinction. I was still me, not arrogant or privileged because that wasn't in my spirit, but I wouldn't deny that I now carried myself with a different degree of confidence. That was also a side effect of being with a man like Kincaid. His haughtiness attached to me on a smaller scale with little to no effort. Its intensity was introduced and bound with my soul each time he kissed my lips or lay between my legs. He was grooming me to align with a man of his stature. I loved and hated what that felt like. My soul was often at war, but Kincaid was destined to win regardless of the battle.

"You're *his* wife. I see it all over you." Joey frowned, and something in his eyes expressed the reason behind it. He didn't like my husband. The way his features hardened was telling of just how deep that ran.

"Why don't you like him?" I studied his face for a minute. "I could sense it that night when you watched him leave. What's up with you two?"

Joey looked off into the distance. We were at the mall, in an open food court area. I had learned a few things about my husband, and one that topped the list was his insane jealousy. I selected a location for our lunch so that there was no question about what moved between Joey and me. I respected Kincaid enough not to give his mind a reason to wander. He never said it, but there were always eyes on me. Initially, I felt it was an invasion, but now it made me feel safe. He wanted me safe and put measures in place to ensure I was.

Joey's eyes slammed on me hard. His face tensed more than it had before. "Do you know who he is?"

"Yes. Why?"

"Then you know you married a monster. A street demon. The type of man who destroys everything in his path and then smiles while he watches it all crumble."

"How do you know so much about him?"

Joey laughed, but there was no humor attached. "I work for him."

"You . . ." I frowned, unable to finish the sentence because I was so confused.

"Not him exactly. Darius, but it's the same. They use Calvetti as a front. Your husband's drugs move through the club, putting money in his pocket . . ." He paused while his eyes slowly moved from my face down my body. It wasn't seductive; it was more introspective. "And the clothes on your back, apparently. Do you know that about him? That's who you married, Nari."

I had an idea about what Kincaid was into, but nothing solid. Either way, I kept my expression neutral. "Why do you care?"

"Because I fucking do. I care about you. I care about what you'll turn into being with him. You're better than that, than *him*."

I was offended. I had no idea what my husband was into, and I didn't care. I should've, but I didn't. I knew him. I could feel him. He was a mixture of dark and light, but he had a heart and was good, even if only to me.

"Are you?"

His eyes narrowed in confusion. "Am I what?"

"Better than my husband. You work for him, right?"

He snorted. "Not the same. I don't have blood on my hands, and I wasn't given a choice. You don't tell a man like Kincaid Akel no. He gives you a command. You keep your head low and handle that shit."

"There's always a choice," was my rebuttal, but deep down inside, I felt he was telling the truth. You didn't tell my husband no without consequences of some kind.

"You really don't know him. You have no idea whose name you're carrying. Ask him about the man who put his hands on you that night. If he won't tell you the truth about them, I will. He's dead, Nari. He killed those two men from the club, and their boss knows. His name is Manchester, and he's just as dangerous as your husband is. He came asking questions. That means a problem for not just Kincaid but you too. You're the reason behind the decision your husband made. Don't be naïve or blind to the world you're now a part of."

"I think I should go." I stood, and so did Joey. His face softened when his hand wrapped around my wrist.

"Wait, don't. Can we at least—"

"No." I lowered my eyes to the place where we were connected. "We're not friends, remember? We're just two people who worked together; now, we don't even have that. Take care, Joey."

I lifted my bags and walked away, not bothering to look back, but I could feel his eyes on me until the crowd swallowed me, and he could no longer see me. My mind was running through a million and one thoughts as I called for the service I used to bring me here. My husband set it up. He knew where I was at all times. I was sure that was by design. That was how he functioned. His presence in my life was a huge contradiction. Subtle and yet so powerful that I could feel him.

I needed a minute to wrap my mind around what Joey was saying about my husband. Did I assume, yes, but hearing it out loud made it feel more real. The same as the day I found out he took two lives because they disrespected me. That was small compared to what I was sure Kincaid was capable of. The things I knew lived in his past. I didn't know before I agreed to be his wife, but I now wore his ring and carried his name, which meant I agreed to accept all of him. Even the things I didn't know. What the hell would I learn about the man I lay with every night while he held me so tight that one would think he feared I would disappear if he loosened his grip, even just a little? It was the same way he looked at me sometimes.

Before I could get out of the car, Alisha was on the porch, smiling at me. She was always genuinely happy to see me. It wasn't the look in her eyes or her smile but her energy. I could feel what her words didn't express. She needed me like I needed her. We were two outsiders in a world built on loyalty and legacies.

When her eyes lowered to the bags I left, her hand flicked in their direction. "I would have gone."

"It was last minute. I needed a few things and hadn't planned on making a day of it."

"Still." She frowned as I entered her home. It was nice. Not as large as the one Kincaid and I would be moving into in less than a week, but it was still very expensive, and the neighborhood held a certain prestige. Her husband might not have been as high on the list as Kincaid, but he was doing well for himself.

"It smells good in here." I lifted my chin, inhaling after she closed and locked the door.

"I made cupcakes." She glanced over her shoulder, leading the way to her kitchen. "I was bored. When I'm bored, I bake."

"See? All that complaining, and you don't need it," I teased, and Alisha narrowed her eyes. She had a staff but no chef.

"Don't get put out. Who the hell wants to be stuck in the kitchen every night? I don't mind cooking, but sometimes I wouldn't mind a break. Feed my husband in the kitchen, clean, feed my husband in the bedroom . . ."

Her lips curled into a smile before she removed a bottle of wine from the rack in the butler's pantry. "Well, I don't mind that part so much. It's actually my favorite part, but you get what I'm saying."

I laughed, reaching for a glass after she filled two with wine. "I do." Sex with Kincaid was one of my favorite things. I couldn't explain it. There were no words, but how he seemed to touch every inch of me was scary. It was like he had been studying the art of pleasing me all his life, but we barely knew each other. One thing I couldn't deny was he knew my body, and I was getting a crash course in his.

"That look right there." She grinned when my eyes found hers. "You're falling fast and hard. It's scary, right?"

"Very." I lifted my glass, taking down some of the wine. It was a red with a bittersweet blend that felt light on my tongue. "And you would know." She and her husband were adorable. The way they loved was intense. I could feel it, which was how I was sure she recognized what was happening with me, regardless of how I tried to deny the direction my heart was taking. "What's the deal with you and Darius? You said it was arranged too, but you never said why."

She crossed the kitchen, opened a cabinet, and removed two small plates, which she placed on the table. One in front of me and one in front of where she had been sitting. I watched as she lifted the glass dome covering a dozen cupcakes. She placed one on each plate and pointed to mine. "It's German chocolate. A perfect blend for this wine."

I nodded, pinching a small piece and popping it into my mouth, waiting. After taking a bite of hers, she chewed slowly and answered my question.

"Darius and I went to college together. I had a huge crush on him. Like massive, but he was so focused. I swear he never looked at me or any other women. He's smart as shit. He and Kincaid are alike in that way. You look at them and just know they're cut from the same cloth. Their roles would be the same, but Darius chose me, and his choice changed everything." Her smile was wide before she got back to her story. "That man was my obsession. I kept trying to get his attention, and eventually, he gave it, but only to tell me that he was engaged and demand that I stop trying." She pushed out an exasperated breath.

"I didn't get it. He was never with anyone, ever. Trust me, I know. I stalked his fine ass all the time, so how the hell was he engaged? It didn't add up. I thought maybe he was lying because he didn't like me, but you know how you feel someone's attraction. When he looked at me, I could see and feel his. It was the way his eyes smiled when they met mine. But he insisted he was engaged, so, eventually, I just said fuck it. I went about my life, met another guy who seemed interested, and we started going on dates. I liked him; however, not like Darius, but Darius didn't want me. One night, I invited Ty to my apartment. We'd been dating for like three months, so I figured it was time. *That time."*

The look she gave explained before she continued. "He showed up, and about ten minutes later, so did Darius. It was the strangest thing ever. He knocked on my door like he had been there a million times before. When I opened it, he pushed past me, walking in like he owned the place. Darius went right up to Ty and punched him in the face. He didn't stop hitting him for a while, and when he did, he lowered close to Ty and said three words. *'I warned you.'* Then he left.

"I was so damn confused and scared as shit. I tried to help Ty, but he wouldn't let me touch him. He left and refused to talk to me. A few weeks later, I couldn't get that night out of my mind, so I tracked down Ty and asked what was going on. He was scared to tell me, but he did. Or at least gave me something. 'Darius is connected. I'm not. Stay away from me.' That's what he said."

She shrugged. "After that, Ty was never on the same part of campus with me, much less the same room, and we had a class together." She laughed, shaking her head.

"So, Darius told him to stay away from you, but he was engaged?"

"Yep. Messed up, right?"

"But you're married. What changed?"

"His mind, I guess. A few months later, my parents visited. They showed up at my apartment *with* Darius. I looked at the three of them trying to figure out what the hell was going on. Short story: Darius wanted to marry me. He approached my parents with that request. How the hell he found them, I still don't know, but he told them I was pregnant, and he wanted to marry me. When my mother said the word *pregnant,* I looked at Darius like he was crazy, and his eyes begged me not to tell the truth, but his smile was so damn arrogant and cocky. I agreed. My parents agreed. And we got married."

"You were pregnant?"

"No. I can't have kids. Car accident when I was younger killed that dream. My parents knew, which was how I was sure something bigger was behind their decision to approve Darius. I suppose when he told them the lie about me carrying his child, my father called him on it, making clear that I couldn't have kids. They made some kind of deal. I don't know what; I don't care. Whatever it was is between them. Darius was supposed to marry someone else. The marriage would've moved his family up in the ranks because of the connection to *her* family. It's why they hate me. He chose me, telling his parents he would marry the woman who carried his child. A child that never happened, that couldn't happen. They don't know the truth, or maybe they do. Doesn't matter. They hate me, but my husband loves me." She shrugged. "This life comes with a lot of secrets. I have mine; you'll eventually have yours. Darius gave up power for love. He has no regrets, and neither do I. We're happy. Be happy, Nari. That's all that really matters when it's all said and done."

"I'm happy." It was the truth. I was unclear about many things connected to my husband, but one truth I wouldn't deny was that he made me happy.

"Good, because you deserve it." Her smile was genuine, which I appreciated. She was the first friend I had who didn't want or need anything from me. Her intentions were pure, so I could honestly say that she was on my side.

"Where are we going?" I glanced at my husband, who was next to me. He had been unusually quiet since he arrived home and told me to change for dinner. I asked what type of dinner, and he said, "*casual*," so I wore jeans, heels, and a sleeveless body suit. My jewelry was simple. Love bangles and hoop earrings, and my hair was pulled up into a bun since my body suit was a mock turtleneck.

Kincaid was in all-black jeans and button-up, with the sleeves rolled up on his forearms. His hair was freshly cut with a sea of curls, which sprouted from his head a little longer than usual. As always, he smelled divine, his scent clean, spicy, and manly. It matched his persona perfectly.

"Dinner." His eyes never left the road as he drove through the city, his speed faster than it should have been. His driving matched his foul mood.

"Where?" I stared at his profile. His eyes met mine for a brief moment before he answered.

"We'll be there soon."

"What's wrong? You seem upset."

His eyes were on me again, and his expression lacked warmth. He simply took me in. His eyes remained steady for a long moment, but he said nothing. One of the things I hated most about Kincaid was that he was unnervingly handsome in a way that was dangerous because his appeal matched his ruthless nature. The combination was a deadly blend.

"We're here." My husband's voice caused my eyes to shoot forward as he turned into a lot. The building was lit up, but there were only two other cars.

"This place looks deserted."

He shut off the engine and tossed his chin toward the building. "I own it."

I took that to mean he shut down for the evening, possibly to have a private dinner with me, but deep down inside, I knew there was more to it. My husband got out and made his way to my side. After he opened my door, he extended a hand to assist me. I stepped out and was pulled to him. I felt him hard against my stomach and smiled when his nose grazed my neck just before I felt his lips. "You always smell so damn good."

Kincaid moved us out of the way so that he could shut the door. His hand moved to the small of my back, directing me through the doors and the building. We stopped outside a private room, where he gripped my chin, kissing my lips. Immediately after, he pushed open the door, and I looked inside. My eyes shot over to Kincaid and then back to the table in the center of the room. Joey sat with a scowl on his face as he glared at Kincaid. Darius was sitting beside him, and Cast was standing near the wall.

"What the hell is this?"

"Dinner with an old friend." Kincaid kissed my cheek and then extended a hand motion for me to move. I didn't.

"Tell me why he's here."

"I figured we would catch up. Discuss what you two talked about earlier today."

"It was nothing." My eyes found Joey before they made it back to my husband.

"Nari, have a seat. If you don't, I might feel you have something to hide."

"I don't."

"Good." He walked to the table and removed a chair, motioning for me to sit. I almost refused but knew that would only make things worse.

"Now, let's get down to business," Kincaid began. Darius stared at me for a minute and then chuckled, shaking his head.

"You two had a productive afternoon." Kincaid motioned with his finger between Joey and me.

"We ran into each other at the mall and had lunch to catch up. What's productive about that?" I sneered, narrowing my eyes at Kincaid. He could've just had a conversation and asked me about meeting Joey. I wouldn't lie because there was nothing to lie about.

"My sweet Nari, you didn't 'run' into Joey. He's been creeping in the shadows, waiting for the perfect moment to get you alone. I'm guessing so that he could convince you that being married to me is a bad idea. It was no coincidence that you saw him today, is it, *Joseph*?" The two had a stare down. Joey's face twisted in anger with every word that Kincaid spoke. My eyes bounced between the two of them before settling on Kincaid.

"What are you talking about?"

"Your good friend here, *Joey*, has a little crush on my wife. One that I don't appreciate, and I warned him about. He's not very obedient."

"You're not my fucking boss," Joey growled at my husband.

"Aren't I, though?" Kincaid smiled in a way that matched his tone . . . threatening, deadly. "Did you think telling my wife I was the big bad wolf would change her last name? Possibly gain you the advantage? She's mine. That's not changing. Not for you or anyone else."

I didn't like the way he said *mine*. It was different than the ways he said it before. To Joey, he presented the term like I was property, something he owned and controlled. When he used it with me, it was like I was something rare, protected, and cherished.

"Point made. Stay away from her. Got it, *boss*." Joey glanced at my husband before his eyes eventually made it to me. He looked as if he were making a point. Confirming what he told me earlier. Kincaid wasn't a good person.

"Not yet, but it will be." He stood and extended a hand to Cast, who handed over a hammer, one I hadn't noticed he was holding until then. Kincaid moved closer to Joey, leaning over the table so that they were eye to eye.

"You touched my wife. You knew better but still put your hand on what belongs to me."

My eyes moved around the room. No one other than me seemed bothered by what was happening—not even Joey. His eyes expressed his hatred for Kincaid, but everything else about him was just as calm as the others in the room.

When my husband's finger tapped the table, Joey lifted a hand and lowered it to that spot. His palm was flat, and his fingers spread wide. He was preparing, and I watched in horror as the hammer landed hard against his thumb with so much force that I heard bones crack. Joey's voice remained locked behind his clenched teeth, but his face showed his pain. My hand flew over my mouth as I shot to my feet.

"What are you doing?"

The only person who reacted to my question was Darius. His eyes met mine, and his head shook so subtly that I would have missed it had I not been paying attention. He was warning me not to intervene.

Kincaid never looked my way. Not even once. The hammer lifted again and came down just as hard, that time on an index finger. Five times. That was how many strikes. Each time, I heard bones shatter.

Joey grunted through the pain, but the words never left his mouth. He struggled but kept his posture straight and his eyes on my husband. When Kincaid was done, he placed the hammer on the table.

"This time, your hand; next time, your soul. Don't you ever in your fucking life touch my wife again. Understood?"

"Understood." Joey barely got the word out through his clenched teeth. Kincaid walked over to me, taking me by the arm, but I pulled away. His eyes narrowed before he barked out his command, "Let's go."

I looked around the room but left. As soon as we were outside near his car, I lost it. For some reason, what I witnessed turned my stomach, and I bent at the waist and expelled its contents.

When I was upright again, Kincaid's eyes were hard on me, staring as if I were his worst enemy. Seconds later, he opened the door and silently waited for me to get in. It took a minute before I did. He rounded the front of the car and settled into the driver's seat, leaning across the center to reach the glove compartment. After removing the napkins, he extended them to me. I stared at his hand for a minute before accepting.

While I wiped my mouth, he brushed a hand down his face and then pressed the button to start his car, turning to me seconds later.

"Nothing touches you, ever. Not without my permission."

Our eyes were steady on each other, shooting deadly bullets. I was the first to retreat, turning to the window, and he followed, pulling out of the parking lot to leave. Neither of us said a word after that, and I hadn't planned on it, at least not anytime soon.

CHAPTER 18

KINCAID.

I didn't sleep much. Maybe an hour at best. My mind wouldn't slow down enough to allow me to. Crazy thoughts were trapped in my head while I watched my wife. She refused to sleep with me, but I told her she didn't have a choice. After she refused to eat the food I ordered, she showered and climbed in bed so close to the edge that one wrong move and she would end up on the floor. I didn't push. It wasn't necessary. She could be angry but would have to do so from my bed.

I watched her sleep. Her face was tense, the muscles around her eyes tight. She was even angry as she slept. That almost made me laugh. My wife was stubborn, but that was a good thing. She needed that type of fire to survive me and everything connected to me.

Now here I was, sitting in the kitchen early as fuck in the morning, tired as hell, infuriated by my actions. Something so simple shouldn't have set me off, but it did. Another man attempting to twist fate in his favor to sway my wife turned me dark in a way I hadn't experienced before. Women were women. Some in my past held my attention, but very few, and even less, stirred things in me. But none had controlled me the way my wife could. I'd never been a jealous man. I didn't think I was capable of the emotion until I met my wife. Just the thought of anyone else doing something as simple as making her smile sent fire through my veins.

Joey had been warned to stay away. I kept eyes on my wife. Subtly so she wouldn't feel suffocated by my life but enough so that no one could get to her. It was how I knew Joey was lurking. I warned him the night at the club to keep his distance. A blind man could see his feelings. He wore them on his sleeve where my wife was concerned, but I understood his obsession. I was battling a similar addiction to Nari. The night at Salacious, when she looked at me, I felt something I had to explore. I didn't want Joey to be an issue, so I warned him to stay away. She was marked; she was *mine*. I had no idea what would happen between us, and until I knew for sure, she was off-limits to anyone other than me.

The fucker was too stupid to suppress his emotions, but because I had experienced Nari, I understood his dilemma. She had a way of putting a spell on you, making you fall when you didn't know you were capable. It was why he pretended to run into her at the mall. I didn't know what was said, but I was sure he delivered a warning. I should've just handled him privately, but I needed my wife to know that even the most innocent things were not fucking innocent.

Exhaling a breath, I lifted my phone and cleared my messages. That was when I felt her. She approached the kitchen and paused at the entrance. I lifted my eyes to hers and took her in. She was wearing a two-piece set, a sleep shirt and plaid shorts. Her own. It was my wife's way of drawing a line in the sand. She was angry with me and needed me to know.

"We should schedule you a doctor's appointment to take a test."

She snorted and rolled her eyes. "I didn't throw up because I'm pregnant. I threw up because seeing you crush a man's hand with a hammer made me sick to my stomach."

Still, you could be.

Nari crossed through the kitchen, moving to the counter where the Keurig was. She was a creature of habit. Coffee first, then breakfast. When her back was to me, I caged her between my body and the counter with one hand on either side, palms flat, pressing against the cool marble. She tensed when I leaned in, resting my chin on her head.

I inhaled her hair, burying my face in the untamed curls. "You're angry with me."

"You're insane."

"You have no fucking idea just how true that is, and the worst part is that I'm not the type of man who understands the meaning of sharing. I'm not wired that way. When anyone crosses that line, I lose all sensibility."

The look I gave expressed what my words danced around. I would kill anyone who breached what was mine. She was mine!

"And that worries me." Her tone was clipped.

The lack of trust hurt, but I understood.

"I will take lives behind you, but never will I lay a violent finger on you."

She turned, giving me her eyes. They were hard and blazing with emotion. "Like that's any better. I don't want to be afraid that any man who looks at me the wrong way will have bones broken—or worse."

Ahhh. Gains and Taylor.

My eyes never left hers. "I'm not the devil. They'll get a fair warning. It's up to them after that."

"You don't get it." She attempted to push me away, but I didn't budge. Too solid, too determined to be in her space.

"No, *you* don't get it. *You* did this. Last night was a consequence of *your* actions."

"*My* actions? I did nothing wrong."

"No, you didn't."

"But you said it was a consequence of my actions. A consequence for what if I did nothing wrong?"

"Making me fall in love with you." It took a minute to register, and when the thought landed, I kissed her forehead. "Get dressed. We're having breakfast with my parents."

I not only left the kitchen, but I also left my truth lingering in the air. I was in love with my wife. I had known for a while, but now she knew too. All I could do was wait and see what she did with that information.

"What did you do?" My mother looked at the two of us and saw our tension. It had to be a superpower of sorts.

"If anything was done, why would you immediately point the finger at me?" I lifted a brow, stepping in after my wife. A kiss was planted on my mother's cheek, but she wasn't buying it. There wasn't enough charm in the world to make her choose my side over Nari's. She was the daughter I could never be. Shoes I couldn't fill. Nari won by default. My mother loved me unconditionally, but my wife was now her new favorite person. It warmed my heart because in the event there was no connection with Nari's biological family, she would always have mine.

"Men are stupid. Whatever has that line drawn between her brows is your fault." My mother hugged my wife but kept her soft-brown orbs on me.

"Such a brilliant woman," Nari said, glaring at me. My mother laughed lightly.

"Come, help me set the table." She glanced over her shoulder at us. "Your father is out back polluting his lungs."

I watched my two hearts create space between us until they bent the corner, and then I traveled in the opposite direction in search of my father. He was out back, enjoying a cigar. My mother hated them, so they were banned from *her* house.

"What's up, old man?"

He cracked a smile, turning to me briefly before his eyes landed out into open space. The air was thick and humid but felt clean other than the richness of his cigar that hung in the air.

"Old? I'm in my prime, youngin."

My hand gripped his shoulder before I filled the seat next to him. We were quiet for a minute before he turned to me. "Kafi called."

"I didn't kill him. Only shot him in the shoulder."

His eyes narrowed on me. The old man wasn't happy. "I heard, but that's not why he called."

"Okay, so what then?"

"First, let me address this issue with Kaber. I made the wrong call. I should've known—"

"How could you? All things moved through me for the past few years. I missed the signs. That's not on you. He fooled us both."

My father nodded but still felt responsible for the deception. I wouldn't put that on him. I took full responsibility.

He moved on. "The vote happened unofficially, but it tells what will be when the time comes. You'll soon begin being groomed to take over for Razi."

I nodded. He made clear that I was his choice after our brief conversation. It wasn't something I asked for or even wanted, but I couldn't turn it down without losing The Families' respect.

"Why me?"

The question was weighted. For them to skip over my father and select me was more or less an insult to him but an honor to me. I wondered how that made him feel.

"You're built to hold the position. I never was. It's a heavy weight to carry, and my back is weak." He grinned before his eyes grew serious. "You, son, you're stronger than me. Always have been. I'm honored it's you. That's good enough. It's always been good enough."

I stared at the side of his face, wondering if that was how he truly felt. Deep down, I was sure those were his true feelings. My father was a great businessman, always had been, but the life and the sins that were required kept him up at night. When the Grim Reaper needed to appear, my father called on me. I slept like a baby. Maybe it wasn't such a good thing, but I couldn't deny it.

"Your wife . . ." He paused and looked at me. "Is she strong enough?"

I laughed at the thought. "She is. She might not know it yet, but she is."

He studied my face for a minute. "Who comes with you?"

"Darius." I gave his name without hesitation.

"He's not ranked. They'll expect it to be someone who is."

"I don't care. I trust him. He's the only one I trust."

"They'll push for O'Neal."

I scoffed at the thought. "He's only ranked because of who he married. Who Darius *could've* married."

"But he didn't. That was his choice."

"And this is mine. It's him or nobody. I can't trust a man to stand for me when I hold the title he feels is rightfully his. It won't work."

"Kincaid . . ."

"No. I'm not moving on that."

My father pushed out a short breath and then put his cigar to his lips. "I'll bring it to Razi."

He was negotiating my terms. As my father, it was expected because he was the person who knew me best—another slight, in my opinion. *We don't choose you, but you can negotiate for your son.*

"Be clear. I'm not bending on that."

He nodded just as Nari stuck her head through the sliding door. "The table's set."

We both turned around, and she smiled at my father, but when her eyes left him and made their way to me, that damn smile dropped. After she was gone, my father stared with a goofy grin while ashing his cigar.

"What?"

"Nothing."

"Say it, old man."

"She's strong enough. I see she's not afraid to challenge you. That tells me all I need to know."

I threw my head back and laughed. My father chuckled lightly, patting my knee before he stood. "Love gives strength the same as it takes it away. When you love, you have the ability to destroy. Those lines often blur, and we hurt those we vowed to protect. Never forget that."

There is not a chance in hell that I can when it's my daily struggle.

After breakfast with my parents, I drove us to Nathan's office. I called and requested he meet me. It was unscheduled, but I paid him enough to be available whenever I called. He knew the rules.

"Divorcing me already?" She shot an evil glare as we stepped off the elevator.

"Do you want me to?" I responded, giving her my eyes, stopping after a few steps.

"Maybe I do." I could see she was on one. All over breaking a few fingers . . .

"Good afternoon, Mrs. Akel. Nice to see you again." Nathan stepped out of his office, addressing my wife first. I was sure he did that only to piss me off for calling him in. He was in the middle of a golf game when I reached out.

"I would say the same, but I'm unsure why I'm here. My husband is being very vague." She cut her eyes at me, and Nathan chuckled, looking past her after she started walking toward the conference room where we sat the night we negotiated her becoming my wife.

"Trouble in paradise?" He snickered like a fucking woman and then followed the same path Nari took. When I entered, I sat next to her, and he filled the chair across from us.

"Is he divorcing me?" she asked Nathan, whose eyes shot over to mine. Seconds later, a slow smile eased in place, and he opened the folder in front of him, removing a stack of papers. He slid them across the table to Nari, who looked down and then back up at Nathan.

It was our agreement—the original one.

"So that's a yes?" She arched a brow, and he shook his head.

"Unfortunately, not. Mr. Akel would like to amend this agreement."

"Amend it? Why?" She frowned at him and then me.

"Apparently, the lovebug has settled in your husband's system. He wants to void the contract completely."

I could see the confusion in her eyes. She didn't understand what he meant.

"I no longer want there to be terms between us. We both stay or leave because it's what we want and not because it's what those papers say we have to do." I motioned to the agreement but kept my eyes on my wife. Hers squinted, and she stared for a long minute before looking toward Nathan.

"What's that mean?"

"It means your marriage is by choice—no more terms. Your only legally binding agreement is your marriage certificate and your shared vows. Anything else is your personal business."

"Why?"

"Because I love you, and I want that to be enough. If it's not, you're free to leave."

"And the money?"

"If you sign the agreement to void all the original terms, you will receive the remaining balance owed to you today," Nathan said.

"So if I sign, saying that the original agreement is void and the only thing binding us is our marriage certificate, you're giving me half a million dollars."

"Pretty much."

"That simple?"

My eyes were steady on hers. "There's nothing simple about love. At least not for me. I'm trusting you with the most invaluable thing I own."

"Which is?"

"Me."

"Can I think about it?"

"For how long?"

Her nose wrinkled. "I don't know. I just want to think about it."

"Take them. Nothing changes until you sign. If you choose not to, then the current agreement remains in place," Nathan said, standing.

She nodded and then looked at me. I stood next, shaking his hand. She followed, and he smiled, tipping his head to her as he left.

"Let's go."

She didn't move right away.

"This is what you want?"

"Yes."

"Are you upset because I want to think about it?"

I studied her face for a minute. "No."

"You sure?"

"I promised never to lie to you, so, no, I'm not upset."

She hesitated again but lifted the papers, and we left. It started one way, but I needed it to continue in a different direction on a different path with new intentions. I chose to be in it and needed my wife to do the same. She had to be in it for the right reasons. I needed to know that I had her fully and completely when things shifted. In my world, loyalty was earned, not given. If the agreement remained the reason we were bonded, I would always feel unsettled, and I couldn't risk even the slightest chance that she could be used against me.

CHAPTER 19

NARI.

"Do you feel at home?" The sound of his voice startled me. That man moved with the grace of a ghost. He always appeared out of nowhere, and it annoyed me to no end because I had no clue how he managed to move so gracefully, undetected.

"Not yet. My name's on all the paperwork. I ordered all the furnishings, and my things fill the closet, but it doesn't feel real for some reason. More or less like I'm visiting or, even worse, suspended in a dream that allows me sight, touch, and smell, but at some point, I'll wake up, and, poof, it's all gone."

Kincaid's body brushed against mine, and a kiss landed at the nape of my neck before I felt his hands close around me. One arm hung loosely around my neck while the other circled my waist. My eyes briefly closed while I inhaled him, and they opened when I felt his chin rest lightly on the crown of my head.

"Dreams are for people who aren't blessed enough to live. This is real. Our home, our lives. Give it time."

We stood on the massive balcony extending from our study and wrapped around the rear and side of the house on the upper level. There were three entrances from our room onto this space—one from the bedroom, one from the study, and another from the

French doors that opened from the bathroom. A bathroom that was bigger than most places I'd ever lived.

"I was one of those people. Kinda still feels like I am." I turned against his tall frame. It was rare that Kincaid wasn't in a suit. It was one of those moments. It had been a relaxed day, just the two of us, so he was in casual athletic wear. Our things were delivered the week before and unpacked by a professional staff. The following week, I spent time adjusting my personal things and attempting to get a feel for my new life. We'd been sleeping in our new home for several weeks, and I still felt like a stranger visiting someone else's space.

"Is there anything I can change to make you more comfortable?"

A laugh burst through that I couldn't contain. "No . . . absolutely not."

His teeth raked his bottom lip as his eyes traveled across my face. "Adamant about that, I see."

"Hell yeah, buddy. If I say yes, you'll call in some expert who specializes in making the poor girl feel at home in her fancy new digs," I joked, but his expression remained frustratingly serious.

"The point of maintaining wealth is to make your life easier. There's a remedy for everything as long as you have the right connections and can afford them."

"My God, I was kidding."

It took a minute, but his smile surfaced. "I know. I just like fucking with you." His hands slipped into the pockets of his track pants while those intense eyes remained locked in place.

"If you're not happy here—"

"You'll buy me another house that seals the deal. I get it; my wish is your command. I'm happy. Just feeling things out while trying to adjust. It's not a big deal. This place is stunning. I love every inch of it. Give me time to settle into my new life, Mr. Akel."

His chin dipped, and I was forced back a step when he advanced. The coolness of the carved stone railing met the small of my back while his hands rested on either side of me, creating a barrier. Kincaid's body leaned into mine while a charming smile spread across his face.

"I can think of a few ways to make the space feel more comfortable if you're game."

My body reacted in several ways, but the most obvious was the throbbing between my thighs and my stomach taking flight. Tempting, but . . .

"You lied to me."

His eyes narrowed, and his face stoned. "I've never lied to you, Nari."

"You have. Before we left Nathan's office, I asked if you were upset that I wanted to think about voiding our agreement, and you said no."

"Because it was the truth. I'm not upset that you want time," he insisted again.

"Then why have you been so distant? You've barely touched me lately. It's like you're only giving me half of you. You're different. I can feel it."

The worst torture ever is to have you, and then the experience be taken away.

"You wanted time, so I'm giving you time—"

"See, there it is. That shift. You might think I don't notice, but I do."

"Let me fucking finish." His voice was low and laced with agitation, but it was eerily calm. The two contradictions had my pulse quickening. "I'm giving you time without my influence."

I wasn't sure what the hell *that* meant, and I supposed my confusion was louder than my silence because he explained.

"I know what I feel. You're still trying to figure it out. I'm a selfish man. I've always been that way. There's no deal I can't negotiate and not come out on top. There's nothing I've ever wanted that I couldn't acquire *until now*. I broker million-dollar deals daily, sometimes hourly. I travel the world, forcing my agendas on people who are sometimes smarter, wealthier, and potentially more powerful, but that only pushes me harder. I thrive when I feel like the underdog and dominate when I know I have the upper hand. In either scenario, I never lose because that's not what I do. I don't fucking lose . . . *until now*."

Until now. He kept saying those two words.

"What do you mean 'until now'?"

"I underestimated my opponent. It is the most formidable mistake ever made in history by anyone. I forced your hand by negotiating terms that gave me the advantage. You didn't stand a chance with me. I was going to win, whatever the hell this thing is between us . . ." He paused, eyes narrowing as they fastened to mine. "Or so I thought. You fucking win, Nari. I can't force your heart to feel what it doesn't feel. There's no price to be placed on something so invaluable. That not only infuriates me, but it also scares the shit out of me because I feel like I'm going to lose the one thing I never deserved in the first place." His stance shifted, his legs spread wider, and his head angled to the side while his shoulders squared in one sharp motion. "*You*."

After a lingering silence, he relaxed his posture some. "The choice has to be yours. That's the only thing that levels us. There's no honor or pleasure with forcing control where you're concerned. I refuse to manipulate the situation to get what I want. Let me be clear . . . I want you." His chin angled toward his chest so that our eyes were level. "However, the decision has to be yours without my influence. Regardless of what that choice is, as devastating as it will be, I can survive the loss. I simply have to know whether it's coming a year from now, three years from now, or never."

My mouth hung open as he turned to leave, crossing the room and out the door. I was stuck with a bunch of truths that I hadn't even considered, and that had my head spinning.

I spent the next hour going back and forth in my head about what my next move would be. Kincaid had exposed a side of himself that I wasn't sure was possible . . .

Weakness.

Vulnerability.

Fear.

And not just any weakness . . . One for me. He was afraid of losing me. Had I not seen the truth in his eyes, I wouldn't have taken him seriously, but there was no denying the sincerity in his confession. That had me faced with my own truth. I was teetering on the same uncertainty.

Weakness.

Vulnerability.

Fear.

We happened so fast and without warning. I fell for a man who was out of my league. He could have any woman of his choosing, and trust me, I'd been face-to-face with one of his choices, and that didn't settle my mind in the least. Regardless, he chose me. To the average person, that wouldn't seem like a big deal, but for me, it was everything. No one had ever chosen me—not even my mother. Sure enough, I'd been told she wanted me, but if that were true, why didn't she come for me? She left her parents and never looked back. Never gave a second thought to looking for me.

Kincaid chose me. That scared me shitless because I didn't know how to be chosen. What did that even mean? What was my role in this? What would I owe? What would be required of me since he'd been the one to make the call? So, yeah, I was scared, and I needed time. I had to figure out if I was willing to accept something or, rather, someone who could totally destroy me if his choice ever changed. He could wake up one day and decide things were different and I was no longer what he wanted. I didn't think I could survive the devastation. You didn't experience a force like *Kincaid Akel* and remain the same. He changed you against your will. Made you feel things you didn't know you were capable of feeling.

People would never look at our story and understand or feel like I got the short end of the stick, even if he changed his mind. They would quickly decide that I was fairly compensated. A million dollars was my payoff. Fair, right? Who couldn't survive a little heartache for the type of money that was on the table? Me, I couldn't. I knew what it meant to be penniless, to be hungry, to go without. I had survived what would break the strongest spirits, but I had never been anyone's choice. Now that I was, I didn't think I could survive the loss. That was my dilemma.

After gathering what I needed, I left our bedroom searching for my husband. I had a little help from a spicy, potent aroma that hung in the air, leading me to his office. His eyes lifted to mine when I surfaced and paused my steps just beyond the doorway. Those brown orbs raked across my body from the top of my head down to my bare feet before he lifted the cigar to his lips and then chased it with whatever brown liquor was in his glass.

"I've never seen you do that."

"What?" His brows pinched.

"Smoke."

"I don't do it often. Today was the exception," he muttered. I could still hear the agitation in his voice, but his eyes were softer now. But only a little.

"I'd like to call a truce."

He snorted. "We're not at war. That doesn't apply, sweetheart."

"I disagree. You're angry."

"Not with you."

"But still angry, and I don't like how your anger feels, even if I'm not the source, so I'm calling a truce, and you have to hear me out."

Those brown orbs surveyed my body once more before he chucked his chin at me. It was my permission to enter, I suppose—such a damn brute.

I crossed the room and stepped around his desk, leaning against it. His long legs were wide, and if I inched forward even a little, I'd be between them, but I chose to maintain distance, pressing against the edge of his desk.

"Here." I lifted the first item I'd brought with me. It took him a minute to react, but even still, Kincaid leaned toward it, reaching beside me to place his glass on the desk. The cigar remained pinched between his fingers when he accepted my offering.

He scanned it and then chuckled.

"Don't laugh. It's totally valid. I had to search the internet to be sure. I've never had this much money in my life. I wasn't informed whether there was a limit to the amount you can write a personal check for."

"No limit, but this amount would typically be handled with a cashier's check or wire transfer. It's not common practice to write or accept a personal check for half a million dollars."

"Well, neither was available to me, so that's what you get."

"This money is yours, Nari. A deal's a deal. I'm a man of my word."

"You are, but I don't want it, so I'm giving it back, which leads me to my second gift."

I lifted the stack of papers I'd left Nathan's office with and laid them in his lap. His eyes lowered and then lifted to me.

"I signed them the night we left his office. I just had one request, which I wasn't sure how to handle. Technically, Nathan is your lawyer. I couldn't figure a way around it without you finding out, so that's why I still have them."

"What's the request?" His eyes remained on the documents in his lap.

"It's there. Read it."

His jaw flexed, telling of his rising irritation, but nevertheless, he leaned forward again. However, he reached around me that time, pulling the ashtray closer. He put his cigar in it before he lifted the documents and flipped through them.

"Green tab," I offered a little assistance to speed things up.

He located it and folded the papers back, and his eyes shot up to mine once more, but that time, that damn signature scowl accompanied it. I shrugged. "I don't want the money. If you agree to keep the money, I agree to void the agreement."

"No."

"Why not?"

"Because a deal's a deal."

"True, but if we're voiding the agreement, then we get rid of all terms, even that part. You're not the only one who feels like they could potentially lose. If I keep that money, then it doesn't feel real. *We* don't feel real. If there's nothing between us but our vows, then you know why I'm here. You'll know with certainty that it's my choice."

"The money isn't a factor. If you tell me this is what you want, then I believe you. Simple as that."

I shook my head. "You're the only person who's ever chosen me. I know you don't understand what that means. All I have is me, and I'm giving you *me* with nothing binding us but my choice to be here. No money, no terms—just me."

Seconds. Minutes. Hours. Possibly years passed while an intense pair of eyes were stapled to mine. All types of thoughts rushed through my mind. What if he'd already changed his mind? What if—

His hands were at my hips, followed by his mouth colliding with mine. When he kissed me, he took me to a place I imagined to be the equivalent of a space between heaven and hell. I felt like I was playing with fire, tempting fate while toeing the line of a nirvana.

Love.

That was all it could be, and as much as I wanted to deny it, I couldn't. I simply didn't have the courage to say the words. And the universe must've felt my hesitation and decided to test my resolve because his phone rang. Once. *Ignored.* Twice. *Ignored.* The third time. *Chaos.*

"What? Slow down. Shot? Who the fuck . . ."

Kincaid broke away from me, facing the wall. His body was rigid from tension. I watched, feeling what he was feeling.

Fear.

I wasn't sure how. Maybe that was the love because I felt it creeping through my spirit, chilling me to the bone.

"I'm coming. I'm leaving now."

When he ended the call and turned to me, his eyes communicated without words. I knew the answer before he delivered the equation.

"My father was shot . . ."

. . . and he died.

CHAPTER 20

KINCAID.

My eyes never left my mother. Nari was at her side. Their hands were stacked, looking as if they were one. Nari's eyes moved around the area with uncertainty. That was new. She didn't know what to think about what she was being exposed to, but her mind wouldn't allow her to dwell on it. Right then, her concern was providing any comfort she could to my mother, and I appreciated her strength. We were in a private sector of the hospital reserved for men of importance. Political and government officials. Our men heavily guarded it. They wore suits and carried guns. No one who wasn't affiliated would be allowed to step off the elevator onto the floor until we gave permission. That was how things worked. That was the type of pull our affiliation bestowed. My father had been pronounced dead upon arrival. So had Razi. Their bodies were riddled with bullets. Neither stood a chance of surviving the attack. Whoever had done it was sending a message. I didn't know what it was as of yet. That would take time. My brain was already working, but it was clouded by the loss, so I wasn't completely focused.

"It wasn't Kaber."

"How do you know?" I kept staring at my mother's face. She hadn't said a word to me. Her body was stiff, her red-rimmed eyes fixated on nothing. She was staring into open space.

"He's dead."

I finally gave Kafi my attention, and the stern expression confirmed.

"Who?"

"We don't know yet. Kaber, your father, and Razi." His index finger touched his thumb, extending the last three.

Rule of three.

Someone was making a statement. The deaths were related somehow.

"You know . . ." Kafi paused because my focus had returned to my mother and my wife. When I gave him my attention, he continued, "It's time."

"No . . ." I glanced at my mother. There was no way I could move into that space right then. She needed me.

"You either forfeit or accept. There is no grace period other than the time allowed to put him to rest. Business doesn't stop, not even for this."

His voice was level, but his gaze was sharp. He was challenging me. I didn't like it, but I understood. The plan was already in place, regardless of whether the vote was unofficial. The title had been passed down. I was in charge.

"Your father was a brilliant man. His mind, always sharp. His hands, always prosperous. There are just some who aren't built to carry certain sins. He never was. We respected your father for what he was great at. You, Kincaid. *You* are built to rule. There was no dishonor in moving down your bloodline to select you over your father. He understood that. He found honor in raising a son who was worthy. This is your place. You earned it, no matter what thoughts challenge the decision. It was always yours, but now, you must walk in faith that it's what you were destined for." While he spoke, my eyes found my wife. Kafi gripped my shoulder and exhaled a short sigh. He read my mind. "Our men will be in place. I'll be in touch."

He left me, walking over to my mother. Kafi placed his hand on her shoulder. Her eyes lifted to him while he spoke softly, offering words of comfort that would fall on deaf ears. She lost her husband, her best friend, her lifeline. I never understood what that meant until now.

My wife.

She was mine. She taught me what it was to feel your heart beat in another person's chest. I had an idea of my mother's pain because of my wife's love.

"Let's go."

After Kafi left, I made my way to my mother. She refused to look at me. There were several reasons why. The loudest one that she refused to speak was that I looked just like him. She couldn't bear to see what she'd lost when she looked into my face or connected with my eyes. It hurt, but I understood.

"Go where? He's here. This is the only place I exist, where my husband is."

I was mentally and physically exhausted, and the journey had only just begun. There was nothing left in me to fight with her. I leaned close, placed a kiss on her forehead, and whispered against it. "Let's go, *now*."

She wouldn't fight with me. My demand left no room for argument. I extended a hand, but she refused it the same way she refused to look at me. Nari's confusion bounced between us briefly before she stood doing the same as I had done, extending a hand to my mother, which she accepted. The rejection felt like a knife in my chest, but again, I understood.

The two of them traveled ahead of me; I followed close behind. Men moved silently with us like ghosts. No sight, no sound, just their presence. It would be one of the hardest battles that either of us faced, but I wouldn't be allowed to give in to the weakness it presented. My future was set, and that meant no cracks in my exterior.

Vengeance, though, replaced the blood in my veins, and no one would be spared. The world wasn't safe until I emptied the arteries of all those involved.

Life moved in a vast contradiction. Fast and slow. It felt like a blink of an eye between the time that my father took his last breath and I was sworn into my new life, but on the other side, it felt like years since my mother had made me feel like her son. She moved robotically like it pained her to accept or give love, but only to me. It was starting to chip away at my resolve. We'd always been close. I had bonded with my parents, but my mother was the one who kept me balanced. Her love had always felt different than my father's. She only wanted me to be happy. He wanted me to be great, sometimes at the cost of my happiness. Deep down inside, I understood to be patient, but she wasn't the only one who lost a piece of herself. Her husband was gone, but so was my father. We were both suffering.

I found myself in a weird space. I shut the world out and focused on business. The only reason why I wasn't working at that very moment was because that day, I had to put my father into the ground. That was one of the hardest things I felt I would ever have to do, but I stood as a man and managed to get through it. He would've been proud.

My parents' home was filled with bodies. Everyone was draped in black as a sign of respect for my father. He was loved and revered as a good man. Their faces all blended together because I couldn't focus on anyone in particular other than hers. *My wife.* She always watched me, waiting for what she called "the shift." That time, the shift would be her way in. I unintentionally shut her out but didn't know how else to survive without breaking.

I refused to let her see me break, so the alternative was to keep her at a distance. It hurt; I could see it in her eyes, but I could feel it more than anything. My wife had a way of speaking to me without words. Her energy seeped through my pores, attacking my senses. I knew what she thought and felt simply from being in her space. She was hurting for me, for my mother, and for herself because I shut her out, but that didn't stop her from being what I needed.

At night, when I climbed between her thighs, she accepted me willingly. When I spilled myself in her womb and then, seconds after, turned my back to sleep or left our bed to work, she never complained. When I sat across from her at the table in silence, eating a meal she prepared, she didn't beg for my voice. She let me remain in whatever space I required to keep from breaking.

It was why I stepped away. People wanted to be there for us. They remained solemn, delivering apologies and condolences that wouldn't change the void we felt. I wanted silence and, more than anything, solitude to deal with my own demons. My father was gone, and I was now the head of our family and about to be thrust into a position I wasn't sure I was prepared for. I stood in his office, quietly battling with the possibility of failing those who depended on me the most. The room felt empty, void of the liveness I used to feel. Void of him . . .

"Hey." A timid tenor lifted into the air. I didn't have the energy to acknowledge her. I knew who it was. She had been lurking all day, and it irritated me to my core.

"I was just checking in."

She continued that time causing me to glance over my shoulder. Aila stood at the entrance of my father's office with a subtle look on her face. Her eyes were expressive as she stared at me, even after I turned back to the window.

"I figured I would find you here. I've been looking for you."

I snorted, slipping my hands into my pockets. "Why?"

"Because you need to lean on someone who understands your feelings. I understand what you're feeling, Kincaid. She's not even trying to support you today. Don't think I haven't noticed the distance. What kind of wife is she?"

One who loves me enough to sacrifice her happiness for mine.

"The only thing you understand is your selfish intent."

Her father was gunned down hours before mine. His funeral came and passed. No one from The Families was present. It was at that moment they chose to make clear he was no longer connected. The message was clear, so there was no way she mistook their absence for anything other than it was . . . disrespect to her family. It was the reason why I couldn't understand her presence today. *Desperation to still belong.*

"That's not true." She moved closer, stepping in front of me. Her eyes softened, carrying a pinkish hue. She'd been crying, but likely for show. Presentation was everything. I wouldn't doubt that she did it to hurt my wife by making it seem as if she somehow had a more significant connection to my family than Nari did. She used fake grief to communicate without words . . .

You don't belong . . . I do.

I noticed how Aila attempted to cling to my mother's side like it was her rightful place. *Fucking pathetic.*

"Why are you here? Wearing that ring? One that you know holds no value. I have a wife—"

"Who was paid to marry you."

My eyes narrowed.

"Yeah, I know. My father told me."

I wasn't sure if he really knew or assumed. Nathan would never leak that information for fear of what it would cost him. I guessed that Kaber assumed it was the only way I found a wife so quickly. She appeared out of nowhere, and he could've easily discovered she worked at Salacious.

"Did he also tell you that he signed you over to me to keep his pockets full? A man who he knew didn't love you and never would. I never once romanticized my investment in marrying you. I requested a term be written to allow me permission to sleep with other women whenever I saw fit, and he didn't even blink before agreeing. Anything that would seal the deal. Your father didn't give a fuck about you, Aila, so you don't understand what I feel right now. You never will."

"Yes, I do. You don't have to be strong; you're allowed to feel things. You're hurting—"

"Yeah, I am. I'm fucking hurting. I lost my father. It's the type of pain that can bring me to my fucking knees. You don't get to act like you understand what that feels like just to get close to me."

Her eyes moved through a range of emotions, but she was determined. Regardless of how deep the truth cut, she still wanted me. As proof, Aila's hands fisted my jacket, and her lips landed hard on mine. It was only a split second before I grabbed her wrist and pushed her away, but she gained more than she would've had I kissed her back. I felt it even before she looked past me, and that victorious smile eased onto her face.

"Some of the guests are leaving. They were looking for you to say goodbye." Nari's voice was calm and deadly. I didn't have to see the look in her eyes to know they were blazing.

"I should go." Aila's regard bounced between me and my wife, like there was some sort of victory on her part. When she tried to step away, I caught her left hand, tugging with enough force to remove the ring. Her eyes went wild, and her mouth hung open when she felt the separation.

"My words haven't been enough. I need you to be clear: there is *no* connection between you and me. Stay the fuck away from me and my family," I warned. Her lips sealed aggressively before she dropped her eyes and hurried out of the room.

"Shut the door."

"No."

"Nari, shut the door."

"You don't get to shut me out, kiss that bitch, spill your heart, and then demand *anything* from me. Not even my time for your half-assed explanation."

Her stare was so focused and deadly that she hadn't realized I was moving until I had an arm around her waist long enough to shut the door and send her against it. She landed hard. My palm pressed flat above her head while my chin angled toward my chest so that I could look down at her.

"That was a failed attempt from a desperate woman attempting to exploit a situation and gain my attention."

"I know what it was, and I don't care. Mission accomplished. It still fucking hurts to see you that open with her when you've been so distant from me. When I asked you to talk to me, to tell me what you were feeling, you gave me nothing. You put up a wall and then carved an opening to let her in. Even if by deception, you allowed another woman in." Her voice trembled, but she stood her ground.

"I've been right here. You've been right here, beside me, in our bed—in *here*." My finger pressed into my chest, but her eyes didn't follow. They remained on me.

"Sharing the same space with someone who ignores you can be even more lonely than suffering their distance. Trust me, thanks to you, I have personal experience with both."

"Nari . . ."

"No, I get it. You lost your father. I don't expect you to be okay, to be the same with me, because it's gotta fucking hurt, but you don't get to give her your emotions and hide them from me. You said more to her than you told me in the past two weeks. You gave your body, but your emotions, which are a direct connection to your heart, you kept locked away until *she* asked you to hand them over. I begged you to be vulnerable with me to let me in, and you said nothing—"

"Baby . . ."

It wasn't the kiss.

She saw an exchange that made her feel like I'd let Aila in when I continuously shut her down. It hadn't been intentional, and it didn't mean a damn thing. It was simply my anger being unleashed on a person who was trying to use my loss for her own gain.

"Your guests are leaving. Please go see them out." For the first time, I noticed what she had been seeing in me. That shift. It had just happened, and it damn sure didn't feel good to be on the receiving end.

I straightened my posture, taking a step back. When she stepped out of the way, my hand moved to the door, but I pressed a kiss to her temple, allowing my eyes to close briefly.

"I love you, and I apologize," I whispered against the spot I kissed before I opened the door and slipped through the open space. That was all I had for now, but I would make it up to her. How ironic that the first thing that filled my head was the last bit of advice my father blessed me with.

When you love, you have the ability to destroy. Those lines often blur, and we hurt those we vowed to protect.

I hear you, old man. I'll make it right. That's my word.

Three days after I buried my father, I was on our private jet to Miami. We would stay for a long weekend, and Nari was with me. When I told her to pack—yes, told her, not asked her—she looked at me like I was crazy. Not once did she ask where we were going or why. She simply continued watching the movie she'd been using as a tool to ignore me. Things with us were in a weird space. She was polite but not welcoming. For the most part, she avoided me, making it clear that I wasn't her favorite person at the moment.

The night after the funeral, she attempted to create distance by sleeping in another room. I hadn't realized it until the wee hours of the morning because I had been in my office working when she showered and settled in. I ended up in the same bed, but she kept her distance by layering pillows between us and, again, sleeping so dangerously close to the edge that she was at risk of a harsh landing if she breathed wrong. The following day, I had one of my guys come dismantle every other bed in our home, leaving only ours. She called me childish, but we slept in our room, together.

"You're cheating." Cast's big ass smiled at my wife, and her face split into a grin returning one. They were in the middle of a game called Go Fish. A fucking child's game, yet she had the nerve to call *me* childish.

"How am I cheating?"

"You just are. I didn't even know how to play. You explained the rules and probably have been changing them as you go because you keep winning."

"She's not cheating," Alisha chimed in. "You just suck at this. You can shoot a gun but can't play a simple card game. Such a waste."

She and Nari found that amusing. They shared a look and broke out in a fit of laughter together. Cast shot them both an evil glare, collecting the cards.

"Let's go again."

I wanted to tell them hell no and drag her to the back so that I could be the center of her attention, but she would have to go kicking and screaming because she was still pissed and . . .

Hurt.

I had to continuously remind myself that my wife was still young and inexperienced with many things. Emotions were at the top of that list, not only due to her age but also because she hadn't been blessed with a family to nurture and support her in a way that built confidence. Nari was always on the defensive, and she didn't trust easily. In her mind, it was Nari against the world. The simplest rifts created a fight-or-flight reaction, so I had to employ patience. I had years of life lessons that guided my ability to trust my gut, but my wife was still learning. It was why she was so quick to shut down. She only agreed to come because I mentioned that Alisha and Darius were both going. He and I had business, and I told him to offer the trip to Alisha as a way to persuade my wife to come. How fucking pathetic was that? I had to *trick* my wife into traveling with me.

It's your own damn fault!

"Easy, killer." Darius chuckled, shaking his head with amusement in his eyes. Mine shot across to him, and he laughed harder.

"Cast doesn't want your wife. He's just as innocent as that damn game they're playing. You trust him with your life—"

"Not with my wife. Not when she's smiling at him and won't even fucking look at me."

"Caid, relax. You fucked up. Give her time."

"I didn't. Aila kissed me, *not* the other way around."

"Didn't you say it wasn't the kiss?" He knew it wasn't. I called him over after the second night when Nari wouldn't let the shit go to ask for advice.

"I talk too damn much," I muttered, annoyed with the entire situation.

"Yeah, you do, but apparently to the wrong people. You hurt her feelings. Women are funny that way. There are some things they hold sacred, and as it stands, your wife doesn't like hearing you bare your soul to other women. You probably could have dicked Aila down and come out better than you did from sharing your heart with her."

"I wasn't sharing my damn heart. She caught me at a bad time, and I messed up and let something personal slip."

"Something you kept from your wife. You told your ex that losing your father hurt and made you feel weak. For a man like you, that's admitting your deepest, darkest secrets." He shrugged nonchalantly. "Give her time, but I suggest you stop baring your soul to anyone other than your wife."

I could've slapped the stupid-ass grin off his face, but he was right. Intentional or not, I understood why it mattered so much. I would take that loss, but Nari was going to stop treating me like I was the devil reincarnated, or I would lose my cool. That wasn't going to be pretty for either of us.

"How do you think this is going to go?"

I considered the meeting we had in two days. "It's a test. They want to know that I can handle myself. I can, but that doesn't mean that they'll like it. Everyone expected consideration, but the decision had already been made. The fact that Razi made sure to have three of the family members present when the unofficial vote happened was intentional. He wanted there to be no confusion that I was his choice . . ." I paused the same thought that had plagued me since the attack happened.

"You think he knew?"

"I can't say for certain, but there was no point in even considering a replacement so soon. I'm the youngest ever. It shouldn't have been a topic at least for the next five to ten years, but the conversation happened behind closed doors for months. There's something to that."

"You ask Kafi and Saulo?"

I exhaled a short breath, my eyes finding Nari as she laughed loudly and Cast threw his cards on the center of the table. He must've lost again. I smiled, enjoying the light in her eyes, even if I wasn't the one who placed it there. It fucking killed me to feel the wall she'd put between us. After a minute or two, I rejoined the conversation.

"They said the choice had been made years ago. The vote was unanimous before it ever took place."

"Makes sense. This shit is in your blood. There was no way it was going to be anybody but you."

He spoke from a place of respect. The lines had been drawn years ago, defining our roles. He was my best friend but would never be respected the way I was. That didn't mean I valued him any less, nor did it take away from his ability to stand beside me or behind me if it were called for. For that reason, I trusted him with my life and always would.

"I wasn't doing this without you. You know that, right?"

He tossed his chin. "I know what it is." His tone was cocky, but only because he understood his value. "Just know that I will not hesitate to drop that muthafucker if he comes at me the wrong way."

I chuckled and nodded. "Noted."

CHAPTER 21

NARI.

"This is nice." Alisha was the first to speak after we entered the beachfront house that would be our home for the weekend. It was beautiful. If I had not been annoyed with Kincaid, I would've been more excited. That place screamed Kincaid Akel. He had selected it ... I was sure. Darius was quiet, the type to go with the flow, but my husband had a penchant for nice things. He wasn't flashy, nothing close to the definition, but he acquired nice things and made no apologies for having expensive taste. I'd grown accustomed to his style, which was how I knew it was all him.

"We have the left side; you guys are right," he grumbled as he adjusted his stance to bring our luggage in. Usually, I would've attempted to help, but I quickly learned that we both had our roles; he was the very capable alpha who could handle all arduous tasks, and I wasn't to lift a finger when in his presence. That took some getting used to for a woman like me who spent her life thuggin' it out on her own. But my husband insisted I allow him to be the man of our duo. Opening doors, ordering meals, carrying luggage, pulling out chairs. I was very capable of all these things, but I had better not dare attempt them in his presence. Honestly, it was part of him that I had a love-hate relationship with. His instinct to cater to me always made me feel appreciated. But at that moment, it irritated the shit out of my entire soul.

Darius and Alisha disappeared on their side of the house while we settled in ours. While Kincaid brought in our luggage, I stepped onto the balcony attached to our room. The view was breathtaking. A cool breeze came off the ocean, bringing a clean, fresh scent that had me closing my eyes and getting lost in the moment. There was something so perfect about the connection to the ocean. It also reminded me of our honeymoon.

"I miss you." His hands didn't touch me because they gripped the metal railing that I was leaning against, but his arms locked me in, and his body leaned into mine, holding me in place. "Tell me what I need to do to fix this. It's fucking killing me to be on the outside."

It would be easy for me to reject him because I could still feel the sting from being shut out, but I missed him too, so I didn't push him away. But I didn't exactly let him in, either. Instead, I inhaled my breath and closed my eyes, enjoying the space I was in.

"Nari?"

His voice was low, tormented. That one word gave away his current state. I could not only feel his stress, but it also flowed with my name.

"It doesn't feel good, does it? Being on the outside and watching others get what you feel belongs to you? Even something as simple as a smile?"

I didn't miss how intently he watched me while we were on the plane. It pissed him off that I would barely acknowledge him while I laughed and smiled with everyone else. It wasn't necessarily intentional . . . until I realized how much it bothered him.

"That's not what—"

"Perception is everything, *sweetheart*. It's how I felt; you can't dismiss my feelings, regardless of your intent. It fucking hurt."

He allowed his chin to rest on the top of my head. Something he'd done a million times, but that time, it was an expression of his defeat. "She will never have anything that belongs to you. *I* belong to you, baby. I need you to let me back in. I can't handle losing anyone else right now."

His parents.

Kincaid's mother was still distant. She and I talked about it. Everyone processed pain in different ways. She lost her husband and had to see his ghost in the flesh. For some, that made them hold on tighter in an effort to experience anything that reminded them of what they lost. But it hurt too much for her, so she kept her distance.

I pushed against his arm to step away but pressed a kiss to his cheek first. "I'm going to take a shower."

He nodded and let me go. As much as I wanted to give in, I stood my ground. While I showered, Kincaid sat on the balcony with his laptop. He was always so serious when his mind was submerged in business. That carved chin of his remained tight while glasses sat on his face. His demeanor was intense. After I was dressed and went to explore for a bit, I returned and settled on the balcony to wait for Kincaid. He showered and dressed, joining me once he was done.

"You ready?"

"Ready for what?" I frowned, turning to face him, unable to hide my smile. It was impossible to look at the man and not be impressed. He wore light jeans and a white polo, matching my maxi dress. I was positive his selection was intentional, but damn if he didn't look good. His brown skin was illuminated by the light of the sun. Not to mention the way his shirt hugged his solid chest and broad shoulders . . . The definition in his pecs and abs peeked from beneath the cotton material.

"Ahh, she smiles." He returned one. "Even if it's superficial."

I laughed, rolling my eyes because he knew I was checking him out and called me on it.

"I like what I see." I shrugged. "No sense in pretending I don't. Where are we all going?"

"Just us."

"What about Alisha and Darius?"

"They left while you were in the shower. You're stuck with me."

"And Cast?" I only mentioned him to irritate my husband.

"No. He's only here for my meeting tomorrow. Sorry to disappoint."

"I'll live."

"Shall we?"

I nodded, stepping inside. After I grabbed my purse and phone, we left in a G-Wagon waiting in the garage. That was when it occurred to me that he seemed very familiar with this place.

"You own this house?"

"Yes. It's *ours*."

Ours, as in what's his is mine.

"I'm not a fan of hotels, so I own properties in cities I frequent."

"Interesting."

"How so?"

"You invest in failing hotels, but you're not a fan of them?"

"As a financial investment, they're ideal, but I prefer the comfort and familiarity of having my own space."

"So you just purchase properties in various cities?"

He glanced at me briefly. "Is that an issue?"

"Could be. A man with that much access might just abuse the privilege."

"If you don't trust me, travel when I do. While I work, you play. When I'm done, I play."

His gaze traveled across my body, but his expression remained neutral. "I'd prefer you with me over the distance anyway."

I snorted. "I'm sure. Where are we going?"

"A little shopping and exploring if that's okay with you."

"Why not? Your dime, my time." He smirked, knowing I wouldn't deny him, even though spending his money wasn't my favorite thing. The fact that I was being cordial was enough to empty his accounts while he also knew that I wasn't for sale. The fact that I'd refused his money was proof. If we were in it, and I mean *really* in it, it had to be for the right reasons, and money couldn't be attached to matters of the heart.

I couldn't, however, complain about the time we spent. The day was perfect. We shopped, or rather, Kincaid shopped for me. Primarily clothes that he picked with selfish intent. I loved his selections but knew they were more for him than me. He chose what he wanted to see me in. The man had impeccable taste, so I was pleased. There were also several stops in jewelry stores where I was gifted overpriced accessories, which I protested but lost the battle each time. I learned not to give much attention to any one thing, or a card was being swiped, and the item was being packaged.

When we reached our destination for dinner, it was well after nine, and I was exhausted and famished. We'd had lunch earlier that day, but with all the walking and moving around, it did little to keep me satisfied because I sat staring at the menu, wanting to sample every item they had.

"I can't decide."

"Then pick a few things." Kincaid had his eyes glued to his phone. I caught a glimpse earlier, realizing he was moving through emails that had piled up since he'd last checked that morning. The man never caught a break.

"No, that's a waste."

It took a minute, but I felt his eyes on me, which I eventually met with mine. "What?"

"You always do that, and I'm sure it's a habit. Nothing you desire is a waste, Nari."

My nose wrinkled, and his eyes narrowed more. "What's the point in ordering a bunch of food I won't eat? Do you know how many people would kill for just one meal?"

"I do because I make it my business to give back as much as I can. I'm privileged; there's no denying that, but I'm not oblivious to the struggles of others. However, that doesn't mean I'm not allowed to enjoy what I've worked hard for."

"You worked hard for it. This life is mine by default." I shifted in my seat. I hated that my new circumstance made me so uncomfortable, but it couldn't be helped.

"Then do something about it. Change the narrative."

I frowned at him, and his expression didn't change. "I won't wake up to empty bank accounts tomorrow or the next day." His cheeks hiked. "Or at least I hope I won't, but the point is, my life is what it is, and *by default*, as you so eloquently put it, that now extends to you, my wife. You earn every penny, in my opinion, with your tolerance of me. I'm not always easy."

"You got that right, buddy."

"Careful," he warned with a teasing tone. "I don't want to change you or erase your history. Contrary to what you might think, I love who you are. Your struggles shaped you into the beautiful woman I see before me. And did a damn good job, I might add." His head tilted while his eyes roamed.

"You're not helping."

He chuckled, nodding. "My point is, use your resources. Refusing the privilege won't make it go away. Find a space that allows you to balance the scale. You know what it feels like to go without and not have support. Use that to find your footing."

"How?"

"Give back. Create something for those traveling the same roads you've traveled, a resource to make their journeys a little easier. You can't save everyone, but you can create a space that lifts them up when life causes them to feel defeated. Wouldn't you have wanted the same available and at your disposal?"

I bit down on my lip, staring blankly. "Yeah."

In my experience, it had always been sink or swim. There were so many times when I felt lost and didn't have anyone to turn to. Not just financially but emotionally. It was hard being alone in a world that has given you its ass to kiss.

"Okay, then, for now, that's your focus."

"That easy, huh?"

"When it comes to you, always."

We shared another moment of silence before he shared something that totally threw me.

"My mother was a foster kid. She hasn't always been the woman you see. She struggled to find her footing in the world my father thrust her into. You two should talk about your past. You'll find she understands you more than you give credit for."

"I didn't know. I would've never guessed . . ." I frowned, attempting to understand how nothing is ever as it seems.

"You wouldn't, but that's the beauty of things. We all have the potential to exceed our wildest dreams when we are open to the possibility. Be open, sweetheart." His eyes communicated something I couldn't understand but could certainly feel. He saw me in ways that I was incapable of seeing myself. "Now, order whatever you want. I hear your stomach all the way over here." He returned to his emails, and I made a mental list of the items I wanted to try.

Hours later, I was full of food and wine. I'd finished off one glass and was working on my second. The semi-tipsy state made me feel incredibly nice.

"Have you dated a lot of women?"

"Define dating." His gaze remained on me while the glass he held firmly slowly met his lips. Those lips. I had missed them. *Shit!* I shook that thought and attempted to focus.

"How many definitions are there of dating?" I squinted a little, and he smiled.

"According to most women, several potentially apply. You tend to have an art of crafting definitions to suit your intentions."

A laugh burst through, but it was more sarcastic than humorous. "You *would* say something so accusatory."

"It's the truth." His expression didn't falter, and the weight of his eyes on me raised my body temperature. "If you're referring to an agreed commitment with two people who are exclusive, then no, I haven't dated much."

"So you were the 'sex with no strings' type? Figures." I lifted my glass, sipping slowly. I was dangerously close to my limit, but the wine he'd selected was hard to deny.

"Yes and no. I spent time with women, but not just in the bedroom. I enjoyed the company of a beautiful woman, but it had to be more than just her body that attracted me. She had to feed my soul as well. For a man like me, an intelligent mind is just as enticing as a well-laid body."

He stared at me long and hard as if assessing my reaction to his words, and then he followed with, "What are you thinking?"

"Does my mind entice you, Mr. Akel?"

Something sinful was reflected in his eyes. Their intensity had me holding my breath, anxious about how he would answer. "Of course. Your potential is dangerous. The minute you stop allowing what you haven't accomplished to hold you back and begin to embrace what you're capable of, it will be hard for me to keep up. I'll have to step up my game, and that's saying a lot. I'm not an average man."

"You're damn sure not," I mumbled before taking another sip of wine.

He laughed lightly, allowing his chin to dip so his eyes leveled with mine. "Neither are you."

"Neither am I what?"

"*Average.* I'm rarely ever wrong about people. The minute you accept that you're meant to be by my side, leaving your mark on the world, there won't be a person or thing powerful enough to keep you confined. Not even me ..." He paused, his eyes moving through something I couldn't decipher but could feel. "... *Mrs. Akel.*"

"And you? Have you dated much?"

"Not hardly. I've had a few boyfriends, but nothing serious. Life kinda got in the way."

"Makes sense."

"What?" My eyes narrowed on his, and a smile moved slowly into place.

"The experiences you have with me are new."

My mouth opened, and my eyes slammed hard against his while my cheeks flushed with embarrassment. "Are you calling me inexperienced?"

"Yes, but that's not a bad thing. In fact, I rather appreciate the innocence of your body. No man wants reminders of his woman's past."

"And no woman wants reminders of her man's past," I sneered. It was true. Kincaid was well versed in pleasing women. I was sure of it because the way he handled me was sinful. There wasn't an inch of my entire being that he hadn't implanted a memory that lingered, even after we left our bed. I wasn't complaining, but deep down inside, I was well aware that others had been his muse, which enhanced his talent. It created a streak of jealousy that I had no right to harbor. Everyone had a past.

"No one's in our bed but the two of us." He said it so calmly yet confidently that I frowned back.

"What's that supposed to mean?"

"It means that my past with other women doesn't play a role in the things I do to you. That's strictly motivated by what I feel. You inspire the way I handle your body."

"So you say."

He snorted, tossing back the remainder of his drink. "I won't lie, especially not about my intimacy with you. In fact, I'm suddenly feeling inspired right now." His eyes lowered, growing intentionally hooded as he stood, extending a hand. I didn't hesitate because I could feel what was coming and wasn't about to deny the privilege.

Kincaid had a stonelike expression while he hovered over me. I felt his intensity, which ignited a lust-fueled spark that exploded in the pit of my stomach and then shot through every inch of my body.

His head lowered, and pillowy soft lips traveled down my neck to my chest. I felt the pinch of his teeth against my nipples, one by one, and the weight of his tongue followed. The descent down my body was slow. I felt tortured by a surge of pleasure that was slowly building each time he touched me. By the time his head hovered between my thighs and his fingers teased my clit, pinching and rolling it between his fingers, I was on the verge of losing it. My back arched away from the bed, and my hands landed on his shoulders. I needed a minute, but his voice thundered over me, causing my hands to still.

"No."

One word paired with a hard gaze had my arms back at my sides. Instead of touching him, I fisted the sheets and struggled not to come undone. My mind focused on the rhythm his fingers created as they dipped in and out of me while his tongue moved to a rhythm of its own. I was definitely his because the minute he lifted his eyes that second time, the command was clear, and my body obeyed. I came hard, lifting my hips in the air, attempting to push harder against his fingers, which remained submerged in me.

Before I had time to recover, he rocked into me deep, seemingly reaching my womb on the first thrust. My fist tightened on the handful of material I clenched, and I gasped, sucking in a deep breath.

"*Uxor mea. Mea agendi ratione.*" *My wife. My inspiration.* There was a wildness to his motions and flickering in his eyes that seemed like he'd lost control. Kincaid was being rough, and his eyes remained fastened to mine. It was like he wanted me to understand why. I did. He was punishing me for being distant since the thing with Aila. He wanted me to feel physically what I had done to him emotionally . . .

Caused pain.

Unfortunately, the two didn't compare. He was delivering the best kind. My insides were an inferno when he dislodged and then returned, burying himself deeper. I arched my back and pushed into his thrusts. He slammed into me harder each time he returned, quickening his pace. Kincaid won. My body conceded, and my second orgasm erupted like a tsunami. It felt as if every nerve in my body responded while my walls pushed and quivered, tightened and released around him.

When my eyes finally peeled open, his were waiting, hard and intense. His motion slowed, and my body relaxed. "I missed you." His voice was low against the side of my neck before I felt a trail of kisses. He continued to penetrate me deeply but with less aggression.

"Me too." Those eyes were on me again, accompanied by a sexy smile just before his mouth clashed with mine. His tongue moved against mine while his body managed restraint to maintain the slow, steady pace he kept. That didn't, however, prevent him from going deep and landing hard each time. I enjoyed every minute of it. He took his time, and when we both gave out, no part of me was left unsatisfied. My mind and body were exhausted, and the last thing I remembered was his voice next to my ear, repeating what he'd said earlier.

"*Uxor mea. Mea agendi ratione.*" *My wife. My inspiration.* I assumed it was Latin but couldn't be sure. I'd ask tomorrow, but at that moment, all I wanted to do was sleep.

"About time." Alisha shot me a snarky grin when I joined her in the kitchen. She was leaning over a plate of something that smelled really good and had my stomach growling.

"Long night?" She pointed to the counter behind me. "Your food's over there. You look like you need it."

I lifted the plastic container and utensils next to it before joining Alisha at the small glass dinette that sat in the corner.

"Mind your own business," I mumbled through a smile while I lifted the lid, smiling at my waffles and cheese eggs.

Courtesy of my husband.

"Oh, honey, as loud as you were last night, you *made* it my business."

"What?" My eyes went wild, and she laughed.

"I'm kidding. There's enough distance from one side to the other to keep your dirty little secrets, but based on how you struggled with those stairs, I'm guessing you and the hubby made up."

"Something like that."

"Definitely something like that. His entire mood was different this morning. The capo is no longer brooding. Thank God. I think he halfway smiled, so whatever you did to him worked."

You mean what he did to me!

I lifted my phone to send a text, reminded of his foreign tongue last night.

Latin?

I placed it back on the table and cut into my waffles, sending a forkful in my mouth. "Did they say where they were going?"

"Yes and no. Business is always the answer. Generic and vague."

I nodded, lowering my eyes to read the text that came through.

Finally up? And yes.

Don't cause the damage and then complain about it. You're the reason I slept in. What did you say?

My goal was not to destroy, and I'm not complaining. This is vacation. Enjoy it however you want. What happened to using your translator?

How is it a vacation when you leave our bed to work? I might need to rethink the translator thing. Apparently, you have to know how to spell the words to translate them.

Ah, that does pose a problem. The offer still stands. I'll teach you, but for now, I'll be your translator . . . My wife. My inspiration.

That time, it wasn't just my cheeks that warmed when visions of last night flooded my mind. My eyes quickly lifted to Alisha when I remembered I wasn't alone. Not that it mattered because she had no clue what I was thinking.

"Oh, don't mind me. Finish your little sexting session with your man, girl."

I laughed, sticking my tongue out at her before returning to my text just as a second one came through.

> We'll only be a few hours; the rest of our time here belongs to you.

> Promises, promises.

Nothing came through after that, so I settled on my breakfast and caught up with Alisha. She and I planned on a lazy beach day while we waited for the guys to return, and then we'd map out the rest of our night with them.

CHAPTER 22

KINCAID.

"**W**hy here?" Cast looked around the building we were approaching, not appreciating how confined the space was.

"Saulo's decision. This is neutral ground. I'm assuming he's already anticipated that O'Neal won't like how this plays out." We moved as a unit. Darius was beside me, while Cast was a few steps behind. His skills were impeccable, and I was sure he had the fastest hand known to man. If anything or anyone around us considered the thought of moving wrong, they'd have a third eye before completing that thought. It was another reason I kept him around.

Darius was the same. He'd drop ten bodies before the first could get their hand on their weapon, but more than anything, I trusted them both without question. I was skilled in the art of war, but those around me also needed to react.

"Gentlemen," Saulo was the first to greet us. He stood in the center of the room while armed, suited men filled each corner.

I approached and shook his hand before he moved to Darius. "This way." He motioned with a flick of his wrist toward a door leading us to the back. When Cast began to move, Saulo paused.

"He must wait here."

I noticed the twitch of his jaw when he looked my way. Cast only answered to me, regardless of who Saulo was. If I didn't approve of him staying behind, he would go wherever I went.

With a nod from me, he stepped back, and we continued through the door. It was metal and locked behind us. Darius glanced over his shoulder and then looked at me. That part was new to him. He wasn't ranked, so he'd never attended meetings like this, but I knew him well enough to know the security measures didn't faze him. I was sure he expected it. Since I'd demanded he be my first in charge, he was stepping into a new facet of the business.

Once we reached the door where the meeting was to take place, Saulo motioned to the suit, who stood guard.

I stepped in front of him, and he patted me down. Darius was next after he handed over his piece. He and Cast were strapped, so I didn't need to be. Once cleared, we were allowed to enter.

O'Neal sat on one side of the table with his guy, Nicolas Martinez, a native Cuban. I didn't fuck with him because I'd heard things about how he moved. His loyalty showed in how the city was being run. Cubans were slowly taking over. O'Neal was stupid to trust him, but that was another reason Razi chose me over him.

Saulo motioned between us but sat on the opposite end of the table. He wouldn't be involved unless things got out of hand. I could tell from the look on O'Neal's face that Saulo would be intervening at some point.

"Why is he here?" His eyes landed on Darius with a smug grin in place. "It's my understanding that only those ranked hold court." He was testing Darius. There was no doubt that O'Neal knew that I hand selected him.

"If that were the case, your wife would be here instead of you, correct? How is she, by the way? She adjusted . . ." he gripped his crotch and smirked before continuing, ". . . to life with you yet?"

"Muthafucker." O'Neal was on his feet, fists clenched at his sides. There was no secret that Darius had been with his wife. They were promised to each other for a year before he backed out of the deal and married Alisha. Yet another reason why O'Neal didn't want him here. Everyone knew that his wife, Charlotte, continued reaching out to Darius even after she married O'Neal. The requests were always sexual. Men talked behind his back.

"Gentlemen, *muestra respeto*." *Gentlemen, show respect*, Saulo warned, and O'Neal returned unwillingly to his seat, but his face didn't change. That muthafucker didn't like one thing about me. I returned a smile, and his face twisted even more.

"Can we talk business, or would you like to continue assessing whose dick is bigger?"

O'Neal's eyes left Darius, who was slouched comfortably in his seat, unbothered, while O'Neal looked like his head was about to explode.

"You don't know shit about business. You still have milk on your breath. You're only sitting in that chair because your father made it his life's mission to kiss ass. You have no respect, just like him." O'Neal was in his early fifties. No doubt he assumed that would grant him favor over me with The Families, but apparently, they disagreed.

Mentioning my father was his way of trying to goad me into showing my age. Young, hotheaded, and irresponsible were his exact words when he spoke about me after the decision had been made. He wanted a reaction to prove his point, but I refused to give it, although my trigger finger was itching even though I had no weapon. I kept my tone even, void of the fury dancing beneath the surface. It wouldn't do me any good to lose control. Like O'Neal, Saulo was testing me, but for a different reason. If I couldn't handle O'Neal, there was no way I could take on the rest of the men who would now answer to me.

"We talking business or what?"

He laughed smugly. "Sure thing, *boss*."

My eyes narrowed on him briefly, amused by how much it bothered him to be under me. It would be wise for O'Neal to do a better job of *not* showing his hand. Instead of addressing the issue, I moved on. "Let's start with the ports."

"What about them?" His tone was already defensive.

"The Cubans have taken over. They're in control when we should be."

"That's a lie." His voice spiked, confirming what I already knew.

I tilted my head to the side, driving my point. "Is it? I have numbers to support what I'm presenting. We can pull them up now if you prefer. The Port of Miami moves larger amounts of guns and drugs through its docks than any other city on the East Coast, which only works in our favor when *we* are controlling that movement. As of late, we haven't been."

His eyes shot over to Saulo, who remained silent. I did, however, notice the hint of a smile that was now in place. I'd done my research, and he approved. I came prepared. O'Neal came with excuses.

"I'm working on it. It's not as easy as—"

"As what? It's your responsibility to manage the ports. If you're incapable, we can move some things around."

Meaning get your ass out of the way and place someone more competent.

"No. That won't be necessary."

"Good. You have thirty days to show an improvement."

His jaw flexed, but he remained quiet.

"There's also an issue with the Haitians. They're noticing the increase in revenue that's leaning toward the Cubans. If they feel undervalued, then they go to war. The last thing we need is them creeping into Biscayne Bay, barging into million-dollar properties to prove a point. Haitians, Dominicans, Cubans, Russians . . . Each group needs to feel valued, or you will lose control of the city because of turf wars. That can't happen. The reason why we line the pockets of politicians, police, and government officials is so that they move how we need them to move. They're targeting the Haitians and turning a blind eye to the Cubans. Fix it—or I will."

The problem was the man sitting next to him. We both knew it, but O'Neal was a pussy who let his first in charge run him. Again, he flexed his jaw, but that time, he spoke up. "I'll handle it. Anything else?"

"For now, no, but what I've addressed is enough to cause concern. It leads to problems that we don't need. Are we understanding each other?"

Before O'Neal could respond, his flunky decided to speak up.

"You're not here. You don't know shit about how things work in *our* city." Martinez's voice was an octave below yelling when he leaned forward, narrowing his eyes, and I had a good mind to break his fucking jaw because of the disrespect, but again, I kept my cool.

"I don't need to be here to understand the natural order of things. Business is business. I also don't need to be here to know that a lack of respect means a lack of control. These people here don't respect you." My eyes left his and moved to O'Neal. "Or you. Find a way to change the climate, or I find a replacement. Poor leadership is a deadly cancer that is currently attacking this city."

I stood, and so did Darius. Saulo's eyes moved between me and O'Neal, but he didn't move immediately.

"We're done here." I turned to leave but paused briefly. "And, Martinez, don't you ever in your fucking life raise your voice at me again, or I'll slit your gotdamn throat."

Darius chuckled, opening the door and allowing me to leave first. Once outside, the guard handed over his gun, and I heard low voices from Saulo first and then O'Neal, who, undoubtedly, was trying to plead his case. It wouldn't do him any justice to lend excuses for his fuckups. That was frowned upon more than anything. As a man, you owned your shit.

We waited until Saulo stepped out, moving with us toward the door that led us there. He stopped and extended a hand. His eyes met mine, and he spoke in his native tongue.

"*Bien hecho. Tu padre estaría orgulloso .*" *Well done. Your father would be proud.*

I shook his hand, and he gripped mine firmly before offering a hand to Darius. "Enjoy the rest of your time here, *caballeros.*" *Gentlemen.*

With a nod, he pressed his finger to the lock, and Darius and I stepped through the door. Cast was still in the same spot where we left him. I hadn't expected him to move.

"Well?" he asked as we crossed the room and exited the building the same way we came.

"Your boy just put us on high alert for the rest of our time here. He cut that man's balls off, shoved them down his throat, and then told him to swallow." Darius laughed, and Cast chuckled from behind us.

I had an enemy before, but O'Neal and Martinez were coming for my head. It made me think of Nari. She would always be a part of the equation. Either way, I wasn't concerned. O'Neal's ego was going to make his wife a widow if it came down to it because I wouldn't hesitate to end him to protect my own.

"You like tempting the fate of others?" My wife smiled when I forced my way onto the lounge that she was in, lifting and lowering her legs across my thighs so that I had more space.

"How so?"

"This." My finger moved from her bikini line up, moving across her skin until I reached the space between her breasts.

"You bought *this*." She shrugged, leaning forward to take the water bottle from my hand. Alisha gave it to me just before Darius dragged her toward their side of the house.

"For me to enjoy."

She swallowed some of the water before her eyes landed on mine again. "Then it's a good thing this section of the beach is private."

"Indeed." My hands began massaging her thighs, moving dangerously close to the thin red material that was covering the space between them. Between the smell of her arousal and the coconut body cream that blended with the ocean water that lingered in the air, my senses were being teased, but one more than the others.

"No suit? I thought you were handling business."

"I was." I leaned in and placed a kiss on her stomach, enjoying the way her body shivered. "I changed before I came out here."

"Oh."

"What have you been doing all day?"

"This." She laughed, waving her hand in the air.

"You like it here?" My fingers inched up her thigh, but she slapped my hand away before I reached my destination.

"Who wouldn't? It's beautiful."

"We can come whenever you want." That time, I tugged at the string holding her bottoms in place, and she wasn't quick enough to stop me.

"What are you doing?" Her eyes bounced around before landing on me.

"This," I offered before I kissed an exposed part of her breast before lifting the top to give me full access.

"Shit," she hissed when I latched on to her nipple. "We're outside."

"We are."

"Kincaid." My name came out in a heavy pant, but I didn't stop what I was doing. Instead, I pushed her thighs apart before I responded.

"We've already established the beach is private. Relax."

"We have guests."

"Who are busy."

"You don't know that." Her fingers wrapped around my wrist just before I was able to send my fingers where I needed them to be.

"Nari, move your hand." My tone was low but firm.

We engaged in a silent war until her fingers slowly released me, and when mine reached their destination, her eyes slammed shut, and her back arched away from the lounge.

"See? That wasn't so hard, now, was it?"

"Fuck . . . no."

One of my favorite things was watching my wife come undone. The way her body yielded to me following the direction in which I guided was fucking toxic to my soul. I was obsessed with every inch of her body and how I could elicit certain reactions. Those were the moments when she was completely unguarded, raw, submissive, and that made my dick so hard it hurt.

My wife's eyes were barely open. Her lips slightly parted while she watched me pleasing her. The closer she drew to the finish line, the deeper I went in between showing attention to her neck, lips, shoulder, and breasts. When I felt her body tremble, I pulled back, watching while she took flight.

So fucking beautiful.

As her breathing slowed, I peppered kisses across her lips and then allowed my tongue to taste hers. She kissed me back, pulling me closer by fisting the sides of my shirt. I smiled against her mouth, landing one last kiss.

"The same way I have an issue sharing, I also have an issue extending control. The sooner you learn that, the happier we'll both be. Agreed?"

"Agreed." She pushed out in a heavy breath.

I lifted the strings hanging at her hip and retied them before I adjusted her top. Once she was covered again, I inched over, taking over the lounge while positioning Nari on top of me. She relaxed against my frame, and we settled in, preparing to spend the next few hours enjoying the same space. I was perfectly content, and after Nari eventually drifted off to sleep, I assumed she was too.

"This place is nice, Darius." Nari leaned forward, placing the fruity drink she'd been drinking back on the table. She'd barely had a few sips, and her nose was turned up each time. I noticed and offered to order wine, but she turned it down, saying what she had was fine.

"Thanks. It's one of my favorites. We just don't get down here enough." He smiled, proud of his accomplishment. Clubs were his thing. He owned several, and we had two together. They served two purposes: legal business ventures and a cover for the drugs we moved through them. Not all of his locations were dirty. This one was entirely legal. It was necessary to switch things up and not create noticeable patterns or trends.

"It's so chic in here. The blue and gray is sexy."

He tossed his chin toward his wife, who was at his side, holding a drink. "That's all Lish. She designs most of them."

"Really?" Nari's eyes shined. She was impressed. "So this is a joint venture. I see you, girl."

"I have many hidden talents." Alisha winked at Nari. "And I'm about to show you another one. Let's dance." She finished her second drink while Nari was still sipping on her first. My eyes lowered to the smile she offered Alisha, moving farther to her stomach.

Are you keeping secrets, sweetheart?

"You dance. I'll move. My skills are a little rusty." My wife laughed before her eyes shot up to me. She was discreetly asking my permission. I was pleased. She was learning protocol. I kissed her temple and looked over at Darius. He was just as overprotective as I was, so I was sure he had men in place. Some likely blended in with the crowd, and others would be more obvious, positioned in specific locations that granted a clear visual from all angles. When he offered me a subtle nod, I relaxed.

"Go, but remember . . ." I paused, standing first and extending a hand to assist. Once she was on her feet, I held her against me. My hands easing down her back and then a little lower before I spoke lowly against her ear. ". . . In color *tui habitu minibus meis.*"

Nari's arms lifted and circled my neck. Her lips brushed mine. "Got it, boss. No blood on your hands tonight. I'll behave." I was sure the words hadn't fully been translated, but she understood one—*color*. My statement about blood on my hands the night we attended our first event as a married couple. I chuckled, bringing her closer, landing a real kiss before she was snatched out of my embrace by a tipsy Alisha.

"Hey, don't make me come get you," Darius warned, and she winked over her shoulder while they traveled away from our area, moving toward the stairs to head to the lower level. He and I moved to the balcony to watch until they reached the dance floor.

"There." He pointed to each corner of the club and acknowledged a few other bodies who moved in closer. "We have eyes on them."

I located my wife and watched as she moved her body to the song's bass that vibrated around us. She wasn't what I would consider a dancer, but her body moved in a way that gained attention from others who were close, partially because of the form-fitting dress that clung to her curvy frame. A thin piece of material connected over one shoulder while the other was bare. There were three ovals cut out of one side, increasing in size, the largest one sitting on her hip. Tasteful but still sexy. She looked amazing, which was another reason why I'd kept her close all night. I noticed men watching my wife and didn't like it. They were issued silent warnings, keeping them at bay, but I knew they enjoyed the view.

"O'Neal is a fucking problem," Darius spoke firmly, but like me, he kept his eyes on his wife. We were a lot alike when it came to our protective ways. I simply never experienced the need to exert the behavior before giving Nari my last name. Once we both had them in our sights and were confident they were fine, we turned our backs, leaning on the railing.

"He's not trustworthy. Martinez is the one running things. O'Neal is a puppet."

"I noticed. How long have you known?"

"For a while. It was never my business. Razi mentioned it several times in confidence. He'd been working on a way to get him out. There wasn't much proof before now. Just a feeling."

"The Cubans are the fucking proof. They're going to be an issue."

"For whom?" I smirked, and he laughed under his breath.

"Definitely not us, but they're going to push."

"They will, and I'll push back. Only one warning." That was my signature. I respected the process, so I allowed a warning so they could make the right call before things went too far. In most cases, it wasn't sanctioned to take lives. Shedding blood was frowned upon. Disputes could be settled through negotiations.

When blood was shed, negotiations stopped, and war began. Wars caused unnecessary loss of time and money. The Families were always focused on making money.

After checking again, I noticed neither Nari nor Alisha were in view. Darius was already making the call. I followed his line of sight as soon as he dialed, noticing one of his men lift a phone.

"Aye." He paused and then nodded, quickly ending the communication.

"Bathroom," he offered as an explanation. I relaxed some but decided to go see for myself. It wouldn't be smart for any random man to approach our women. There were rules, but there was also no guarantees that someone wouldn't be ballsy enough to break them.

When we reached the hallway that led to the bathroom of the floor they were on, Darius nodded to one of his guys. He'd likely moved when Alisha and Nari moved. Just as the ladies stepped out of the bathroom, I noticed a figure dressed in all black. He peeled from the wall, blocking their way.

I moved at the same time, but he spoke before I could reach them.

"*Una puta y un ladrón asesino. Partes hechos en el cielo.*" *A whore and a murdering thief. Match made in heaven.* He lifted his eyes from my wife, and they landed on me. I wasted no time positioning her behind me before I responded.

"*Y tu eres un hombre muerto caminando frente al portero del infierno.*" *And you are a dead man walking, facing the gatekeeper to hell.*

He smiled and went for his gun, but there was one already pressed to his temple before he was able to get his hand on it.

"You can't kill me. I know the *reglas*." *Rules.*

He was tagged and no doubt related to Martinez. His words were specific. *Murdering thief.* They felt as if I stole the rank I had just been given, and he also knew I had blood on my hands.

My expression remained neutral. "Rules only apply when they're respected on both sides." I moved closer. "You violated them." I reached for his gun and dislodged the clip, which I dropped in my pocket. Seconds after, I gripped the weapon firmly, and it crashed hard to his face, repeatedly, until he dropped to his knees. Blood spilled, and a few broken teeth landed on the floor. When I grabbed his shirt and pushed the barrel under his chin, knowing that one bullet remained in the chamber, I made my point clear.

"Where my wife is concerned, there's only one rule: there are none."

I landed one last blow that sent him crashing to the floor. "Tell your people that this is their only warning. It's been wasted on you. I wonder if they'll think you're worth it."

When his eyes lifted to mine, I smirked and handed his gun to Darius's guy and went to my wife. Our eyes connected, and I noticed something I hadn't seen before. *Fear.* What bothered me the most was that I couldn't tell if she was afraid of what happened or afraid of me. I didn't ask. Instead, I placed my hand at her back and motioned for her to move. It was time to leave. That didn't mean a conversation wouldn't take place. It simply wasn't happening right then at that very moment.

CHAPTER 23

NARI.

By the time morning came, I was exhausted. Neither of us slept much, but we remained quiet. When I did drift, it wasn't peaceful sleep. I tossed and turned, but Kincaid was there, pulling me closer, resting his chin on my head while my back rested against his chest. He hadn't said much. Maybe ten words passed between us once we left the club, and none of them were concerning what happened.

I watched my husband beat a man with a gun and then threaten to kill him. It was violent, but not once did Kincaid seem affected. His body was relaxed, his face and voice as deadly as his hands when assaulting that man, but he moved as if he'd been in the same position a million times before. *Violently beating a man.* Once it was over, he coolly moved us through the club as if the reason was him simply stating it was late and we should go versus knocking a man's teeth out who clearly meant me harm. *Puta.* He called me a whore. I knew that word, and my husband he referred to as a murdering thief. It was why I didn't ask questions. I needed time to process. We came home, showered, and climbed into bed. Kincaid asked me if I was okay. I nodded, and we settled into silence. He was angry. I could feel it radiating from his body. I could feel him. We had that weird-ass connection that I still couldn't understand, but it was there.

After I noticed I was in bed alone, I sat up, raising my arms above my head for a stretch before heading to the bathroom. I emptied my bladder and then freshened up before going to find my husband. Since I'd slept in one of his shirts, I slipped on a pair of shorts since we had other guests and took the stairs, finding him in the kitchen, phone to his ear. Cast startled me with a low rumble of *Good morning* from the living room.

"Good morning." I smiled politely. "I didn't know you were here."

"Change of plans," was all he offered before returning to focusing on his phone.

As I entered the kitchen, Kincaid lifted an arm, motioning for me to join him. He had crossed his ankles, and one arm folded over his chest while the other was bent at the elbow to hold his phone. He unlatched his body, opening the space for me when I reached him. A kiss landed on the top of my head while he spoke to his caller.

"I need to hit you back. My wife is up."

I angled my head back, and his eyes were on me while he listened a few seconds longer and then ended the call.

"You're dressed." My eyes swept his frame.

"Yeah, I've been up for a while."

"Oh."

He stared at me in an odd manner. I couldn't tell what was on his mind, but it was as if he were studying me.

"What's wrong?"

"Nothing. How do you feel?"

"Tired. I didn't sleep much." Our eyes locked in an intense stare before he nodded.

"You didn't. You were restless."

"And you were up early," I added before pulling away to get water. His loaded gaze stayed with me until I was done, but he remained elusive, saying nothing.

"Why are you watching me like that? I'm fine if you're worried." I assumed his mood was about last night. It was as if he were brooding, his expression tight and body tense.

"Come holla at me for a minute." He motioned to the upper level. "Upstairs."

"Is something wrong?"

"No."

"Are Alisha and Darius still asleep?" My eyes swept the space. Everything seemed untouched, unlike other mornings, where reminders of our guests were sprinkled about. Empty cups, food containers, or random articles of clothing were usually left behind.

"No. They're gone. Left this morning."

"They left this morning?"

I frowned as my foot reached the first stair. Kincaid was ahead of me but didn't stop. "Yes. We're leaving later today after the jet returns. We have one more thing to take care of."

"Oh, more business?" I asked after I entered the room and sat at the foot of the bed, sipping my water.

"No, personal." I frowned again, tilting my head to the side.

"You're being weird. If this is about last night—"

"No. We'll get to that. First, I need you to do something for me."

"What?"

"Take a pregnancy test."

"What? Why?" I paused, my water midair, and he was staring so hard it was like I could physically feel his eyes on me.

"You didn't drink at the club. You didn't make coffee this morning." He motioned to the bottle of water in my hand. "You also didn't drink with dinner last night."

"And I had wine the night before. Why are you alluding to my drinking not being normal? I'm not keeping secrets." That was a partial truth. I woke up yesterday morning, and the smell of the coffee I prepared made me extremely nauseated. I ended up pouring it out. Also, right after I finished my breakfast, it came back up before I could dress for the beach. I wasn't sure, but there was a possibility . . . but then, the rest of the day, I was fine. No issues. I even managed dinner without problems, so it could've been nothing.

"I'm not alluding to anything, but you've been drinking socially, which is why you need to take the test. You shouldn't be consuming alcohol if you're pregnant. You *won't* be drinking if you're pregnant." His expression and eyes turned hard.

"I wouldn't harm my baby." I felt as if he were accusing me of something. It was why I didn't drink with dinner or at the club last night. I wasn't sure, so I wanted to be safe.

"*Our* baby, and I'm not accusing you of anything, sweetheart. Just looking for clarification. We need to know."

"We don't have a test."

He pointed to the dresser. There was a bag there. *How the hell did I miss that?*

"I went this morning. I considered flying Dr. Chandler in, but figured you'd feel ambushed. We can see her as soon as we get back."

"And that's *not* being ambushed?" I frowned, pointing to the bag of what I now knew were tests.

"I'm not forcing you. I'm asking. I would assume you would like to know as much as I do. No?" His chin dipped, and those eyes were on me again, challenging me to disagree.

"You're right. You do have an issue with control," I sneered, walking to the dresser and then heading to the bathroom. I half expected him to hold the damn test while I peed on it, but he remained in the room. I used both and took my time, even after reading positive results. I had missed a few days with my pills, but for the most part, I was consistent and still . . .

I was having a baby.

Kincaid's baby.

What the hell?

Did I even want that?

As soon as I stepped into the room, our eyes met. It took him a minute to observe me, but a smile spread across his face. I hadn't said one word.

He was on me quickly and lifted me from the floor, my legs around his waist, and I ended up on the dresser with his body pressed between my thighs.

"Honesty, agreed?"

I nodded, and he asked his first question. "How do you feel?"

"I don't know." It was the truth. I wasn't happy, sad, scared, or really anything for that matter. Just . . .

Processing.

"We never discussed kids. Not in-depth. Is that something you're opposed to?"

I snorted. "A little late for that."

"There are measures—" He said the words, but I could see the truth in his eyes. There was no way in hell he would agree to me not having this kid. He wanted this; I could feel it.

Abortion.

Adoption.

"I wouldn't do that. I don't think I could."

"Good, but I need you to be honest. You can be unsure, you can be afraid, you can even be angry, but you have to be honest, no matter what."

"Okay."

"We'll see Dr. Chandler when you get home to make sure everything is good with both of you." Kincaid was taking charge.

Statement, not a question.

"Okay."

"Nari . . ." My eyes lifted to his, and he studied my face again. "We're okay."

It wasn't presented as a question, but from the look in his eyes, I understood he was asking. I nodded again, smiling subtly, and he kissed my forehead. Then he lifted me off the dresser and placed me on my feet.

"Get dressed. We have someone to meet."

"Who?"

"I'll tell you on the way." There was that look again. He was holding back, which made me anxious. I just didn't have time to focus on it because this baby was now my bigger issue.

I am going to be a mother.

My mind was in a fog as I sat beside my husband while he sped through the streets of Miami. He knew this place well. It was clear that he visited often. Before my thoughts could go rampant, a text came through from Alisha.

Hey, you okay? Last night was crazy.

I glanced at Kincaid, who seemed stuck in his thoughts.

It was more than crazy. I don't know how I should feel.

I would tell you not to worry, but things have changed. Your husband has moved up, and his position makes him a target. That makes you a target. They'll use you to try to make him weak. Don't let them. Trust his word and do whatever he asks.

I will, but it's still hard to wrap my mind around.

It will get better. It's sad to admit that those acts will eventually be a part of your expectation of being married to Caid. Gotta go. We'll hang out when you get back.

Okay. I'll call you.

His voice startled me when I locked my phone and stared out the window.

"Talk to me, not Alisha. If you have questions, I'll answer them." I didn't bother turning my head when I responded.

"Will you?"

"As best I can. There are some things—"

"That you can't tell me. Got it."

"Not because I want to keep secrets. Only because what you don't know keeps you safe."

"Does it?" I challenged when I finally gave him my full attention.

"Regardless of whether you believe it, yes, it does."

"He called me a whore and you a murdering thief."

Ladrón asesino. That I had to look up, and after multiple misspellings, I finally got it right. There was bad blood between the two. That much I also understood.

Kincaid stared at me hard before he snorted and turned toward the road. "And I told him that he was a dead man walking who was facing the gatekeeper to hell. No one touches you, ever."

"Is that a promise you can truly make?"

"Yes." The word was quick, without hesitation, and the affirmation reached his eyes.

"I believe you."

"You should." His eyes lowered to my ring and then lifted to my stomach. We were both silent for the rest of the drive. I was so caught up in everything that had been going on that I hadn't thought to ask who we were meeting until we were parked at a small Mexican restaurant. There weren't many cars in the lot, and the ambiance didn't match the elegance of places I expected of Kincaid. It wasn't until then that I also noticed that Cast pulled up beside us.

"Why is he here? I thought it wasn't business."

"It's not."

"Then who are we meeting?"

"Your mother."

"My . . ." My eyes narrowed and then slammed into the building before they bounced back to Kincaid. "My mother? You found her? She's in there?"

"Yes. I met her this morning to be sure. We talked, and I asked if she would be open to meeting you . . ."

"She said yes?"

He nodded, but his expression was cautious. "Only if you want to. We can leave."

"No." My eyes landed hard on the building again. "I want to meet her, but don't tell her . . ." I paused, still staring at the building, "about the baby. Not yet, please."

"I won't. You can tell her if and when you're ready."

We got out, and I felt my hands shaking. Once we reached the door, I paused and waited. Cast was behind us, but neither of them said a word. Kincaid only kissed my temple and waited for me to move. He was following my lead. I appreciated that.

The place was empty. Aside from the employees behind the counter, she was the only one there. I watched Kincaid nod at an older guy and realized he'd likely arranged that somehow. It was something he would do. *Privacy!*

My mother stared at me the minute we entered. She sat at a corner table with her hands resting on it. The first thing I noticed was how short she was and that she looked a little thin. She also had my face. Her hair was wild all over her head, looking like mine when I wore it free and in its natural state. That day, however, mine was pulled on the top of my head and twisted in a messy bun. I wondered if she was making the same observations about me as I was with her.

"I'll wait here." My eyes shot up to Kincaid, and I shook my head.

"Can you sit with me?"

He nodded and pulled out my chair, filling the one next to it after I was seated. His hand rested on my thigh and mine on the table, mirroring her position. It wasn't purposeful. Just felt natural.

"You're beautiful," she spoke lowly and smiled.

"I look like you."

A nervous laugh escaped her lips. My stomach was in knots. That was my mother. The woman I never thought I would ever meet.

"You do. Thank you for coming. I didn't think you would," she almost whispered.

"Why?" I frowned, and her eyes left me, moving to Kincaid.

"Wasn't really sure if you'd want to, but more than anything, he wasn't sure if he would let you. Your husband's really protective. That's good. I like that about him. When he asked if I'd like to meet you, I said yes. He made clear that he'd think about it but didn't know how he felt or how you would feel. You know, because I've been gone so long."

"Yeah." I felt anxious. "You didn't look for me."

Her eyes lowered, and then they met with mine again. "No. I couldn't at first."

"You could've, but you didn't."

Her head shook softly. "When I left home, I was sixteen. If I had looked for you, they would've known. My parents. They could've forced me to come home by law because I wasn't old enough to be on my own—"

"Why not find me when you were old enough? You could've then."

"Two years had passed. By then, I didn't think it was fair. You had a family—"

"I didn't," I cut her off.

"But I thought you did. They lied to me. I didn't know back then. They told me that a family would adopt you. A married couple that wanted kids but couldn't have them. I thought you were happy. I didn't have anything to make you happy. I barely had my mind most days. I was so depressed I would cry for hours, and when I wasn't crying, all I could do was sleep. My parents told me I needed to get over it and that nothing was wrong with me, but there was, which I found out years later. I've been taking medication to manage it. Depression. My doctors think having you made it worse. Triggered something in me."

"Is that why you didn't come lookin' for me? I made things worse for you?"

"No, sweetheart. No." Her head was shaking fast. "I wanted you, but my parents told me I couldn't keep you. I was a kid. I didn't have anything, but I swear I thought you were with a family, being cared for, being loved. Getting the love I couldn't give you. I didn't know until now that you weren't happy or being loved. He told me."

I looked up at Kincaid, whose eyes were already waiting. He was studying me intently like I would somehow break, and he was going to catch the moment right before I did to prevent it.

"Why are you here, in Miami?"

"I live here. I have for years."

"Alone?"

"Yes."

"Do you have other kids?"

God, please say no. I won't be able to handle anything else.

"No, just you. I . . ." She paused. "I didn't think it was fair just to move on like you never existed."

"But you did," I snapped and found myself getting angry.

"I know it feels that way, but I didn't. I couldn't."

"Yeah. Just like you couldn't come looking for me."

She looked up at Kincaid and then back to me, but my mind was floating. I felt like I was no longer able to breathe. "We should go."

He didn't hesitate. My husband stood and nodded at my mother. "Thank you for coming."

She seemed anxious but timid as she stood. "Can I hug you before you go?"

I nodded, and she moved to me, arms open, until I was between them. She trembled as she held on tight, and I barely hugged her back. I couldn't. My mind was still floating, and I couldn't fucking breathe. Before she let go, my mother whispered, "I'm here if you want to try this again. On your terms. Whenever you want."

Stepping away, I nodded and simply said okay.

Everything that happened after that was a blur. I remained quiet, and Kincaid allowed me to. He didn't ask questions. We drove back to the house, packed our things, and then he and Cast loaded them in the SUV that arrived shortly after. On the jet, Kincaid and Cast talked while I slept. He watched me until I drifted off to sleep. When we got home was the first time we discussed the meeting with my mother. He sat, working on his laptop in the study off from our room while I unpacked our suitcases when he decided to bring it up.

"I have her information if you want to reach out."

"Why didn't you tell me when you found her?"

"Because I needed to be sure before I put you two together. You would've never met her had I felt she wasn't worthy of being in your life."

"Is that why you took me with you to Miami?"

His eyes narrowed a bit. "Not the only reason, but it influenced my decision. It would've been just as easy for me to fly her here. I wanted to spend the weekend with you, away from all the other bullshit that was going on."

"Since I wasn't talking to you?" I smirked, knowing he meant the friction after the episode with his ex.

His cheeks hiked. "Yeah, that too."

I crossed the room and climbed in his lap. He accepted my presence, moving his laptop to the side to make room for me.

"You're not obligated to get to know her. That's completely up to you, which I made clear. She doesn't know how to contact you. That's why I didn't want to bring her to the beach house. That way, there were no ties between the two of you and no way for her to go around me."

Always being protective.

"I do want to get to know her—well, part of me does, but then I pull back the thought because it could be the same as it was with my cousin."

I'd been burned by my so-called family. What if my mother had an agenda? I couldn't ignore what my life must've looked like. There was no way to experience Kincaid and not see dollar signs. He was my husband, which meant, by default, I was attached to whatever he had.

"I don't believe she wants anything other than a relationship with you. If I sensed anything different, you wouldn't have met her."

I curled my body against his, finding comfort in his arms and the familiarity of his scent. I hated how much I looked forward to those things, but I loved how they made me feel like I belonged. "Thank you for today. I can't believe you found her."

"Technically, I didn't. My people did."

"But only because you asked them to. Do you think you can find my father too?"

"Depends." He kissed my forehead. "We'll have to see what she can tell us about him. His name wasn't on your birth certificate. That's the first place we start."

"I'll ask."

"You're going to talk to her?" He was attempting to remain neutral. I could feel it by how he hesitated and didn't push.

"I am. Maybe we could visit again."

"We can, and I can bring her here anytime you want. Just let me know."

I nodded, and he hooked my chin. "We call Dr. Chandler tomorrow, eh?"

"Sure thing, boss," I teased, causing him to chuckle before his lips covered mine, and our tongues began to dance. So much, so fast. I met my mother, and I was about to become one. I needed a minute to catch up.

CHAPTER 24

KINCAID.

"Mr. Akel, my family is not prepared to hand over our life's work."

I exhaled an irritated sigh, reclining back farther in my chair while I unbuttoned my suit jacket. "Mr. Margaux, I understand your hesitation, and I'm sure your family is attempting to balance the idea of losing what used to be your legacy."

"Not used to—*is*," he made clear, attempting to assert himself. The effort was plausible but still, nonetheless, amusing.

"You've exhausted all possibilities. Had I not done my homework, I wouldn't be here. What I'm offering is fair. It's me or the banks. Either way, you lose. Chateau Margaux is no longer your legacy outside of the memories created throughout the years. I can save your family financially. Sign, and the money will be wired to your account within the hour. Chateau Margaux will be mine. Refuse, and by the end of the week, I will make this same deal with the banks, and Chateau Margaux will still be mine. You can't change the course of things. At this point, it would be best to bow out gracefully. Tell your children and their children whatever fables you need to in order to save face, but this is happening. How it's happening depends on your decision. I'll be here in New York for the rest of the day. If I don't hear from you by then, I'll begin negotiations with the bank when my jet returns home tomorrow morning."

His face flushed red with anger, but he remained quiet, watching through thin eyes as I stood to leave.

"Send my regards to your grandfather," I announced on my way to leave his office. I paused briefly, giving him my final thoughts. "Your family put up a tremendous fight to hold on to its legacy, but sometimes, we must know when to fight and when to concede. You can't win. Don't make this harder on your family than it needs to be."

Without waiting for a response, I was gone. Cast fell in step with me, and we left his building, not speaking until we were back in the car. He drove while I filled the passenger's seat.

"He sign?"

"No, but he will. I'm not concerned. This is simply his way of protecting his ego. Margaux knows that I'm his best option."

"You might be, but it's still a gut punch. You walked your ass in there and told him, 'Hands up.' I'm sure they didn't see that coming."

I smirked and nodded, removing my phone and responding while I pulled up the text I'd missed from my wife.

"A Black man with money is a threat. A Black man with money and intelligence is a promise. I'm their worst nightmare because I understand the value of knowing when someone underestimates their opponent. They see my face and guess wrong every time, landing on the losing side of things. A *threat* can be managed, but a *promise*, that's an entirely different beast. I'm the beast they never see coming. They have no defense against what I bring to the table, a table I built, tripled the value, and then sold that muthafucker back to them, only to sit on the other side and make them sign over their life's work."

Cast chuckled, nodding while I answered a call from my wife.

"Impeccable timing. I just finished a meeting."

"What type of meeting?"

"We'll soon be purchasing a chain of French hotels."

She snorted. "You say that so casually. Who the hell speaks that dismissively about purchasing a chain of hotels? I'm sure it costs a fortune."

My cheeks hiked. "It did, but it's money well spent. Our return will triple what I invested within the first year we open."

"Our?"

"Yes, sweetheart. Half of what I own belongs to you, but enough about that. How are *you* feeling?"

"Besides lonely, perfectly fine. No issues on my end with this little guy other than my inability to stomach the smell of coffee. I'm not sure if me and this kid are going to get along."

Guy! As much as I'd love to have a son, I was equally thrilled with the idea of our firstborn being a daughter who would undoubtedly have me wrapped around her tiny little fingers the same as her mother had already done.

"Guy? Let's not be presumptuous. We still have time before we know for sure."

"Guy as in baby, not gender. Maybe I should rephrase. How about itty bitty?"

I chuckled and smiled. "I like the sound of that, and Dr. Chandler suggested you not overdo things with your caffeine intake anyway."

Nari groaned, and I was sure her eyes rolled. "She didn't say I couldn't have any."

"No, she didn't, but apparently, our itty bitty isn't on board with your indulgence."

"This kid is already running things. I'm not sure how I feel about that."

"You're still in charge, sweetheart. Now, let's discuss your being lonely. I thought you invited my mother to stay."

"I did, and she's been wonderful. I think this was good for both of us, but regardless of how nice it's been having her this week, her presence doesn't match yours. I'm not sleeping well."

Ahh, I see.

"I'll be home tomorrow, and my priority will be putting you to sleep." My dick swelled at the thought. I mirrored her sentiment of being lonely. I was in the same boat. I missed my wife.

"Promises, promises," she teased.

"Of which you have proof that I never fail to deliver. Agreed?"

"Agreed."

"I'll call you later. I'm at my next meeting and have to go."

"I suppose those millions aren't going to make themselves."

"Actually, they do. Our money is making money as we speak."

"Of course it is. I talked to my mother today."

"Oh yeah? How did that go?"

The two had been communicating. I kept my distance but remained protectively close. I felt personally responsible for my wife's well-being.

"Good. She seems genuinely interested in getting to know me."

"Give her a chance, sweetheart."

"I am."

"I want you to feel whole, and part of that is feeling connected to your roots. I'll call you as soon as I'm situated later."

"Got it, boss."

She ended the call, and I turned to Cast, who had parked and was grinning at me with that fucking amusement that seemed to take over each time he was around, and I talked to my wife.

"What?"

"Nothing. Just trying to figure out who the hell you are because you're damn sure not the Kincaid I've always known."

"When it comes to some things, I would have to agree, but don't get shit twisted and get caught up by underestimating me."

"Never. I know better, but still, this shit is fucking hilarious." He tossed his chin, and we got out. Cast remained a few steps behind me as we entered the building and took the elevator to the third floor. As soon as we stepped inside, Cast posted up, and I was escorted to Mayor Adler's office. He wasn't going to be happy to see me, but I didn't give a damn.

"Kincaid," he greeted with a hand extended as soon as his door closed and I was in front of his desk.

"Carl," I returned before taking a seat.

"I didn't know we had a meeting scheduled." His face expressed annoyance from having his day interrupted.

"We didn't, but I felt it necessary. There should never be a time when you leave issues on the table for too long."

"Issues?" His brows pinched at the same time the muscles in his fluffy jaws flexed beneath the surface.

"Let's have a little history lesson."

His ice-blue eyes narrowed on me, but he didn't speak. He knew better. Regardless of my new title, Carl Adler was well versed in my authority. I had been at the table with him several times over the years, handling business for The Families, but now, he answered directly to me.

"There are ten major airports and ten major seaports located along the East Coast, all of which are easily accessible from I-95. I-95 is the key overland route, which travels the East Coast and connects all the high-intensity drug traffic areas from one end to the next. Guess what has a direct connection to I-95?"

His eyes narrowed more, so I continued. "JFK, Newark, Liberty, and LaGuardia. Those are yours to police, correct?"

"Yes, but I still don't see the issue."

"The issue is that six of the last twenty-three flights which have landed in those airports have been held up or confiscated by New York authorities."

"I have to present the appearance that I'm fighting this shit. The war on drugs has become a big conversation with the big boys in DC. I can't just let everything through."

"Agreed, but six shipments is excessive. The product also hasn't been rerouted. Thus, my mention of I-95. Once you have your dog-and-pony show for the media to prove that you're doing your job as mayor, those shipments should be on their way down I-95, heading south. They haven't. Why is that?"

"Red tape. It's not as easy as you think to—"

I cut him off, delivering a verbal warning before continuing. "First of all, I don't have to think a gotdamn thing. Otherwise, there wouldn't be need to line your pockets. I suggest you find a way to make that shit easy."

It wasn't necessary to raise my voice. I rarely ever did. A look, a motion of my head, a shift in my stance were enough to get my point across.

"I'll get it done."

"You will also loosen the restraints at the port. Port of New York/New Jersey hosts the largest complex of containers on the East Coast. Two hundred sixty-six billion dollars in international cargo moves through there within a year's time. Do you understand how much money we lose when your people don't do their fucking jobs?"

"We're doing what we can without compromising the integrity of the system. If I allow too much leniency, we create suspicion, and they'll be on our asses. What the fuck do you expect me to do?" His face flushed red, but he was smart enough not to raise his voice.

"I expect you to do what we pay you to do. What you *assured* us you were capable of handling. Our money pays for your three yachts, your private jet, and your children's private schools. Not that laughable salary you earn for this bullshit title." I lifted the nameplate from his desk and hurled it across the room. "The election is next year. I'll begin vetting for your replacement just in case it's necessary. Now, it's up to you who we back when the time comes."

I stood and adjusted my suit jacket, standing with my shoulders squared, hands crossed in front of me.

"Let me be perfectly clear so that we don't have this issue moving forward. I don't like unnecessary visits. You're taking time away from my personal affairs just for me to remind you of your fucking incompetence. Get your shit together, Carl, and do it fast. We're always watching—always. Be sure to mention to your wife that blue isn't her color. Her skin is too pale, and it does her no justice."

His face showed alarm at the mention of his wife. No doubt his thoughts went to what she wore while she had lunch at their daughter's school earlier that day. I tossed my chin his way before leaving the office. Once I was in my car, I sent Adler a photo of his family. The image was of his wife kissing their daughter on the cheek. They were safe because it went against regulations to harm women and children, and I personally had lines I refused to cross, but it was a reminder to Adler there wasn't a part of his life that we didn't have access to. The realization would be enough to light a fire under his ass or suffer consequences of crossing the wrong people.

"I haven't pleasured myself using my own hands since my early teens. There's never been a need to."

"You're such a liar." Nari laughed, and the sweet sound of her voice had me wishing that Margaux hadn't called me hours ago, requesting I see him in the morning before my scheduled flight. He was ready to close the deal. Apparently, his grandfather insisted that he stop fighting on his behalf. I was their only option. That I knew, but I understood his need to give it his all.

"One thing I will never be is a liar."

"So you don't lie, ever?"

"I'm not saying that. I've bent the truth on occasion, and I'm notorious for excluding details when it suits my position; however, with you, you will always get the truth."

"Now I really don't trust you when you're away. You're insatiable, which means that you're either lying or finding an alternative. The only alternative is another woman."

"Nari, sweetheart, I will never cheat on you. As insatiable as I am when it comes to your delectable body, I am a man who has no issues implementing control. My dick will never rule my actions."

"So when you think about me, and I'm not around, you just deal with it. No touching, no self-exploration?"

"No, but I am curious as to how *you* handle the same challenge."

"I have fingers and toys. Both do a decent job, but none compare to you."

I snorted. "They better not, or I'm losing my edge."

"So arrogant."

"I've earned the right, wouldn't you agree?"

The line went quiet.

"Nari?"

"Oh, sorry. I was going to test that theory, but maybe I'll wait until we're off the phone."

My teeth raked across my lip while my dick inflated instantly. "Your teasing is going to cost you when I get home."

"Good. That's precisely what I was hoping." She laughed at the same time my doorbell sounded.

A frown creased my face as I traveled through the living room and pressed the monitor to see who was at my front door. Brushing my palm down my face, I went back to my call.

"Nari, let me call you back."

"Hmmm, do you need to go so you do *not* use your hands?" she teased, bringing a smile to my face.

"No, I meant what I said. The only relief I will enjoy is between your thighs."

"So you say."

I chuckled. "Give me an hour, and I'll call you back. Don't go to sleep."

"No promises, buddy."

Luckily, she ended the call before Val pressed the doorbell again. With my proximity to the door, there was no way Nari wouldn't have heard the notification.

Val's back was to me when I pulled the door open. It allowed me a minute to take in the temptation I hadn't seen in a few months. Thin waist and a round ass sitting nicely and on full display due to the bodycon dress that hugged her curves.

When she turned and smiled, I was almost tempted. Almost. She wasn't my wife, so she wasn't getting my attention.

"It's been awhile." She smiled and stepped inside, not bothering to wait for an invite. I shut the door, watching as she moved deeper into the space, turning again to face me.

"How did you know I was in town?"

"Word travels fast when Kincaid Akel touches down. I'm a little disappointed. You didn't call me."

"Why would I? If the streets are whispering about me being in the city, then I'm sure they've been yelling about the recent changes in my life."

Her eyes lowered to my left hand before they rolled.

"That's circumstantial. You and I both know it doesn't change a thing with us."

I smirked. "That's where you would be wrong. It changes everything. I love my wife. I won't cheat on her, not even with you."

I could see the confusion first and then surprise flicker behind her eyes. Val and I had been acquainted for years. She lived in New York and traveled to Atlanta for business. On every occasion we were in the same city, we spent time together. The night I proposed to Aila, Val was in my bed after I left the engagement party. That was how she and I functioned, so to hear that I was married and presuming to be faithful had to come as a shock.

"You're kidding, right?"

"No. I'm very serious. My marriage to Nari is real. I will not break my vows."

"I don't believe that." She walked closer, attempting to place her arms around my waist, but I caught her wrists to subdue her gently.

"You should because that's a line I'm not going to cross. It's best if you leave."

"You're asking me to leave. *Me?*"

I smiled at her arrogance. "What makes you think that you hold privilege over any of the other women I've spent time with? There were several, of which you're well aware."

Her feelings were hurt. I could see the disappointment in her eyes reminding me of the conversation I had with Nari about my dating history. Val had formulated one of those definitions, which she assumed granted her favor over the other women I entertained.

"I guess I misunderstood my position in your life." Our eyes locked before she forced a smile. "It was good to see you, Kincaid. If your position changes, you know how to find me."

"I do," was all I gave. There was no point in reiterating what I'd already made clear.

After she was gone, I called my wife back but didn't get an answer. It was just after midnight, and not much time had passed, so I tried again. When I didn't get a response, I decided to get some work done. I would be home before lunch so that my wife could be my lunch.

CHAPTER 25

NARI.

He was all over me—his touch, his scent, his emotions. I could feel them so intensely. The way he moved inside me was beautiful. How else could I describe the way he handled my body besides . . .

Beautiful!

My husband was a gentle beast who spared no expense in making me feel everything he had to offer. He was with me and in me, branding my soul and my flesh with his virility and possessiveness.

Kincaid lifted just enough to balance his weight on his arms so that our eyes were level. His teeth raked across his bottom lip, and my head whipped left when I heard his knuckles crack. Both hands were balled into fists, which matched the scowl that was etched in place. I would've been surprised that he was reacting to my current state of mind, but over the months, that man had learned my every mood. He could feel me the same as I could feel him, which was how he knew things weren't right. It had been a week and a half since he returned from New York, and *I* was the one who implemented a shift. I hadn't meant to, but it happened.

She caused it!

"Stop fucking pulling away," he growled at the same time another hard thrust landed between my thighs. I hadn't physically retracted, so he meant mentally. He could feel the disconnect.

"I'm not," I lied.

"You are." His eyes narrowed before his mouth came down with force against mine. His tongue explored in long strokes. My husband was feeling needy because his pace was no longer tender. It was intense, quick, and hard. He was attempting to reach that place inside me which would alter my mood and shift me back into accord with him. It wouldn't happen. I had already shut down, but my mind was racing with anticipation of the pleasure that was budding in my core.

He controlled my body, but my heart, I would keep that distance. He hit me with long, hard thrusts that forced my thighs to spread and my hips to open wider. I shut my eyes and allowed him to guide us both to that place. That beautiful place where nothing mattered but the two of us, inching toward the brink of delirium that we both traveled to when our bodies became one.

Each time he pulled back and landed with more force, my mind took flight. I was so close. My husband was in me so deep, long, and thick that there was no denying his presence. I felt him pulsing and hard, moving with a skill that brought tears to my eyes.

Had she *been in this same place? Did he make* her *lose her mind like I was surely losing mine?*

I gasped at the thought and then swallowed the cry that threatened to escape. His fingers gripped my chin, forcing my eyes to his. "Baby, tell me. Stop hiding." His voice was low, tortured, begging, but I refused. Instead, I lifted my head and sent my tongue into his mouth. He paused but accepted. I was sure he wanted my voice instead. He wanted to know why I was emotionally disconnecting, but he became distracted when my body began to tremble and spasm beneath him. I exploded, and only a moment passed before he spilled into me. I could feel his release, hot and heavy, shooting into me with aggression. Closing my eyes, I held firmly to his strong arms, which eventually pulled me into his solid frame after he rolled over onto his back.

"Your mouth can lie, but your body can't. Tell me," he demanded, but I refused. I gently kissed his lips and smiled. It was forced but still a smile.

"You have to go. You're going to be late."

"I don't give a damn about that shit. This . . ." He frowned hard, "whatever is going on with you—with us—I need fixed."

He was frustrated. Kincaid was used to being in control, even with me and my emotions. Right then, he wasn't, which had the brooding alpha spiraling, angry and unsure of himself.

"Stop trying to create a problem that doesn't exist. I'm fine." I tried to peel my body from his, but he held firmly, locking corded arms around me. After a long minute, I pushed out his name.

"Kincaid, please. You're going to be late, and so am I." He had a meeting with someone important. I wasn't sure who, but I'd heard him on the phone in my half-lucid state. The call woke him from a restful sleep, and after his phone was back on the nightstand, he rolled over between my thighs, and my body came alive when he entered me.

After a minute, he gave in. I slipped away first, padding to the bathroom, but I felt the burn of his eyes on me, moving introspectively across my skin. By the time I was almost done in the shower, he joined me. His body brushed mine, and his palms landed flat against my stomach. After he kissed the back of my neck, I rinsed and stepped out of the glass enclosure, never giving him my eyes, but his were on me.

Before he could finish his shower, I dressed in jeans, a fitted hoodie, and sneakers, then grabbed my things before leaving. I managed to get out of the house before having to face him again, and that was when I came undone. My hands trembled as I gripped the steering wheel, and the sobs caused my body to jerk. How was I here? How did I allow myself to fall into his trap? I had been warned and saw all the signs, but I still trusted that this would be safe. He would be different. Kincaid would somehow manage to be the only person in my life who didn't let me down, someone I could feel protected with, but no, he was just like everyone else.

An hour later, I was sitting in front of Nathan. He was dressed casually. I had called him and demanded a meeting on Saturday morning. His clothes didn't matter as long as he could do what he'd promised months ago.

"Good morning," I began, my eyes landing hard on my phone, which had an incoming call from my husband. I silenced it and then focused on Nathan.

"Good morning. What's this emergency that you called about?" His brows were pinched together, his eyes thin as they narrowed on me. Had I not been around him several times before, I would've assumed he was angry versus just serious. Nathan was always serious, businesslike—a trait he and my husband shared in common.

"You told me that you would represent my interest when negotiating."

"Have I not?"

My head bounced up and down, agreeing. "You have, but I need one more thing. You have to do this for me and not consider the fact that my husband is the one who pays you. You promised to be fair and consider what was best for me as well as him. Does that still apply?"

He frowned, giving thought to the question. Nathan didn't like me being there, demanding his assistance in my husband's absence, his real client.

"Where's Kincaid?"

"Not here, and if that's a problem, then I'll go, but you promised . . ."

"I did. How can I help you, Mrs. Akel?"

I snorted at the reference. He was making clear that his interest leaned toward my husband.

"These." I tossed the papers onto his desk. His eyes lowered and then lifted to me.

"I don't understand."

"I signed them, but I want to add a provision. I no longer want to void the original agreement. I do, however, want to change one thing."

His greenish-brown eyes narrowed a bit more. "Which is?"

"We are allowed to see other people."

"I can't make that change without both of you agreeing."

I laughed smugly, lifting my phone. "My husband has already agreed. Even if by default."

I pulled up my social media, located the recording sent to me a week ago, and pressed play, holding up my phone so that Nathan could hear clearly.

"*Val, sweetheart, I'm not sure what you want me to say. What we have is what we have; however, you know that ring on her finger changes nothing between us, so stop bringing it up. You were in my bed the night I proposed. I'm only in New York for a few more hours before I head home. Are you going to come take care of me or not?*"

"*I want more than this.*"

"*I can't give you more. I've already explained how things have to be moving forward, but truthfully, I never promised you anything other than what we are. Our agenda is clear. Consensual sex between two adults. If it's not you, it will be someone else. The decision is yours.*"

"*Consensual sex with me but not the woman who's wearing your ring?*"

"*You don't need to worry about what I have with her. She's just a means to an end. It's business, sweetheart. Now, should I be expecting you or not?*"

"I'm on my way."

"I'll see you soon."

After the recording ended, I proceeded to read the message that accompanied the recording this Val woman sent to me. My memory drifted to the night he and I were on a call, and he abruptly ended our communication, promising to call me back. It didn't register then, but the minute I received her message, it all clicked.

> *I was with him the night he put that ring on your finger. I was with him last week in New York, and I will be with him whenever I choose. As long as you know your place, you and I won't have any issues. Men don't change. They simply get better at hiding their true selves.*

When I finished playing the message, my eyes landed hard on Nathan.

"Now, are you going to make the changes I need?"

He hesitated, and I could see the internal battle taking place. His loyalty was with Kincaid, but I could tell he didn't like what he heard any more than I did because I won. Seconds passed before he nodded.

"I'll take care of it."

"Good. I'll wait." I leaned back, prepared to sit until this was done. Moving forward, I would look out for myself because, apparently, no one else would.

My entire life was centered around this man. I was carrying his child, hiding away in his penthouse or our home, using the money he'd provided to feed myself and our unborn baby. Everything about me was directly connected to him. I wondered if he'd done that on purpose. Kincaid was a calculated man. He moved with purpose. Maybe the dependency had been a part of his plan all along. It rendered me helpless to anything but a need for him. Kincaid made clear that he had issues with control. If my entire life rotated around him, he was always in control.

My chest tightened with the realization as I sat in the center of his bed, legs crossed at the ankles, while I stared into blank space. I had been such a fool. Why would I ever think a man like him would love and respect a woman like me? Not that I wasn't worthy; I was, but he did what he wanted, which included taking what he wanted. He took me, stole me like a thief in the night, with promises of security, trust, and love.

Bullshit.

He was a brilliant man. Kincaid was a master at knowing his opponent so that he could manipulate the situation to sway results in his favor. I'd seen him do it plenty of times before. It was how he handled business. My husband was a master manipulator and had shared that with me. Yet, I fell right into his trap. I couldn't run. Kincaid would never allow that. Not with me carrying his baby. I did, however, need time to rid myself of the emotions he'd created so that I could reposition myself in his life. My role would be more defined and not ruled by the fantasy he created. It was business. I was a *means to an end*—his exact words.

A bubble of emotion threatened to escape by way of another sob, but I swallowed it down. I refused to make things any worse than they already were. I had to stay focused and get my mind right. If I didn't, he would win. All was fair in love and war . . . right? Well, it wasn't love, not anymore, just war, survival of the fittest, and I was the one who needed to strap on my boots and prepare for battle.

When the concierge phone rang, my eyes shot over to it, and my fingers lifted but hesitated. I wouldn't have answered, but my husband wouldn't need to call. He had full access to this place, and I was sure he'd be here dragging me back to our palace as soon as he figured out where I was. That caveman nature suited him well. I wouldn't have a choice. He would win, but that didn't mean I had to fall back into the role I'd been in. I refused.

Pushing out a short sigh, I lifted the phone and placed it to my ear.

"Mrs. Akel, a guest is here requesting to see you."

I frowned, wondering who the hell would be asking to see me here, at his penthouse.

"Did they give you a name?"

"No name, but he says he's your father. Shall I send him up?"

"My . . . he . . . Did he say that word specifically? *Father?*"

"Yes, ma'am."

"Can you ask him a question for me, please?"

"Absolutely."

"Ask him to give you my mother's name."

"Will do, hold please."

My fingers trembled while I held the phone. Had Kincaid found my father and kept it from me? Maybe he'd planned to meet him here, first, before allowing me to meet him. He'd done that with my mother, so it would make sense.

"Mrs. Akel?"

"Yes . . ."

"He said your mother's name is Endia Renee Collette. If there is a problem, I can get your husband on the line."

"No, please, that won't be necessary. I'll come down," I almost whispered the response, but he heard me because seconds after, it was followed by his voice.

"Sure thing. I'll let him know you're on your way." I heard a shuffle and then, "Mrs. Akel will meet you in the lobby. She's on her way down now," just before the call ended.

I climbed off the bed, smoothing my palms over my ponytail and down the front of my jeans. I felt anxious and nervous about meeting him, still in a daze that this was really happening.

After checking my reflection in the mirror affixed to the dresser, I crossed the room, removing the gun I knew Kincaid kept in the nightstand on his side of the bed. He'd introduced me to it, explaining how to remove the safety and how to hold and aim it. The man claimed to be my father, and he possibly could be, but one thing I'd learned about being connected to my husband was that one could never be too sure. With the small chrome handgun tucked in the pocket of my hoodie, I left to meet the person who claimed to be my father.

Once I reached the lobby and stepped off the elevator, I noticed a man dressed in a suit standing in the open space. He turned to me at the same time my eyes found him, and I relaxed when he smiled.

"You look just like her." His smile was friendly and warm, reaching his eyes, but the way he took me in was as if he were seeing a ghost. *My mother's ghost.*

"We can talk in there." I motioned to the small coffee shop to our left, but still in the lobby. His gaze moved toward the glass front before he nodded and extended a hand, motioning for me to go first. I did after allowing my eyes to sweep the space around us. Security was stationed a few feet away, and several people were moving about. There weren't any customers in the coffee shop, but two women were positioned behind the counter. They smiled and greeted us when we entered, taking a spot near the front.

"Did my husband find you?"

His face tensed briefly while his eyes narrowed some. "No."

"Then how did you find me?"

"Your mother. I hadn't seen or heard from her in years. When she contacted me through one of my offices, I almost didn't believe it was Endy. She and I had a complicated past. It makes sense that she up and disappeared the way she did."

He has a nickname for her. Endy.

"Did you know about me?"

"No, not until she called out of the blue and told me you found her."

"My husband did. Not me."

"But you met your mother. She told me that you came to visit and asked about me."

"When did she tell you this?" I frowned because she hadn't mentioned him. We talked a few times a week but never about him. When I asked who he was, she would always change the subject. She never gave me a name or any details about him other than he was older and someone she had no business getting involved with.

"A few weeks ago. She gave me your name, and I did a little research."

"But how did you know *where* to find me?"

"Your husband."

"But you said he's not the one who found you."

"He didn't; however, he led me to you, just not intentionally. The name Akel is what brought me here."

"You know him?"

"I do, and I also know he owns a penthouse in the building."

But we don't live here anymore. My hand lowered beneath the table and eased into my hoodie pocket.

"And you just decided to pop up, *today*?" My brows pinched.

"No, I received notification that you were here, alone. Your husband is a resourceful man, but so am I. You're my daughter. I wanted to meet you. You wanted to meet me, so here I am."

"You said alone? Why point that out?"

A voice suddenly answered. "Because he knows that I wouldn't let him anywhere near you. Isn't that right?"

Kincaid appeared out of nowhere. Maybe I was too caught up in the man who identified himself as my father to notice when my husband entered the coffee shop, but he was there, sitting next to me with a gun, which he lowered to the tiny wooden table. His hand was on the sleek black metal, and his finger was against the trigger. It was aimed across from us with specific intentions. *I will shoot you if you blink wrong.* My body stiffened at the reality of what was happening.

My husband and my father were on different sides of the fence, placing me between them. How was I supposed to handle a past I didn't know about and a future I was uncertain of? These men were both asserting their demand to have me in their lives.

"That's not for you to decide. She's your wife, but she's my flesh and blood. How do you think it will change the nature of things between you if my blood somehow ends up on your hands? Her husband killing her father. That can't end well for you."

"That's a risk I'm willing to take. *My wife* sometimes makes decisions driven by her emotions. That's not always safe or smart. She will have all the facts where you're concerned." Kincaid's response housed a double meaning. He was not only speaking to my father but also to me as well. My separation and ignoring him was being blamed on my emotions and not facts. One thing I didn't miss was that my controlling husband was leaving no room for any misinterpretation about where he stood on me having a relationship with the man whose DNA I carried.

My father smirked and lifted a hand, which he eased into this suit jacket. The act had me placing mine on top of my husband's. I had no idea what was going on between the two, but I wasn't about to allow a bullet to end whatever it was. Not there in the coffee shop in front of me.

Seconds passed before a business card was placed on the table. My father used a finger to move it closer to me.

"I'm open to whatever you decide. That's how you can find me, but even if you lose it, I'm sure your husband knows how to get in touch." His eyes lifted to mine before he stood and adjusted his suit jacket, slipping his hands into the pockets of his slacks. A cocky grin was now in place while he made a point of giving attention to Kincaid. It was brief but deliberate, and he addressed me again right after.

"When you're ready, I'll make myself available," he spoke with an affinity that had my husband's body radiating a type of force that I had never experienced from him before, and if looks could kill . . .

My father would no longer be breathing.

"You're testing the restraints of my patience. It would be wise of you not to tempt fate." Kincaid's voice was unnervingly cold and detached. The threat was delivered with ease, and both men seemed confident in their positions. That was what worried me the most. There was no middle ground between them, not even me.

"Always a pleasure, Akel. I'm sure I'll see you around." His tone was mocking, which didn't sit well with me.

My eyes remained focused on my father until he was no longer in sight. A kiss on my temple brought me back to my current reality. "Let's go, sweetheart. I see there's a lot we need to discuss."

I had no idea what the hell just happened, but what I did know with certainty was that my husband wouldn't hesitate to end my father's life, and the sentiment was returned by him as well. That only meant that my life had just become a million times more complicated than it already was, and thus far, I was barely holding on. I wasn't sure how much more I could take, but I was about to find out. The Akels were at war and not just with each other, but apparently, my husband now had his own battle . . .

with my father . . .

TO BE CONTINUED . . .

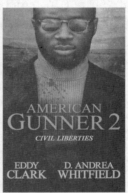

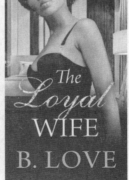